Forced Conversion

Forced Conversion

Donald J. Bingle

Five Star • Waterville, Maine

First Edition
First Printing: November 2004

Published in 2004 in conjunction with Tekno Books and Ed Gorman.

Set in 11 pt. Plantin by Al Chase.

Printed in the United States on permanent paper.

Library of Congress Cataloging-in-Publication Data

Bingle, Donald J.
    Forced conversion / by Donald J. Bingle.
      p. cm.
    ISBN 1-59414-254-8 (hc : alk. paper)
    1. Virtual reality—Fiction.   2. Immortalism—Fiction.
  3. Soldiers—Fiction. I. Title.
  PS3602.I545F67 2004
  813′.6—dc22   2004057956

Dedication

To Mom and Dad

Acknowledgments

I hadn't really planned on writing a book. It's actually Jean Rabe's fault I did.

Jean encouraged my first foray into fiction, a tournament scenario for the *Paranoia* role playing game system. More tournaments followed, for the *Paranoia*, *Bond*, *Timemaster*, *Chill*, *Advanced Dungeons & Dragons*, *Dream Park*, and even *Battle Cattle* game systems. All were an outgrowth of my activity on the RAGA® (Role Playing Game Association) Network's sanctioned tournament circuit (where I was the top-ranked player in the world for fifteen years). Many of the tournaments were specifically requested by Jean. These led to writing adventures and source material for various of the role playing game companies, many with Jean as an instigator, editor, or collaborator. I eventually converted one of the game tournaments into a screenplay and started doing movie reviews for *Knights of the Dinner Table*, a comic book for role playing gamers.

When I turned to short stories, again Jean was there. She published a science fiction story of mine in *MechForce®️ Quarterly* and, with a few changes, got another published in an anthology edited by Margaret Weis (*Earth, Wind, Fire, Water: Tales of the Eternal Archives # 2*). More stories (one of novella length) followed in more anthologies (*Civil War Fantastic*, *Historical Hauntings*, *The Search for Magic*, *Sol's Children*, *The Players of Gilean*, *Carnival*, *Renaissance Faire*, and *All Hell Breaking Loose*), some of which stories were edited by Jean (or someone I met through her) and some of which were simply instigated by her. These anthologies resulted in my introduction to John Helfers at Tekno Books. Between these sporadic stories, I worked on a treatment for a science fiction television series and on my second screenplay, *Extreme Global Warming*.

Finally, it was Jean who convinced me to attend World Horror Con in 2002 and sign up for one of the pitch sessions with a science fiction editor, even though I had no book to pitch, nothing but a couple-page outline of an old story idea set in a world with a fair amount of backstory. The editor seemed so interested that it motivated me to actually write the book, this book. My contacts through Jean paid off again when John Helfers agreed to read my book and quickly connected me up with Five Star.

Of course, you don't go from a pitch to a book without a lot of help in between. Special thanks go to all of those who read and made comments on drafts of the book: Lenora Anderson, Bob and Terri Bielinski, James Bingle, Linda Bingle, Dewey Frech, John Helfers, Randall Lemon, Barb and Rich Letterman, Jean Rabe, Paul Stevens, Susan Wagner-Fleming, Tim White, and Mary Zalapi. Thanks also to: Cheryl Frech, Ken Ritchart, Beth Vaughan, and Patty Villasenor, as well as to all my gaming friends in Chicago, Denver, and elsewhere, my family, my colleagues and clients at Bell, Boyd & Lloyd (where I work as a corporate and securities lawyer), and my fellow writers at the St. Charles Writers Group for their support and encouragement during the process.

John Helfers has been the most relaxed, open, friendly, decisive, and helpful editor you could possibly imagine. Even more, he has incredibly fast turnaround and always is there when you need him.

I couldn't possibly have written this book or anything else

without the support and encouragement of my lovely and creative wife, Linda, who tolerated with good grace the hours I spent apart from her, cooped up in my office with the computer, unable to be disturbed in any way, because I was in "writer mode." She also helped enormously by commenting on numerous drafts and by making suggestions and drawings for several possible cover ideas. Hugs also go to Smoosh, Mauka, and Makai for sleeping by my feet while I was typing and not insisting on going for walks too often.

Finally, thanks to Tekno Books and Five Star Publishing for being willing to take a chance on a first novel. Please support them and all of their authors by buying their fine products or convincing your local library to do so.

Donald J. Bingle
March 2004

Chapter 1

Derek hated firefights with religious zealots. They never gave up. Even when they faced certain death, they thought that meant they had won, that their reward in heaven was close at hand and even more glorious if they took you with them.

The scene looked peaceful enough: a shallow mountain creek cutting its way through the soil and detritus of a broad valley floor. A scattering of aging Ponderosa pines whispered and swayed lazily in the breeze above, while the buffalo grass baked and dried in the naked glare of the sun.

But the sun and the trees lied when they whispered peace. Violence stalked this place. The bear and mountain lion tracks crisscrossing a bar of silt nearby bore silent witness to the danger. The pleasant gurgle of the creek's bright, flowing water tried, but could not mask the truth of the mountain wilds. Kill-or-be-killed was nature's way.

And today . . . today there would be violence here of a type never shown in the nature vids.

There were at least three mals on the far side of the creek. His enemy was hiding in the more plentiful pines and bushy undergrowth on the north side of the valley. Derek couldn't see them, hadn't seen them even during the coordinated burst of automatic weapon fire that forced him to dive for the dirt several minutes ago, but he knew that they were there. They were spread out along the outside of a U-shaped bend in the coldwater creek. That way they would have a clear shot at anyone fool enough to charge down the loose gravel bank, cross the shin-high water, and attempt to scramble up the opposite side.

Derek wasn't a fool and he certainly wasn't gung-ho enough about this mission, any mission, to charge forward on his own. Instead, he hunkered down behind one of the bigger Ponderosa pines. He gulped for air, breathing in the sweet smell of the sticky sap oozing from where a bullet had scored the trunk only moments before. The sugary scent mixed with the salty tang of his own sweat and the whiff of powder still in the air from his untargeted return fire. His mouth tasted of mud, tinged with metal.

He glanced furtively about for hostiles, then sat with his back to the trunk as he checked his ammunition and waited impatiently for the rest of the squad to move up. They'd heard the gunfire. There was no reason to risk moving back to report. Still, he counted the seconds and yearned for a radio to call for help.

He'd learned many things in the course of his training: military maneuvers, survival techniques, PsyOps methods. Things he otherwise never would have thought about back home; things Katy would never know or understand; things he would never tell her when he saw her again after his service was complete. But he had never learned why the squad couldn't use a damn radio to communicate on patrol, not even a radio with an encrypted signal. Their vehicle had laser communications gear, but out in the field they used hand motions. So he sat, frozen in place, imagining a hand motion he would love to give whoever had banned the radios, and waited for reinforcement.

He heard the squad before he saw them, which didn't say much for their training, or, more accurately, their leadership. A.K., the hulking squad commander, crashed forward, barely bothering to crouch as he moved quickly through the buffalo grass. Sandoval, slightly pudgy and sweating profusely, trailed diagonally on A.K.'s right, just ahead of Pancek, who moved in the calm, deliberate manner of a professional soldier. Manning, short and wiry, moved quickly and furtively in a mirror position to A.K.'s left, along with Digger, who was older, taller, and considerably more laconic in his movements and his attitude. Back and center, their resident techno-geek, Wires, crept forward awkwardly with his conversion equipment.

Derek swung his rifle around the side of the trunk and let off a burst into the trees across the creek, both to give the squad some cover and to make sure they knew exactly where he was. The squad would know the sound of his rifle; the ConFoe suppressor rifles made a deep, dull bark—the result of the rubber bullets. The mals used a variety of weaponry—everything from ancient Kalashnikovs to collapsible Uzi submachine pistols, but they all had the sharp yelp and bite of real ammunition made of brass and lead and designed to tear a ragged hole out of your sinew when they hit.

The mal religious fanatics didn't have to play by the rules regarding lethal force. Only the ConFoes were supposed to do that. It's what almost made it an even fight, despite the superior numbers, training, equipment, and transportation of the ConFoes. The Conversion Forces were tasked to locate, capture, orient, persuade, and convert the malcontents, forcibly if necessary. The ConFoes could only use lethal force in defense; the mals used it all the time.

A.K. halted the group's advance in a brief hollow behind a small deadfall. "Bareback," he growled. Pancek, Manning, Sandoval, and Digger simultaneously popped out their ammo magazines and snicked in fresh ones from their belts with smooth, practiced motions. Wires merely continued his slow, burdened effort to catch up; he didn't even carry a gun.

Derek knew that A.K. had no need to switch; he never

used rubber, despite the regulations.

Derek made no move to switch magazines either, but for a different reason. "There's no need for that, A.K.," he hissed back to his squad-mates. "We outnumber 'em."

"To hell with that. Damn mals need to learn to run back to their hidey-holes when A.K. comes to town," the squad leader boasted, louder than he needed to. He obviously didn't care if the mals heard.

"There's only three . . ." Derek argued back.

A.K. fixed him with a steely gaze, the muscles tensing in his jaw. "You only saw three." He looked up toward the shade of the more densely packed trees across the creek. The sunlight dappling through the swaying pine branches was the only thing that moved within his gaze. "They only showed you three." His tanned face crinkled slightly as he took in a long deep breath, then loosed a practiced stream of spittle through his teeth. "I smell one behind every tree."

He motioned, first to Sandoval, then to Manning. The signs were quick and precise and ended with a curt nod. Sandoval moved back and downstream, Manning back and upstream. They would cross the creek a hundred yards on either side of their advancing leader and attempt to flank the enemy. Derek had less than three minutes to get with the program before all hell broke loose.

Swearing below his breath, he ejected the partially expended magazine of rubber bullets and replaced it with the real thing. He stuck a couple extra magazines into the waistband of his camouflage pants for ready access and counted the grenades hanging off his belt: three stunners on his right, two incendiaries on his left.

Unfortunately, the mals decided not to wait to be flanked. They opened up on Derek with apocalyptic abandon before he could even turn back around toward them and get his bearings. Bursts of automatic fire tore up the ground in arcs to his left and his right, zeroing in on him as steady fire from the front pounded into the soft wood of the Ponderosa pine, chewing through it, sending wood and splinters flying into his neck.

He knew better than to have remained stationary this long after having been spotted by an enemy, especially with his back to them. Now they had fully triangulated their fire on his position. It was only a matter of seconds. . . .

With a bellow, A.K. vaulted over the deadfall and charged forward to the left of Derek's untenable position. In A.K.'s left paw, a gleaming silver machine pistol spat out a stream of fire and death at the position of the left-most attacker. In his right, an automatic heavy rifle did the same. A.K.'s taut muscles absorbed the recoil of each shot and his shoulders strained to keep the weapons level despite their thundering rate of fire. Even with the dual targeting and his quick movement forward, A.K.'s aim remained remarkably true, pummeling both positions without respite.

More splinters exploded from Derek's tree as A.K. drew even and passed his position, still firing to both sides, his arms outstretched, his chest full and wide toward the center mal, who had been punishing the side of Derek's cover facing the creek.

Pancek and Digger flung themselves wide to either side, each firing in short bursts at the mal nearest them as they gained speed in an effort to rush and jump the creek.

Derek's tree stopped vibrating as the center shooter began to veer his fire toward the charging A.K. It was up to Derek to save the belligerent asshole. He reached down with his right hand to his left side and loosed a grenade, flicking the pin out with his thumb as he had been drilled in boot. He drew his arm back, then flung his arm upward as he twisted around the right side of the tree to fastball the weapon into the thicket directly across the creek.

As the explosion rocked the previously peaceful valley, Derek threw himself toward a large pine to his right, trusting the dust and chaos of the explosion to cover his movement and staying low to avoid the steady stream of lead that A.K. continued to spew in both directions. The tree he chose was half-undercut by the eroding bank of the creek and leaned out at a forty-five degree angle across the water. If he could clamber atop it and sprint across, he could drop down on the other side before he was re-targeted and capture their center opponent.

Derek attempted to shoulder his weapon to leave his hands free and planted his left foot hard to push up onto the angled pine. As he did, the earth gave way beneath him and his leg dropped into a void until his crotch shockingly halted the fall by colliding with a wide tree root. His rifle slipped off his right shoulder as he spun and jerked painfully downward to his left. Blackness and flashes of light flooded Derek's vision as his plan disintegrated with the eroding earth. He scraped his face on the tree trunk as he fell, wrenching his lower back and twisting his right knee in the process.

Derek gritted his teeth to avoid crying out and struggled to remain conscious. The bank had undercut the old pine more than he had realized and his leg had punched through a layer of dirt between two gnarled roots. His left leg now dangled helplessly below the angled tree without purchase. His gun was out of reach, in the open to his right. Shots rang out on three sides of him, but the tree blocked his view of the firefight raging about him. Mud spattered against his exposed leg as slugs slammed into the bank. The automatic fire approached him from the left in a stream so thick that he knew his leg would be chewed off when the dum-dum bullets cut through his flesh, leaving his blood to course down into the pristine water of the creek.

He tried to marshal his thoughts and figure out what to do, but the only thing that could permeate the haze of pain was that this was surely an asinine way to die. Even more so, because only mals died at all anymore.

That was the beauty of conversion.

Where was that damn slowpoke, Wires, when you really needed him?

Icy slivers of water sliced into Derek's face and splashed across his shoulders and chest. He opened his eyes into utter blackness. His body ached, the pain throbbing outward from his privates and his lower back to his legs, chest, shoulders, arms, and face and somehow out further into infinity, his agony reaching out further than his appendages. His head throbbed in time with the spasms of his back. His tongue was swollen and thick, his lips cracked and crusted with mud and sweat. He tasted blood and grit and bile with the sharp metallic aftertaste that always accompanied a burst of adrenaline.

This wasn't what they promised in the conversion brochures. This isn't what they told people, well mals, during orientation. Either they'd lied or he had died. Maybe the religious freaks were right about an afterlife, just wrong about what it contained.

He drifted back into blackness.

Stinging cold assaulted Derek's face again. This time, when he opened his eyes, the flickering of a small flame broke the blackness. It snapped off as foul smoke and ash assaulted his nostrils. A circular red, white, and gray glow appeared from behind the smoke where the flame had been a moment before.

"If he closes his eyes, splash 'im again, Manning," grumbled the leering visage of A.K. behind his cigar. "He'll either wake up or drown. Either way suits me."

Shapes and shadows came into focus among the trees that blocked and scattered the dim moonlight. Another flame, this a campfire off to his left, crackled and snapped as the pitch of the pine branches boiled and burned.

"I tol' you," said Sandoval's voice somewhere behind Derek. "I tol' you, Wires, that you was wastin' your time setting up the machinery. No way 'ee needs to be converted yet. Poor bastard has to finish 'ees service in the ConFoes, just like the rest of us."

Derek saw Wires, to his far right, unpacking and assembling the scanner in a small clearing. Even in the dark, the techno-geek's hands moved deftly, with quick certainty, snapping components together, toggling nuts onto well-oiled bolts, and plugging connections in with alacrity. He looked over to Sandoval without pausing at all in his tasks. His voice was soft and emotionless, "Just the same, I will continue. He looks terrible and you know this process takes some time. I'd prefer to be ready in case my services are needed."

Digger squatted next to the crackling campfire, squinting into the flames and breathing in the pungent, piney smoke without coughing as he warmed his leathery hands. "If it's all the same," he drawled, "I'll wait and see. Friggin' bedrock's too close to the surface hereabouts. No use diggin' a hole, less'n you need it."

"I'd try to live if I were you," chuckled Manning, fingering another canteen full of cold water. "Wires ain't ready yet, Digger doesn't want to be bothered to bury you, and A.K. ain't even got around to chewing you out over your lame-ass assault technique."

It came to Derek that he had neither been converted nor

had he died. Instead, his life in the squad and his tour of duty in the Conversion Forces continued. Perhaps it was the pain, or even the drugs that Manning had undoubtedly given him in an unsuccessful effort to dull his searing agony into an all-consuming full-body ache, but Derek felt no joy in discovering he was alive. No joy at all.

"What, what about the mals?" he croaked out raggedly, his words slurred and slow, his throat cracking with the effort.

Manning chuckled again. "Two wasted. Me on the one side—A.K. drove him headlong straight into me. It was bee-yoo-ti-ful! Pancek got the one on the other side."

"Hey, man, I keeled him too," interjected Sandoval. "Why do you think he run so slow? Shot him in the ol' rumpola. Come next spring," he continued, gesturing expansively at the clearing about him, "his ass will be grass!"

A.K. stopped sucking on his cigar and smiled thuggishly. "Pegged the bastard in the middle, too, but he got away. Wires was screaming for help so loud I had to come back and take care of you just to shut 'im up." He blew a putrid smoke ring into the thin, clear alpine air. "We'll follow the blood-trail to verify the kill come morning." He stuck the stogie back into his mouth and inhaled deeply. Like most smokers these days, he always fired up the strongest, most loathsome, extra-nicotine laced chubbies he could get his hands on and sucked the smoke deep into his lungs, holding it there as long as possible before exhaling. After all, fouling your lungs really didn't matter anymore.

Which was a good thing, Derek thought, as he pulled the asbestos coated emergency blanket up to his chin to stave off the cold 'til dawn.

Derek still felt like crap in the morning, but Manning's

19

drugs had taken hold enough to make him ambulatory. Just barely. He wouldn't want to jog uphill with a full pack or take on a mal in hand-to-hand, but he could move as fast as Wires could with all his equipment. That meant the squad was back in business.

Getting going wasn't easy, though. Not only was Derek stiff and sore, but his hands were so numb from the drugs he had been given that he actually had to look to see if his fingers were gripping the zipper of his fly when he unzipped to take a morning piss. Even with the powerful drugs, he still winced in pain, then gritted his teeth as he fumbled gingerly at his crotch. His privates were swollen and discolored in ways never intended and not at all amorous. There was blood in his urine and pissing hurt like a son-of-a-bitch.

It was a good thing his equipment was no longer needed for procreation. Like others of the unconverted, he used his recreationally from time to time, but it would be weeks before that would be enjoyable again. Derek zipped up and headed back toward the camp.

Pancek, quiet and reserved as always, greeted Derek on his return with only a brief nod. Pancek's dark brow was furrowed like he had a headache and he had bags under his gray eyes; no doubt he had been on perimeter guard duty most of the night. But Pancek didn't complain. He simply shouldered his pack and kicked dirt into the smoldering remains of the campfire. Then he walked calmly to the stream, stooping to fill his canteen. Finally, he stood, patiently waiting for the others to be ready to move out, as he screwed the cap back on the ConFoe-issued container.

A.K. came back into the campsite after reconnoitering ahead. "Bleeding like a stuck pig . . ." he sneered, gesturing to a clear trail through the buffalo grass.

"I don't think their religion allows them to bleed like

pigs," smirked Manning.

"I don't think peegs are a problem for thees religion, Manning," replied Sandoval as he hefted his pack and slung his rifle.

"Pigs, cows, chickens . . . all these religious types are wacko. The government offers them heaven . . . whatever heaven they choose, but they're too stupid to take it," complained Manning, "which is why, ladies, we have to sleep on the friggin' ground and haul our sorry asses up a friggin' mountain."

"Manning, my friend," said Digger as he put a friendly arm around his small, wiry squad-mate. "Perhaps they do not know that heaven awaits them. It is our job to bring them the truth, to orient them to the possibilities, to let them choose, to give them an opportunity to convert. Not missionaries, but on a mission for their good and ours."

Most of the squad winced visibly at Digger's sarcastic recitation of text from their Conversion Forces training manual.

"I don't haul this equipment around for nothing, you know," noted Wires quietly. He had finished disassembling the conversion scanner with one hand as he had eaten his breakfast with the other.

". . . And, if they reject our generous offer of eternal life, then we'll just hafta' blow their asses to kingdom come," retorted Manning, patting his automatic rifle like a faithful dog.

"In which case, I get to do my job," finished Digger as they headed out, trying to keep pace with the ever-aggressive A.K.

Derek held his tongue during the exchange and wondered for the thousandth time what a misguided sense of duty and a slick recruiting vid had gotten him into. Back in his real life, before the Conversion Forces, he had been told he was a good-looking guy: average height, brown hair, with an athletic build from playing sports and a broad, white smile. And, back then, he had a bright future ahead of him in one of the new worlds, just like everyone else.

Now look at him. Dirty, banged up, and bruised, with greasy, unkempt hair that looked almost black, three day's worth of stubble, and a hobbled, bent-over gait that reminded him of his grandfather. And he couldn't remember the last time he had smiled.

Worse yet, he couldn't imagine the next time he would smile.

He had a violent, miserable, and dangerous job. And the future, at least the immediate future, didn't look all that promising. In fact, it looked like hell.

He hated firefights with religious zealots. The gangs and the loners could be vicious opponents, too, but at least those mals mostly fought in a straightforward, military way. They would battle to protect turf or supplies or to cover while their wounded were evacuated to safety. Occasionally, they would simply run away in retreat. Sometimes, the gangs and the loners would even peaceably surrender.

But the zealots never surrendered. They feared conversion more than anyone else, more than anything else. They not only fought for their lives, they fought for their eternal souls.

Chapter 2

The injured mal made pretty good distance for a guy who had bled so much, but, then, he hadn't stopped for the night as they had. Adrenaline had obviously kept him going. Or fervor. It didn't really matter which.

A.K. had Manning take up the trail when it got more difficult to follow. The grass and alpine shrubs gave way to rocks and occasional patches of clean, white snow as the mal headed up toward a low mountain pass. Pancek suggested that the group would make better time if it just hiked up to the saddle of the pass, the obvious destination of anyone headed this way, but A.K. insisted that Manning actually track their quarry—whether because he was truly concerned about the remote possibility of the mal doubling back and slipping away or because it just felt more like a hunt that way, Derek didn't know and didn't care. He ached from the climb, even at their slow pace, and his lungs burned from sucking in the cold, dry, and all too sparse air as they gained altitude.

Manning sniffed and poked and focused his beady eyes in an effort to discern a trail, then scampered from rock to rock to repeat the effort like the little ferret he resembled. He clearly delighted in showing off in front of A.K. and A.K. let him do it. Their Neanderthal leader stood watching in a relaxed slouch, mashing an unlit cigar with his teeth and smiling a disgustingly yellow smile whenever Manning picked up the trail again.

At the top of the pass, the squad stopped. A.K. scanned the area with his digital ocular scope while Manning searched for further signs of the blood-trail. Each seemed to be taking considerable time.

Digger dropped his pack and paced nervously below the near edge of the ridge, squinting up at A.K. "You know, you make a wonderful friggin' target silhouetted against the sky at the top of the pass," he finally called out, disgusted at the lack of combat sense or, perhaps, the unmitigated macho gall of A.K., who continued his ocular scan.

Pancek held up a finger to test the wind. "Even with a Kalashnikov, a decent sniper could easily take him out from more than five hundred meters," he observed, but not loudly enough for A.K. to hear.

Sandoval, Wires, and Derek sat unceremoniously on the ground to rest, each one leaning against the nearest convenient rock slab or boulder. Sandoval began to idly inspect the gray and black patterns of his rock slab and the contours of the green and pink lichens splotched over its rough granite surface, then stopped, as if suddenly fearful that such a pastime would make him look inattentive to the tactical situation, at best, and sensitive and girlish, at worst. Derek was too tired and starved for oxygen to care, either about the pleasing variegation of the rock face or Sandoval's homophobia. Sure, they were only at about 11,000 feet or so, but he was tired, dehydrated, and not fully acclimated to the altitude.

Finally, ferret-boy conferred with A.K., and the two rambled down-slope to talk to the rest of the squad.

"Our quarry dressed his wound. Manning thinks someone met him here."

"You see," interjected Manning proudly, "the blood-trail stops, but the lichens have been disturbed on the rocks, both along the ridge to the south and downhill to the west. Given the distance between strides . . ."

"Yeah, why don't you go calculate that again, sport?" ordered their squad leader dismissively, then waited while Manning retreated back up the hilltop to repeat his routine.

"Look, Derek, Manning's gonna take you and Wires and Sandoval and follow the injured guy down-slope." He paused as they nodded their assent, then added, "You girls might be able to move fast enough to catch someone half-dead who hasn't slept, at least if he keeps heading downhill."

He motioned with his head for Pancek and Digger to follow him. "The rest of us will follow his contact along the ridge and take care of that problem."

Wires frowned as he stood and gathered his equipment. "Shouldn't I stay here so I can move to whichever party needs the conversion equipment quickly?"

A.K. looked at Wires, a hard, stern look of disgust usually reserved for stupid children or dogs that passed gas while he was eating. He motioned toward Digger. "I have who I'll need when we catch the bastard." He turned and walked quickly away, Pancek and Digger quickly falling in line behind him.

As soon as they moved out, Manning abandoned his pretense of repeating his tracking observations and gathered his troops. "Lock and load, ladies," he ordered curtly, enjoying his authority. "Remember, no birth control. It's against their religion." He giggled in his nasal, ferret-like way at the joke, even though they had all heard it a million times.

Derek sighed and switched out the rubber ammunition yet again.

Maria moved quickly along the ridge to the south.

She followed it as it angled up toward the peak of a snow-capped mountain until she reached the snowline, then veered off to the west. She jogged steadily, skirting just below the ice and sharp-edged rocks to make her way around the peak, toward the ridgeline and valleys beyond. Her taut body was lithe and strong and conditioned to the thin mountain air. She moved quickly without breathing hard, her dark, shoulder-length hair bouncing as she darted around granite slabs and mounds of loose scree.

Her plain gray jumpsuit provided some camouflage on the mountain slopes and covered her too-pale skin from the burning ultraviolet rays of the sun as it peeked at her over the top of the mountain. The standard-issue garment also protected her from the cold of her alpine journey, as well as the cool darkness of Sanctuary. The turned up collar of the jumpsuit did not quite cover a thin, light scar running down and forward from her right ear just below the angular line of her jaw. She ran her right thumb lightly along the scar as she considered the situation during a brief pause in her scrambling flight.

She hated that she had left Joshua behind to fend for himself. He was surely too weak to escape the advancing ConFoe squad for long. He had lost too much blood. He was exhausted and dehydrated. He had barely made it to the top of the pass where she had waited on lookout.

Maria had tended to Joshua's wounds and given him her canteen, but it would not be enough. Fatigue and exposure nipped at his heels and the ConFoe squad was close behind. Joshua had attacked the ConFoes in an effort to protect Sanctuary. Now she knew he struggled merely to live long enough to draw their enemy away while she ran home to raise the alarm. She continued on.

Maria would not see Joshua again on this world, but she had been taught that she would in the next. Between deep breaths of cool, clear air, she muttered a prayer that Joshua would not be converted before he died.

★ ★ ★ ★ ★

A.K. loped along the ridge top, drawing ahead of the more methodically-paced movements of Pancek and Digger. He knew the tactics were all wrong—at least according to the asshole training sergeant back at boot. He could trip a booby-trap or be caught alone in an ambush or even simply fall off a cliff and break his ever-lovin' neck. To hell with that. This, this was the thrill of the hunt—you didn't have that if you were careful and proper and followed candy-ass procedures.

Besides, it was always more fun to catch them when you were alone. There were no witnesses that way.

He stopped shortly after he passed the snowline. Something was wrong. There were no tracks. He swore vehemently—a string of short, descriptive, and foul expletives punctuating his thudding steps as he backtracked looking for where his quarry had altered her course.

Yeah, he knew it was a she. The length of stride had suggested it, but the tiny boot-print in a muddy depression not far back had confirmed it. She couldn't have turned off too long ago.

Rather than squat down and examine the scratches on the rock-face or disturbed lichens or gravel, he stopped and looked around the mountain to either side. After all, there were only two directions to go—east and west. East led back towards the direction of yesterday's firefight, a possibility if the mals they met had been protecting something—a cabin or a campsite—and she was making her way back there.

But he doubted it. She had met the injured mal a fair distance from the firefight—a fair distance *west* of the firefight. A.K. stopped and turned southwest and craned his neck to the right. His black eyes narrowed, attempting to pierce through the hazy glare along the snowline as it curved around the peak and continued on. A slight movement of gray against gray caught his attention.

There. There she was.

He lifted his rifle, aimed casually, and fired off a short burst. There was no way he could hit her, not from this distance, not even if he'd taken his time and used a sniper-scope, but he might get lucky.

Besides, he just liked the idea of terrorizing the bitch.

Maria instinctively dove sharply to the right as she heard the report of the automatic weapon. She rolled as her shoulder hit the hard slope, then spread her arms and legs to slow her tumble before it became an uncontrolled fall down the jagged face of the mountainside.

Once her slide was stopped, she scrambled behind a nearby car-sized boulder, peering back to pinpoint her attacker. Bright red trickled from a gash in her forehead, tracing an irregular path down the pale whiteness of her cheek to the edge of her scar as she poked her head cautiously out from the up-slope side of the hunk of granite. A gust of wind blew her dark hair forward, fluttering the strands before her sharp blue eyes briefly, then failed, leaving the tresses to fall back into her face and mat against the jagged, red trickle on her cheek.

Her face flushed with embarrassment when she saw the brute, far back along the ridgeline, raising his rifle with one hand above his head and pumping it in the primitive celebration of all self-congratulatory killers, amateur or professional.

He was too far away still to be a threat, unless, of course, she broke a leg or flung herself off a cliff-side because of his macho display of aggression and firepower.

She felt stupid, but not too stupid. She could tell from the high-pitched crack of the burst that the ConFoe hadn't been firing rubber projectiles.

Had they changed the regulations to make the Conversion Forces more lethal yet again? That information was yet another reason to make it back to Sanctuary alive. It might mandate an acceleration of the Plan.

Maria got her feet under her and scrambled away in a crouch, south and slightly downhill. The valley where Sanctuary lay hidden beneath the trees was not far now. A cool north breeze raced her down-slope.

The second faction of ConFoes moved as a group. It wasn't that Manning was any less bloodthirsty than A.K., who the vicious ferret-boy sought to emulate in the ways of searching and destroying. The maniacal little chicken-shit was just too cowardly (he actually wore a Kevlar vest all the time) to truly go off on his own and too much of a show-off to not want the squad to see what he would do to this traitorous, blaspheming mal terrorist when they caught up to him.

Sandoval helped from time to time as the obviously still-hurting Derek struggled down the uneven slope, though Sandoval made no offer to assist the similarly slow-moving and encumbered Wires.

Wires didn't notice, or at least didn't respond to, the slight.

Derek didn't care about the inequity at the moment. The drugs were wearing off and his numb tiredness had grown into a throbbing ache that was now turning into a staccato of painful jolts streaking out from his groin and back as his combat boots thudded hard down the tortuous terrain.

The slow pace didn't matter. Their quarry had little hope of escape. Shortly after they had passed through the tree-line, the blood-trail had started up again. One of the ragged, twisty, stunted trees had apparently snagged the unlucky mal's dressing and poked into the blood and pus of the bullet wound, causing it to flow freely yet again. Manning made a show of tracking from his point position, but Derek could have followed the trail himself, even through the haze and shooting lights of his increasing pain. Hell, Wires could have followed the trail and everybody knew Converters didn't even get combat training.

Joshua was light-headed and it wasn't from the altitude. He rested against the tree trunk of a dark, tall spruce, his labored breath coming in shuddering rasps. He had never really hoped to escape, but he had hoped to lead them further away, away from his beloved Sanctuary.

He had prayed for strength all through his trek from the creek-side firefight. A less faithful man would have thought that his prayers had gone unanswered. Joshua knew that it had only been his prayers that had gotten him this far.

He drank deeply from his canteen, then poured the rest of the contents over his head and face, the cold liquid splashing him to greater alertness. He would have no further use of the water. It was time to make his last stand. If he somehow killed all of the ConFoes, it would not matter that he had not led them further from his home.

He found a thicket of thorny bushes growing in a depression behind a stony outcropping amidst the thick, dark spruces. The thorns tore at his jumpsuit and skin as he crawled in, but did not slow him. Either his pale, bluish skin was losing feeling or the hot fire from his freely flowing wound drowned out all competing sensation in its ferocity. Neither was a good sign.

He positioned his Kalashnikov in a V-shaped crack in the face of the outcropping, facing back along the way he had come. Then Joshua settled in to wait. He prayed that his pursuers would not be too slow in overtaking his position. He knew that he didn't have too much time.

"Crap! I crawled faster than this when I was a baby!" Manning tapped his foot exaggeratedly as he stood looking back at the straggling members of his command. "I could swim upstream faster than you wusses can walk down a friggin' hill!"

"Let me kick you in the balls a few times and see how fast you move," said Derek, under his breath. Wires looked at Manning with a stare that implied something similar about seeing how fast the loathsome asshole would move schlepping around over a hundred pounds of bulky equipment, but he verbalized none of it. Sandoval just shrugged and kept moving.

Manning didn't let his lack of motivational skills affect his self-perception of his leadership. "Oh, hell, ladies. Take a break. From the looks of this blood-trail, he'll be dead when we find him anyway." He turned and sat with his back to the squad, his rifle resting in his lap as his eyes scanned the forest, looking, hoping, for trouble.

Dead bodies weren't any fun . . . well, not much fun anyway.

Joshua opened his eyes, jerking his head up from the grainy dirt where his chin and cheek had rested, his drool wetting it into a pasty spot of mud that clung to his face as he peered out from his hiding spot.

"Christ, they're slow," he muttered aloud before quickly becoming embarrassed by his language and mouthing a short prayer asking forgiveness.

If he'd known that they would be this slow, perhaps he

could have gotten away or led them further away or set a booby-trap or two before taking up his covered position. Not now, though. Now his legs no longer responded when he tried to shift position. Bless it, he wanted to take some of them with him.

The next time Joshua awoke, he was laying on his back and warm, foul liquid was streaming into his face. The shadows were lengthening and he was no longer surrounded by thorny bushes.

"See," bragged Manning, zipping up his trousers. "I told you the bastard was still alive." Sandoval looked away, muttering to himself, while Wires matter-of-factly reached for his equipment.

"I'll set up," he said quietly.

Derek had moved to rush at Manning as the twisted bastard had begun his barbaric method of bringing their prisoner to consciousness. An evil grin playing below Manning's beady dark eyes had betrayed the prick's intentions a moment before he straddled their captive to gratify his foul imagination. But a crescendo of pain had overtaken Derek as he tensed to move—he wasn't capable of stopping Manning tonight, not with his hands.

Manning still straddled Joshua, his gun slung on his right shoulder and held by his right hand so that the barrel waved lazily in front of the sputtering mal's contorted face. His left hand fingered the snap holding his hunting knife in its sheath on the left side of his belt. He nudged the partially bandaged wound in Joshua's right side with his left, steel-toed, muddy, combat hiking boot.

"You know, don't you, mal, that the first to convert, I mean after the techno-geeks, were terminal patients and those . . ." he dug the toe of his boot into the wound, pressing into the yielding flesh until he met the stiff resistance of a rib, ". . . with severe, chronic pain."

"Back off," yelled Derek, his teeth gritted with his own pain. "Wires isn't even set up. You have to give him a chance to convert."

Wires' hands moved nimbly over his unpacked equipment, assembling it with precision in the dappled light filtering down between the swaying boughs of the thick trees. A steady northerly breeze snatched away any reply he might have made as he worked methodically and quickly at his task.

Manning glanced at Derek with undisguised disgust. "You're the one that got hurt. Don't you want to get in on the fun?"

Gasping for breath, Derek shook his head violently, both in response to Manning and in an attempt to clear the darkness caused by the pain searing through his body.

"You have to give him a chance to convert," Derek choked out again.

Manning sighed heavily and looked down at his disabled prey. He smiled sickly and started to speak in his most sweetly sarcastic tone, "Do you know that heaven awaits you if you convert? Any heaven you want, if you convert."

Joshua made no response, but merely stared at Manning leering maniacally down at him. Spittle hung from the corner of his tormentor's mouth.

"He doesn't understand! Orient him," gasped Derek as he fought his own battle for consciousness.

Manning snorted in derision. "He understands," he threw back to Derek over his shoulder. Looking down, he continued, "Don't you, mal? You understand what conversion is, don't you?" The mal continued to stare up at him, his mouth open, laboring to breathe.

Manning jerked his left boot hard, crunching through the

rib-bone that had blocked it before. The ragged edge of the bone punched back and up, puncturing a lung and causing yet another wave of severe pain to course through Joshua's trembling body. "Don't you?"

Sandoval turned away and stumbled hurriedly into the woods. "I theenk I'll take perimeter watch."

Manning twisted his boot, like he was stamping out an extra-nicotine laced cig.

"Don't you?"

"Yes," hissed Joshua, "I know . . . I know what conversion is . . ."

Wires continued his efficient assembly of the conversion scanning equipment. "I'll be ready in just a bit. Hold on, will you?" he said, without a clear indication of whether he was talking to Manning or the mal.

"He gets a choice," Derek shouted weakly against the growing breeze. Still hazy, even Derek didn't know if he was guided by moral outrage or simple military discipline in protesting Manning's actions. "You can't destroy a defenseless mal without giving him the choice."

Manning didn't know what he hated more, this pathetic mal, the stupid, coddling, pro-choice regulations of the Conversion Forces, or his own cowardice for not moving ahead of the squad and having his fun unencumbered by Derek's implied threat of reporting him. A.K. would never have put up with this crap. He would just do what he wanted, and bad-boy A.K. was definitely pro-death. But, then, Manning wasn't A.K.

Manning looked down at his quivering captive with detestation. "Then choose, asshole. Do you choose to let Wires here convert you?"

Life ebbed out of Joshua. Blackness flittered through his

consciousness. Even the pain seemed to subside, though it never really seemed to dull or lessen—it just seemed to no longer affect him. He almost felt as if he was watching himself. This wasn't how it was supposed to happen. He wasn't taking any of them with him.

"I . . . I . . . choose . . ." he whispered between ragged breaths.

Manning saw the mal's lips move, but couldn't really hear what he was saying. He bent low to try to hear. Whether the wretch abandoned his religion at the last instant or pronounced his own death-warrant, either way was a win from Manning's perspective.

"I . . . choose . . ."

Joshua drew in a last breath, deep into his only functioning lung, coarsely dislodging the phlegm and blood in his throat, and spat toward the leering ConFoe's face. Close as his target was, the green and red-streaked glob still fell short of the startled ConFoe's visage and plopped onto Joshua's chin. The mal didn't even have enough strength for a last gesture of defiance, but the result of his effort was the same as if he had been successful.

A millisecond later a burst of automatic weapon fire smashed into Joshua's face and neck.

"Fuck," spat Manning as he wiped his now blood-spattered face with his sleeve and staggered abruptly away from the pile of meat that had been his prisoner. "He chose not to."

As Derek slipped into unconsciousness, Wires calmly reversed his motions and started disassembling his equipment.

Damn, but that wisp of a girl was fast.

A.K. stopped on the southern slope of whatever godforsaken mountain he was on and looked down into a valley thick with evergreens and dry grass. Even without waiting for the more methodical pace of Digger and Pancek, he wasn't sure the bitch wasn't outrunning him.

He surveyed the valley from his vantage point as he caught his breath. His mouth was already dry from the increasing tempo of the arid mountain wind and the warmth of the afternoon as he moved into the lower elevations, but miles of thick brush and forest still lay ahead of him, crowded on either side by sheer walls of rock. The hard lie of the terrain dictated his tactics. She couldn't move laterally, but he would have to be careful or she might double back as he tried to chase her through the forest to the opposite end of the valley.

He got out his digital ocular scope to see if he could discern a path leading out of the opposite end of the canyon.

He peered through his sophisticated equipment, toggling up the magnification and enhancement to full power. It was hard on the battery, but necessary given the haze of the mountains and the distance involved, not to mention the narrow and indistinct path he sought. Minutes passed as he scanned and re-scanned the area.

Finally, he lowered the scope and whistled softly. He stuck a finger in his mouth, then held it above his head in the breeze.

"Game over, baby. Game over."

Maria gazed back at her pursuer. She did so from behind a tree, even though she didn't really think that he would be able to see her in the dense brush, even with his superior ConFoe equipment. Even if it had infrared enhancement, she was okay. Now that they were no longer in the rarified air of the peaks and passes, the day was too hot for her body temp to stand out clearly, even in the shade of the trees. The needles of the evergreens were dry and brittle; the arid ground had warmed all day in the bright sun. Besides, he seemed to be looking well past her position. Maybe he thought she was even faster than she was.

Despite her lack of imminent danger, Maria was still disappointed in her situation. She would surely make Sanctuary safely, but she had hoped to lose the ConFoes before they had followed her to this place. She could have moved past the valley in an effort to lead the loping gorilla following her to some other place, but then there was a chance that Sanctuary might not know that the ConFoes were in the sector, that there had been a firefight, that they were using lethal ammunition, and that Joshua was, at best, dead.

They had to know; they had to have warning. Too much depended on it. She would muster a force when she arrived at Sanctuary and ambush her pursuers. They had to die, all of them. No one could live to report back, to identify this valley, or the Believers all faced certain destruction or, worse yet, eternal damnation, should they be converted by the heathen ConFoes.

Pancek and Digger weren't loafing, they just didn't have the same joy in their work as A.K. Still, once A.K. stopped chasing the elusive mal, it wasn't too long before they caught up with him. They were a bit wary all the same, though, as they approached. Their squad leader was squatting near a deadfall yards into the thick of the forest, his rifle slung over his shoulder. He was looking down and appeared to have something small in his right hand. Digger motioned for Pancek to fan out to the right in case there were unfriendlies about, but as he did A.K. started to speak, without turning back to them.

"Hell, Pancek, I don't know which is louder, your boots

scrambling over loose rock or Digger's shovel banging into his canteen every other step." He stood and turned, casually tossing a grenade in a wide arc toward Digger's feet.

"Incoming!" yelled Pancek instinctively, as he dove into a depression to his right. He reflexively began to sight his weapon on A.K. even as he hit the dirt.

Digger started to laugh as the grenade angled toward him. He had been around A.K. longer than most of the squad and was used to the jerk's sense of humor. Then he noticed that the grenade had no pin in it.

He lunged to catch it and fling it away, but he moved too late and with too much panic. Instead of catching it, Digger's callused hand merely grazed the grenade, deflecting it downward as he became entangled with his shovel and fell face-first into the dirt. As he closed his eyes and waited for the inevitable, he realized, to his confusion and grateful relief, that the grenade not only had no pin in it, it had no top to it at all.

Pancek kept his face low, waiting for the explosion before popping up to waste their traitorous squad leader, but the thunder never came. All he heard was the thud as Digger hit the ground coincident with the grenade and the guttural, barking laughter of A.K. When Pancek finally dared to look up, Digger was sitting on the ground, holding the topless grenade upside down, as A.K. strode up the hill toward them roaring at his own joke, a wad of gray cloth in his beefy grip.

He tossed a pair of regulation briefs at Digger. "Here, you probably need these."

"Pardon the crap out of me, sir," said Digger with venom disguised as disgust, "but what the hell are you doing?"

"Needed the powder," remarked A.K. jovially. "Opened it up . . . carefully . . . and poured it out in a line just short of that deadfall."

Pancek took his finger off the trigger of his assault rifle and toggled the safety back on. Apparently he was not going to die today, at least not at the hands of his maniacal squad leader. At least not at the moment. He stood up and brushed the detritus of his dive off his fatigues as he scanned the woods behind their approaching leader. Someone ought to be paying attention to their enemy. Someone ought to take their mission seriously.

"Okay," said Digger dejectedly. "I give up. What for?"

A.K. jerked his thumb back toward the wooded valley behind him. "Box canyon. Plenty of dry grass and sap-filled wood. Good stiff breeze from the north."

Pancek understood, but Digger still hadn't parsed it out as A.K. reached him and extended a hand to help him up. In the opposite hand, A.K. held up the ancient Zippo that he used to fire up his nicotine chubbies.

"Time for a barbecue."

Maria made the appropriate birdcalls at the appointed places as she approached the entrance to Sanctuary. First a magpie, then a lark bunting, then a Steller's jay.

She received no response. The watchmen and guards never responded. It could give away their position.

Finally, she arrived at the camouflaged entrance to the mine-shaft, set low into the eastern cliff-face of the canyon. She entered Sanctuary and quickly set off to assemble a military force to eradicate her grinning, loathsome, government pursuers.

Pancek thought that A.K. enjoyed setting the forest fire just a bit too much. Of course, A.K. seemed to revel in all forms of mayhem more than a bit too much for Pancek's taste. It was just a job. Put in your time, do your duty, then convert and get the hell out of Dodge, that was Pancek's approach. He looked around uneasily. He didn't really like being this far away from Wires and his equipment. What if something were to happen?

Pancek was glad to see that Digger didn't make any effort to help A.K. with the blaze. He didn't need it and he didn't deserve it.

The small line of black powder from the grenade touched off the fire nicely, but hadn't really been necessary. Fast upon ignition, the grass burned fiercely, driven by the wind. Then, the burgeoning fire reached the deadfall and the tangle of branches flared up, giving the flames access to the branches of the trees. From there, the hot storm grew with exponential speed.

The oily sap of the wood and the low flash point of the needles quickly turned the peaceful trees into hellish candles of death. The spruces burned white-hot, the growing north wind driving the arson forward into the valley, flames leaping heavenward as thick, sweet smoke billowed up into the clear blue sky.

And, while the spruces burned with vigorous intensity, the occasional Ponderosa pines interspersed in the forest literally exploded when the now fast-moving wall of fire hit them, showering flaming debris in shooting arcs, ensuring that the path of the conflagration widened to cover the canyon wall to wall.

As twilight fell, the ash and sparks and flames made for an apocalyptic vision. Spinning, wheeling vortices of smoke and flame writhed outward from the advancing wall of superheated annihilation, spreading the main furnace of the fire in erratic and explosive thrusts.

"Hell," said Digger and A.K. nodded and grinned in agreement before Digger could even continue his thought.

"How do you know this fire's going to stay contained in this canyon? I heard tell of these things rushing up-slope faster than a horse can run, then jumpin' fifty, sixty yards over rock and water or whatnot to move onto the next ridge." He stared at the firestorm as he spoke.

A.K. shrugged his shoulders unconcernedly. "Who gives a shit? Ain't no Sierra Clubbers about no more, now is there? They're all off in their little Sierra Club world where no one pollutes with their cars, 'cause there ain't none, and no one has to worry about where they put their garbage, 'cause they don't produce any. Hell, I don't think they let cows fart in their world. So who the fuck cares if the whole state of Colorado goes up in flames?" He reflected on the possibility a few moments. "It would probably optimize satellite reconnaissance. So, you tell me, who the fuck really cares?"

Pancek hesitated, then spoke up.

"The rest of the squad might care. Any guess where they are by now?"

"Crap!" growled A.K. "You suck the fun right out of everything, you know that?"

Chapter 3

It took a few moments for Maria's eyes to adjust to the dim light inside Sanctuary, but she didn't slow at all. She moved past the defensive positions near the entryway without needing to see or think; she had been this way countless times during her life in this place, this abandoned mine. She bore left along the main gangway to the large, carved room where many of the largest mineshafts and tunnels converged. They called it "Grand Central," but it also served as the main barracks for the Believers' fighting forces. It was close to the main entrance and stood between the outside and all that they treasured in the rooms and tunnels below—their knowledge, their religious items, and, most importantly, the living areas for the mothers and children.

Maria walked briskly toward Grand Central, the sweat from the heat and exertion of her flight back to Sanctuary chilling quickly. A cool breeze flowed out of the depths below as the mine exhaled due to the natural changes in the barometric pressure outside.

The abandoned mines were a perfect place to hide from the ConFoes. The steady, cool temperature refreshed the Believers in the heat of the summer and protected them from the harsh coldness of the winters. The hard bedrock shielded them from the prying eyes of the ConFoe satellites and the dangers posed by any heavy weaponry that might be brought to bear. A dependable and inexhaustible supply of clear water could be found deep in the flooded lower levels of the mine, far from any source of tampering or contamination from their enemies. Lights and generators and first aid stations and the like had been installed in days bygone at some mining company's expense. There was even some mineable ore left from which spare parts and weapons could be fashioned. The wilderness outside provided berries, roots, and game.

Over the years, they had made quite a hospitable place of the old mine, bringing in scavenged furniture and fixtures for living quarters, kitchen facilities, and the like. There was even a cavern large enough for recreational and sporting activities, with plank bleachers along one wall for spectators.

The most spectacular room in Sanctuary was a natural cave that intersected with the mine shafts. The room had a towering ceiling and glittering quartz walls. It was quickly and unsurprisingly designated the chapel for the Believers. The chapel couldn't hold quite everyone at once, but there were plenty of services. Besides, some people had to be on guard at any given time.

In this world at this time, it wasn't enough to save your soul by mere belief, you also had to protect it from the ultimate temptation, the soul-sucking perversion that was conversion. That's what Sanctuary was all about. The miles of cramped tunnels and quarters, the stockpiling of supplies, and the training of guards and warriors; they were all motivated by the need to protect the souls of the Believers from forced conversion by the evil ConFoes.

The Believers had made Sanctuary as pleasant as they could for a hidden, underground fortress, but it certainly wasn't heaven. They would all go to heaven some day, of course, if the ConFoes didn't forcibly convert them first. But their defenses were strong and their beliefs were stronger.

Still, there was no need to test either right now. If she could lead a counter-attack that eliminated the ConFoes on her tail, Sanctuary could continue unbothered and untested for many more years. In that time, the Plan could be perfected. Maybe it would never have to be implemented at all. Perhaps the evil bastards that comprised the Conversion Forces would retreat to their own unnatural sanctuaries and leave the Believers alone. Then the meek truly would inherit the earth. But until the last of the dreaded ConFoes left, her people, the Believers, would fight to survive. They would battle to continue in this world, along with all the other misfits, scavengers, gangs, and cults that chose not to convert.

In the eyes of the Conversion Forces, they were all malcontents . . . mals. Yet, they were the ones that were content with the world. It was everyone else that had forsaken it.

She brushed aside her meandering philosophic thoughts as she entered Grand Central and began issuing terse commands. Pre-packed supplies and ready weapons were quickly grabbed up by the men and women of Sanctuary's fighting force. The troops were keyed up and ready even before she had arrived. The sentries had reported hearing distant gunfire the day before and communication had been lost with one patrol; they knew without being told that this was not a drill.

Maria could have debriefed and stayed behind. She certainly was spent from her efforts to outrun her pursuers. But the adrenaline still coursed hot within her, despite the familiar surroundings and the air-conditioned feel of the air about her. Besides, she was a Believer and her assigned task was to defend the faith and the faithful by force of arms.

More importantly, she was the one who had led the heathen ConFoes here.

She was the one who knew where they had been and how many there were.

She was the one who had abandoned Joshua to their bloodthirst and torture.

She was the one who seen the grinning glee of the ape that led the ConFoe pursuit.

She was the one who, due to an incident long ago in the city, would never . . . could never . . . join the mothers in the rooms below, caring for their children.

She was the one who could never contribute to the gene pool, who had nothing to contribute to the future of Sanctuary but to offer her life for the taking of the Believers' enemies.

She was the one who was destined to be the martyr.

Her momentary reverie was interrupted by the appearance of Sanctuary's Commander of Resistance, General Fontana. The sentries had alerted the General of her return and he had hurried to Grand Central as quickly as possible.

"Lieutenant Casini?" said Fontana softly as she turned and saw him. Maria saluted briskly, but did not wait for Fontana's cursory return salute before launching into her situation report. She spoke quickly, without emotion, or even adjectives. "ConFoe intrusion northeast, on a vector from the highway."

"How many?" asked Fontana, with an arched eyebrow.

"Seven, sir, at least according to Joshua. His squad engaged the enemy in a firefight along Fortymile Creek."

The General frowned. "A bit rash, given that he was outnumbered. Why didn't he fall back for reinforcements?"

Maria shook her head briefly. "I can't say, sir. All I know is that the other two members of the squad are dead."

"Dead?"

"They're using real ammo, Sir. Hollow point, by the look of it. And grenades . . . and not just stunners."

The General's face hardened. He nodded for her to continue.

"Joshua . . . Sergeant Czerwinski was severely wounded and is attempting to lead the enemy away from Sanctuary. Unfortunately, a portion of the ConFoe patrol is on my track.

I am about to take a strike force out to eliminate those ConFoes and, then, track back to relieve the Sergeant . . . or avenge him."

The General gave a curt nod of concurrence. "Get to it, then, Lieutenant. Dismissed," he said as he saluted and began to move back into the deeper tunnels to report this latest danger to the political leaders of the Believers.

Maria saluted back and quickly went about fulfilling her duties with the professionalism of a soldier and the enthusiastic determination of a zealot.

It was now Maria's turn to prove herself in organized combat as the General had back in the years before Sanctuary, the chaotic years of food and energy shortages, civil unrest, gang dominance, and declining population. Those years had been the turning point, the years in which conversion had mutated from a highly prized option for the few to an officially-encouraged government program and, then, ultimately, to the brutally-enforced, soul-sucking mandate it now was.

The intensity of recent events and the crucial nature of her immediate responsibilities quickly forced thoughts of history aside, however, and focused her concentration on upcoming tactical issues. She turned back to her troops, barked a few terse commands, and began quickly to walk toward the entryway. A formidable fighting force followed close on her heels, ready to cleanse the blasphemous ConFoes from the Believers' hidden and hitherto peaceful valley.

Unintelligible shouts from the entryway spurred Maria and her forces into double-time. A score of safeties clicked off almost simultaneously, the soft, sharp sound of each reverberating with the booted footfalls of the soldiers off the strong, sure walls of the main shaft.

As the doorway came into view of the anxious troops, a

scene of panic and pandemonium greeted them. Sentries and outside workers were streaming in the already partially shut metal door that would seal the mine.

Maria was about to protest that their enemies were few and that she had the forces to claim victory over them, when she realized that her kindred were not fleeing any mortal foe. Cries of "Fire!" drowned out all more detailed explanations and, as she raced ahead of her now somewhat confused troops, she saw that the simple word "fire" was insufficient to describe the nightmarish conflagration that was coursing quickly along the valley floor toward their precious Sanctuary, like the torrent from a burst dam in hell itself.

A continuous low roar rumbled from the rampaging wall of flames. A stiff rush of air from up-valley and even from the mine itself was sucked unceasingly toward the base of the firestorm, feeding it. Orange and yellow vortices whirled madly about the advancing line of incineration, reaching high into the thick smoke billowing into the sky and occasionally bending down to torch off a tree or spark another leap forward.

A lone sentry rushed in a heedless, yet exhausted, panic from the hot agony and death that bore down upon him. He flung himself toward the closing door and collapsed to the ground just inside the entrance at Maria's feet. His chest heaved for breath. "I'm . . . I'm . . . the last," he gasped between long, sucking breaths. His arm moved to comfort a painful stitch in his side as he attempted to focus and calm his thoughts.

He saw Maria staring down at him as the giant door continued to close.

"Intentional," he rasped as he exhaled. Seeing no comprehension on Maria's face, he gathered his thoughts anew and tried again. "They . . . the ConFoes . . . they set it."

Without another thought or word, Maria leapt out the closing door an instant before it clanged shut with finality. The dancing red and yellow and orange of the approaching fire was already reflected in the door's dull, weathered surface, but she paid it no mind as she raced away, southeast and upward, hoping, praying to stay ahead of the flames.

She had moved by instinct, before she had even thought it through consciously, but her racing thoughts matched the tempo and heat of the flames pursuing her as she put the tactical situation together during her new flight for a new sanctuary.

If the ConFoes set the fire, they were most probably not caught by it. The ConFoes tracking her were alive. The fire had been set to kill her. That meant they would now leave this place and report. Soon someone would investigate, and the entrances and ventilation shafts of Sanctuary, denuded of their cover of peaceful pines and scraggly undergrowth, would be noticed. And then the dreaded ConFoes would bring in whatever force they needed to destroy her home. They had to. Their entire ConFoe philosophy demanded it. Anyone who could not be converted, must be destroyed.

No exceptions. No survivors.

A rabbit streaked in front of her in wild-eyed panic, soon to be yet another innocent casualty of the ConFoes' philosophy of destruction.

Her instincts, her hind-brain, demanded that she flee blindly ahead, too. But she forced herself to stop, to think, to survey the terrain. The firestorm would certainly consume the valley; it would probably jump the lower ridge at the south end and careen on until the approaching weather slowed or stopped it. She needed to move out of its path, not before it. She needed to find a place where the rock and snow were free of fuel for the flames, where she could withstand the passing of the hellfire that consumed the valley and move back, back north and east toward the bastards who started this so she could stop them before they reported in.

Her eyes fixed upon a steep, barren patch of exposed rock well up the ridge wall. If she could clamber up fast enough and anchor herself somehow in the middle of the bare expanse and hide beneath her emergency blanket (courtesy of another ConFoe she had "met" since she had come to Sanctuary many years ago) while the fiery tumult scorched everything about her, she just might make it.

The door to Sanctuary remained firmly shut.

"I can't believe she did that," said the first watchman, shaking his head over Maria's foolhardy behavior. "She'll never survive."

"Anything's possible," responded his colleague in genuine awe of the display of faith he had just witnessed. "God works in mysterious ways."

All the next day, Derek staggered, zombie-like, through smoke and haze and falling ash back, east-southeast toward the rendezvous point, where they had left their vehicles to commence this misbegotten mission. The heavy smoke and ash of the unexplained forest fire to the southwest irritated his throat as he sucked in breath with a wheezing sound.

Several of his squad-mates held damp kerchiefs (or, in Manning's case, women's panties) over their mouths as they trudged along, but Derek had abandoned that tactic. He was too tired to hold his hand up to his mouth as he walked. Besides, any covering reduced the already meager amount of oxygen needed to fuel his muscles and what was left of his pain-racked brain.

He stopped for a moment and bent over, leaning on his

weapon like a cane, coughing flecks of blood onto the gray soot and ash that covered the low, lacy vegetation that held fast to the rocky ground. His life in the Conversion Forces had managed once again to reach a new low. The only thing he could imagine worse than this miserable mission would be to have to do it over and over again, like the damn training exercises back at boot. Then he heard A.K. and Manning somewhere ahead, greeting each other with tales of fire and conquest and death, and he knew he had been wrong. Bad as this had been, and it had been bad—physically, emotionally, and morally bad beyond all comprehension—the two psychopaths ahead would make the next mission even worse and the next and the next and the next.

Macho bullshit A.K. and his evil little ferret-boy, Manning, had made each and every day of his life in this squad worse than the day before for more days than he could remember. And the steady slide of life in the squad into an abyss of pain and torture and mayhem was rapidly accelerating. Maybe it wouldn't be forever, but it would be for a long, long time. Longer than he could possibly bear.

"Yo, Derek!" barked A.K. from up ahead, his graphic pleasantries with Manning apparently concluded for the moment. No doubt the gruesome debriefing and rehashing of the hellhole of a mission would be continued later at a conveniently amusing time, like over a meal. "Get your ass in gear," boomed their squad leader. "We gotta get the gear stowed and move out, find some clear air for the Hummer's laser relay link-up and report."

Derek was in no mood to move, much less comply.

"I'll provide look-out while Wires moves up and unloads," he shouted weakly, as Wires passed his position. The Converter moved slowly, but steadily, under his burden of equipment toward the vehicles.

Derek heard a string of expletives from A.K. as foul as the air about him.

"Fuckin' Wires. Can anybody tell me why we even bother to bring him along?"

Pancek felt obligated to fill the ensuing silence. "According to . . ."

"Shut up, moron!" A.K. immediately interrupted. "If I ever really need some asshole to quote regs to me, you'll know. I'll put a gun to your head and give you the time between when I pull the trigger and when the round enters your friggin' brain."

"You tell 'em," giggled Manning.

"You shut up, too, maggot! I'll kill you just for sport."

Sandoval showed some uncharacteristic *cojones* by distracting his violent companions. "Hey, man, let's chow down before we spleet."

Chow, now that might be worth making it back to the trucks. Still, Derek waited for a few minutes so he wouldn't have to help carry stuff. Finally, he heard the group begin to unload the Hummer, then a minor commotion and a string of curses from Manning, punctuated with "Gimme that back, you thief!"

That was the last discernable thing Derek heard of the squad, until the explosion.

Maria did not hear the last conversation between Derek and his squad-mates. She was too far away. But she did hear the explosion.

She had waited to hear and see the explosion.

Even though she knew it was coming, she involuntarily flinched at the sight of the blast. The fireball from the Hummer's fuel tank expanded in a hemisphere of orange-hued death before collapsing back upon itself and morphing into a black pillar of oily smoke. The greasy dark plume contrasted sharply with the lighter, cooler, pine-scented miasma of yellow smoke hanging over the wilds from the still-raging forest fire miles away to the west and south.

Her time on the steep, barren slab of granite the day before was still too fresh in her mind for her not to flinch at the sight of fire. It was only yesterday that the scorching orange death had sought her out, surrounding and attempting to crush in upon her as she took refuge under her blanket and breathed and re-breathed the air caught in her knapsack at the last moment before scrambling under the foil and asbestos cover.

It was a miracle that yesterday's fire had not consumed her, that she was even alive to flinch at the sight of today's fiery explosion. The purloined ConFoe blanket had, thank God, not failed her. In fact, it had performed remarkably well, reflecting and minimizing the transfer of heat from three sides as she was suspended in what seemed to be a lava lake in Hades itself.

Technology can be a wonderful thing when it's not ruining the world completely.

The first-degree burn on one side of her body was testimony that her plan had not been perfect, however. And even the relatively minor pain of that burn was too fresh and too closely associated with the searing flames of the orange death for her hind-brain not to scream for her to flee at the sight of this new fireball.

The granite on which she had pressed herself during the firestorm, already warm from the sun, had heated like a pizza stone in the conflagration, searing her as she pressed against it. Yet she had no choice but to press fiercely against the scalding rock, no ability to ease up and raise her body off it even a fraction of an inch, lest she dislodge the blanket or loose herself from her precarious perch and move from the frying pan into the howling fire.

In those minutes that seemed like ages, the fire also forged her soul, hardening her for the task ahead. She would not be the martyr. They would be martyrs. She would be the instrument of their martyrdom.

In one way, the fire made her task easier. Once the wall of flame had passed and she was able to move again, the smoke gave her cover. Her newly tempered resolve gave her speed. At first, she merely kept pace with the group of ConFoes that had pursued her as they returned the direction from whence they came. But, they had eventually stopped for the night and set watch, while she had continued on, past them, toward the highway, where their vehicles would be. As dawn broke, she had spied their trucks, even at some distance, during a period of relative air clarity. The sight had hastened her steps and made it easy to beat the plodding soldiers to the vehicles.

She had little in the way of special equipment with her, but a bit of wire, an opened gas tank, and a small electrical spark was all she had really needed.

When the pyre devouring the fuel and ammo and plastic and rubber that had once constituted the ConFoe vehicles died down and the smoke cleared, she would go back and check to make sure that they were all dead, that they were all martyrs to their unholy, blasphemous, technological cause.

After all, their godless technology had destroyed the world and now it was trying to destroy heaven.

Chapter 4

In the very instant of the flash of the explosion, Derek decided. He made no move, no flicker of a motion, toward his squad-mates.

In the moments that followed the showy destruction of the blast, while hunks of burning plastic and metal still rained down from the sky in a circle around the resulting crater, he consciously confirmed what his subconscious had decided unbidden. He closed his eyes only a second in thought, his retinas still retaining the after-image of the fireball that consumed the ConFoe equipment and personnel.

He would not make a move to save any of them. Not to tend their wounds and burns, not to comfort or convert them as they died, and certainly not to risk life and limb—even if he were not already himself a physical disaster—to pull them from the fiery wreckage. Not even if they called out in pain or screamed in writhing agony. He wrote them all off the second the explosion occurred.

He had not a scintilla of hesitation over A.K. or Manning.

A.K. was no more than a brutal thug, a gleeful hunter and exterminator of his fellow man, and a wannabe warlord of the most amoral type. He represented what the Conversion Forces had become as the number and quality of souls who were unconverted had dwindled. Men who served not from duty or obligation or honor, or even from stupidity in falling for the damn recruitment vids, but from bloodlust for the hunt and the megalomania that springs from the power of life and death. Derek felt no sorrow from the fact that apparently one of A.K.'s prey had successfully turned on the hunter. He imagined a squirrel—a sinewy gray and black squirrel like they had here in the west, not the chestnut, bushy-tailed things that had back east when he was a kid—dropping a round into a mortar tube and chittering gleefully as the round popped out of the tube and dropped through one of A.K.'s putrid smoke-rings, right into the bastard's lap.

He wouldn't . . . couldn't ever . . . lift a finger to save A.K., not if the asshole was screaming for help as he burned right in front of him. It's not that Derek wanted to hear the screams, but it would somehow be satisfying to know that the macho jerk screamed like a little girl.

As for Manning, well Manning aspired to be a macho amoral asshole like A.K., but he didn't have the strength or the skill or the cunning or the discipline or the self-control or, quite frankly, the quality of character to be a ruthless, amoral hunter. No, Manning was a whiny, vicious, pathetic, immoral psychopath. He was the type of individual who graduated from incinerating ants with a magnifying glass to pulling the wings off flies to exploding frogs with firecrackers and then turned mean. He was the kid you always suspected when a cherished family pet went missing and who always acted as a brainless henchman for the biggest bully in school. He was the guy you would never trust alone with your girl, with any girl. He was the maniac you always thought about when you heard a news story about a rooftop sniper or a string of grisly serial murders. He represented what the Conversion Forces were becoming—a corps of evil sadists, delighting in torturing and annihilating the weak, the passive resisters, the moralists, and the religious types—the better humans who remained unconverted—just for the sheer sick pleasure of creating and causing terror.

No, if Manning was roasting vigorously right before him,

Derek would pour kerosene on the fire and piss on the ashes only after they stopped smoldering. There was not a single thing that could have improved Derek's life . . . or what remained of life in this world . . . more at this moment than for the psycho little bastard to be blown straight to hell.

Derek did have some modicum of remorse for Digger, Pancek, and Sandoval. Each was, in his own manner, like him, just trying to get along and do his duty as a member of the Conversion Forces. Digger in his relaxed good ol' boy way, Pancek doing his quiet, professional best, and Sandoval trying to fit in, but hating himself for doing it. But Derek knew, also like him, they all would just keep marching forward and following orders and doing what they were told to do without having the gumption or the backbone or the strength of character to resist the accelerating slide of the Conversion Forces into the terror death squads that Manning had wet dreams about.

But, it was also because they were just like him that Derek had only a tinge of remorse or sympathy for the trio. He knew deep in his mind (only mals believed they had souls) that, like him, they never would have forsaken their duty or taken action to check out of this world with pills or a gun or a rope, but that they all wished on most days that somehow it would happen. They craved death because they hated their duty, they hated their life, and they hated that they didn't have the integrity or the character or the courage to do anything about it.

No, if any of the three of them were aflame before his eyes, he wouldn't move to save them, because it was clear to him that they wanted to escape this world. And death, even an agonizing, tortured death, was the only way to escape the ConFoes, absent unauthorized conversion. Even if Derek had his gun in his hand as they burned and sizzled close before him and even if his tired, quivering muscles could hold the weapon steady enough to shorten their trip into nonexistence, he would probably not even attempt that mercy, because he knew that, like him, they also recognized that they deserved to suffer for what they had done. More accurately, what they had allowed to be done.

Wires caused Derek the only hesitation—a second or two before he confirmed by deliberation what his mind had instantly determined. It's not that Wires was an order of magnitude more noble or moral or brave than Digger or Pancek or Sandoval. He, too, had kept his nose to his own responsibilities when terrible things had occurred, yet he had always endeavored to make conversion readily available. No one had died or been beaten to death or destroyed because Wires was slow or the equipment was not being efficiently handled or assembled.

Wires had made some effort in his own quiet, limited way, but he still shared the responsibility and likely the mindset of Digger, Pancek, and Sandoval. No, Derek had a few second's hesitation in rethinking Wires' pain-wracked demise only because killing a Converter was like killing a non-combatant, like offing a priest, back when priests were respected and revered by civilized society. Wires' only purpose on the squad was to orient the mals, give them a choice, and allow them to convert if they so chose.

But Wires was a throwback to what the Conversion Forces had once been meant to be. He had not converted anyone in months, and between the tactics of the ConFoes and the recalcitrance of the remaining mals, it wasn't likely he would have converted anyone anytime soon. Wires no longer had a place here. Derek would not make a move to keep him here.

If Derek were a better man, maybe, just maybe, he would have tried to save Wires. He might have been able to save the tech and use his bulky scanner to convert him if Derek were strong and brave and had high ideals. But none of that was true. Derek was weak and tired and injured and depressed physically, emotionally, and morally. Besides, if poor, diligent Wires was blown to smithereens, Derek was convinced that Wires' precious scanner was burning alongside him. Better to let fate take its course.

Derek wasn't sure how he had really decided all this, when he had written off every friend he had left in this world. Perhaps it was intuitive. He certainly had no memory of ever thinking it all through beforehand. Yet the mind is quicker and deeper than one's conscious thoughts. It could have been simulating hypothetical scenarios on its own accord during his body's arduous treks up and down mountainsides searching for their elusive and misguided quarry.

Perhaps none of it had been decided before the flash of the explosion. Perhaps he was simply a coward, a man without enough character to care for his squad-mates, and it had merely taken a few moments after the manifestation of his inherent character flaw for his clever mind to fix upon a series of plausible and comforting rationalizations as to why abandoning his comrades was the correct thing to do.

His combat sense, the part of him that had been trained and drilled and instructed in military maneuvers at ConFoe boot-camp, knew that it was likely that the enemy was here . . . now . . . and that it was also likely that the mals did not know that Derek was in the vicinity. If they did know, surely they would have waited to trigger the explosion until he had joined the others.

Of course, it was also quite possible that the detonation was an unmanned booby-trap and he had just been lucky enough not to be at the wrong place at the wrong time. Still again, the mals could be watching the vehicles and his companions burn right now from cover. Any move he would make to save his companions or even to cry out in anguish over their wretched demise would bring the enemy upon him.

And as much as he was in pain and despised his miserable existence and loathed himself for failing to instinctively move to save his companions, right now he chose life. To do anything other than to hunker down and wait and see was not a rational choice for continuing that life.

He tenderly lowered himself into the waist-high, dry, wheat-colored buffalo grass, as the acrid, thick haze of the vehicle fires rolled vigorously by. He would wait and see.

It was many hours 'til dark and there was nothing he dared do before then.

Maria never thought or rethought for a nanosecond about lifting a finger to rescue or relieve the suffering of the savage ConFoes. If she had been close enough to hear their screams, their horror would not have affected her one iota. She had done her duty in a war . . . a war that was a matter of more than life and death to the Believers . . . a war that was a matter of life and life after death.

The torment of the ConFoes in this world was nothing compared to the anguish that faced their heathen souls in the afterlife. They had long since chosen that terror by their words, their actions, their non-beliefs. Now they were martyrs to non-belief.

But then, martyrs have always abounded in religious wars.

At some point, when she was sure she was safe from any survivors, as well as from detonations from any of smoldering ammunition and provisions that remained, Maria would inspect her handiwork, count the bodies—Joshua had been sure there had been seven—and return to Sanctuary.

Right now she was tired. Dead tired. Killing tired.

She slept the sleep of the righteous . . . the exhausted, wounded, and seemingly victorious righteous.

She awoke thoroughly pissed off.

Chapter 5

Again Derek awoke in blackness and in pain. It had not been a good night. Swirling black smoke and unseen, sinister forces had tormented him in his dreams and his muscles had stiffened in odd positions as he lay sprawled in the buffalo grass. He absently brushed the gnats away from his face and vowed to check himself thoroughly for chiggers and deer ticks when it was light. Yeah, the insects were inheriting the world, but they didn't need to do it at his expense.

He cautiously raised his head above the level of the grass. A gentle northwesterly breeze had arisen anew during the night and pushed the haze of A.K.'s wildfire away from the abandoned highway. The destroyed ConFoe vehicles were no doubt long since burnt out, too, as he could see stars twinkling in the sky in that direction.

It was good to have awoken before daybreak—the darkness would give him cover to investigate the site of yesterday's destruction and recover any useable supplies without being noticed by any mal watchers on the far ridges.

Supplies or no, though, he wasn't sure his aching body was up for the challenges he now faced, alone in the Rockies—one of the last bastions of the mals—with no transportation. But his difficulties would only increase if the mals saw him. The highway, nestled into valleys and passes in the shadow of majestic mountain peaks, was too easily seen and too closely watched to be safe without the weapons and manpower with which the ConFoe team had first arrived.

He had best get on with it.

Making his way quickly down the slope on the faint game trail his squad-mates had followed the day before, Derek scanned the scrubby bushes and young pines that littered the area for movement. Something, after all, had made this trail and he no more wished to meet a mountain lion or black bear than he did a mal patrol.

There was, however, no movement save his own and the murmur of the gentle breeze.

Finally, he followed the game trail around the corner of an erosion ridge and came in view of the highway. Even in the starlight, the wide ribbon of Interstate 70 gleamed a ghostly gray as it stretched through the wilderness, marred only by the burned out hulks of the two ConFoe Hummers smack-dab in the middle of the westbound passing lane. There had been no reason to pull off onto the shoulder before parking, not anymore. Besides, the placement of the vehicles would force any attacker closing on them to traverse open ground, making the squad's parking selection one of the few tactical military decisions that A.K. had gotten right this mission.

Surrounding the vehicles were various hard-to-recognize lumps of debris, charred supplies, and other things best left unidentified. Derek gathered up a few scorched MREs he found scattered about. One of the boxes had apparently been open when the blast occurred, propelling the nutritious but pasty military meals in a wide arc near the edge of the debris line. Heavier items had been consumed by the fireball and resulting inferno. His erstwhile comrades fell in that category, he was sure.

It was dark and there wasn't much he could readily scrounge, but along with the MREs he did find a partially burned topographical map of the area, an extra canteen, and a working flashlight. He tested the flashlight by hunching his body over it and flipping the switch with the beam pressed against his thigh, so as to not reveal his presence. He was about to give up his search for additional items when a metallic glint caught his eye, down the road a ways, behind the guardrail in the center median.

He arced to his left, edging slightly closer, his eyes peeled on the position of the brief glimmer of light. There it was again, a momentary flicker of some sort. He froze and moved his head back and forth slowly, trying to recreate the angle. Finally he managed to catch it again. Straining, he finally made out that the light was merely a reflection of the stars from an irregular three-foot high lump leaning against the backside of the guardrail.

He watched for several minutes, but the lump was motionless—more motionless than he could have remained even with his ConFoe training. He unslung his weapon, fingered off the safety with slow, even pressure, and moved toward the lump, ready to fire the second it twitched.

No twitch came as he approached, however, and Derek eventually discerned that the lump was an emergency blanket draped over something or someone. Stepping carefully over the guardrail ten feet west of the object, he crept stealthily forward.

Finally, his left hand trembling as he reached forward, still attempting with his right to keep his rifle trained on the target, he grasped and flung the blanket up and to his left over the guardrail revealing . . .

. . . Wires' conversion equipment pack.

The meticulous Converter had apparently set the valuable equipment aside while the crew had unloaded boxes of food for a quick snack before departure. Mindful of the effects of sun and dust on the machinery, he had no doubt draped his own emergency blanket over the pack, before joining the others in preparing foodstuff. Now the pack was all that remained intact of the squad's extensive equipment and supplies.

The scanner would be a bitch to carry. Heavy, unwieldy, and somewhat fragile, it would be a definite burden for Derek. But it was ConFoe equipment, he was still on a mission, and it would be against regulations to leave it behind or destroy it, not that the latter would prevent him from hiding behind the bulky machinery for cover if he got into another firefight. The conversion scanner also included an integrated, short-range laser communications device, which could come in handy when he got within line-of-sight of a ConFoe facility. Besides, the equipment in this pack was what the Conversion Forces were supposed to be all about. Conversion was the essence of their mission. And he believed in their mission, at least the idealized version of their mission, even though the reality of service had become increasingly brutal and shameful.

Derek sat in the dirt, shouldered on the bulky pack, and pushed himself upright, using the dull and pitted metal guardrail for support. He slung his weapon as best he could given the wide pack, stepped back over the guardrail, and headed northeasterly off the highway. The interstate was too dangerous and, from the glow on the horizon in that direction, A.K.'s fire raged on somewhere to the southwest.

He would head northeast and figure things out with more precision come daybreak.

As he looked back at the devastation one last time, he was sure this was a scene that would never be in a recruitment vid.

Maria stirred from her well-deserved slumber and her emergency blanket reflected not starlight, but the glaring rays of the mid-day sun.

She was pissed. Not at the sun, but at herself. She had

slept well into the day, much longer than she intended. She berated herself mentally and gazed down upon the scene of yesterday's destruction. All was silent. All was still.

She took care of her necessary biological functions, then sat for a bit, still irked at her dereliction. She watched the highway while she nibbled at some rations and swigged a bit of water. Still, there was no sign of movement, no sign of life or rescue on its way.

Finally, she made her way down to the scene, itself. Maybe she could find some food or salvage some equipment or find some information of use to Sanctuary. Of course, before she could do any of that, she had to verify her kills. It's not that she gloried in the body count or made notches in her gun stock, it was simply a matter of good military tactics.

It was neither an easy nor a pleasant task.

The first four bodies were grisly, but not that difficult to verify. She guessed that the largest one was the ape that had shot at her and most likely torched Sanctuary's valley. He had been in the driver's seat of the lead vehicle when the explosion occurred. The body was black, the skin and muscle charred and cindered by the fire that had consumed the vehicle. Unfortunately, the ape's neck was also broken. The bastard had probably been killed by the initial concussion and had not suffered at all, certainly not enough. If she were lucky, though, his neck might have broken, but left him conscious, to watch in terror as his unfeeling, motionless body grilled like a well-done steak.

The other three of the four easily confirmed kills had apparently been standing near the back of the lead truck when the explosion occurred. The shock wave had propelled the three soldiers hard into the front of the second truck and trapped them in the inferno that consumed both vehicles. From the position of their bodies, she guessed that they all had died even before the time of the secondary explosions from the rear vehicle and its stores of ammunition. She didn't look for dogtags. The ConFoes disdained them, given their superior firepower and attitude. Besides, the names of these heathens meant nothing to her. To her, they were indistinguishable from one another, except that one had apparently carried a shovel.

The next two kills were much harder to find. She widened her search outward from the vehicles until she came across an unburned body in the ditch on the north side of the roadway, well behind the vehicles. Apparently, this one had been on the highway outside of the radius of the fireball. Maybe he had even had time to dive for cover, but he had been unsuccessful in that effort. A jagged piece of shrapnel protruded from his neck and the dirt was sticky and wet beneath his head, his blue eyes staring up vacantly into the sky. This was the one that had always carried the heavy pack, though she could see no sign of it now. She knew that it marked him as a high priest of their godforsaken technology and, therefore, made him more dangerous than the sadists and hunters and torturers and murderers that accompanied him. This one endangered the soul.

The bastard had almost gotten away. It was proof of the divine that a single hunk of metal had taken him out so thoroughly. She was glad he was dead and prayed that his satanic equipment was one of the heaps of molten slag that littered the scene. She hoped even more fervently that his two missing companions were also among the heaps of molten slag.

When she found no more corpses at the outer limit of the blast radius, she was forced to work her way back in, more slowly, more methodically, to see if she had missed anything. The arsenal in the back of the rear truck had done a lot of damage; it could be that there was not much left to find. She resigned herself that she might be looking for nothing more than body parts, then trying to figure how many different bodies they came from.

Finally, late in the afternoon, she found the evidence she had sought so ardently. It wasn't much—a blood soaked spot, remnants of a bloody ConFoe jacket, a bit of hair, and some small bone fragments in the scorched crater beneath the back of the second transport. A small man had apparently sought refuge underneath the chassis when the lead truck had exploded. Even with the high clearance of the ConFoe Hummers, he would have to have been wiry and nimble to have taken cover so quickly.

Trapped by the flaming fuel and plastic that surrounded him and set the second truck ablaze, he had, she mused, probably pulled his jacket over his head in a desperate and futile attempt to escape the heat and smoke. Odds are he was already dead from the fire or smoke inhalation when the arsenal above him had gone off and his inert body had been pummeled repeatedly into the asphalt by a crate of bullets and a collection of satchel charges. Finally, she guessed, the grisly remains had been incinerated by the burning fuel and then pulverized or dispersed when the rack of armor-piercing mortars blew, leaving nothing but a greasy red smear and a tuft of hair mixed with gray matter on the cratered pavement beneath the rear axle.

Bad choice, small guy.

That made six.

Joshua had said there were seven in the patrol. She thought that she had confirmed Joshua's count when she had sighted the fragments of the squad as she moved past her foe from a distance, though it was difficult to tell for sure through the dappled light and intervening branches of the pine forest.

Six.

She took a break, then gathered up a few salvageable MREs and ate one of the bland, unrecognizable entrees as she thought.

Maybe her count was wrong. Maybe Joshua had killed one of the ConFoes before he had died. She had to know. She could not return to Sanctuary not knowing.

The sun was already heading for the peaks in the west. Damn! Why had she slept away so much of the day? The coming darkness was no friend to any of the possibilities that faced her.

Finally she strode rapidly to the outer perimeter of the area she had searched. She wasn't the best tracker in Sanctuary, but she was probably good enough to tell if anyone had left this place. If not, she could always attempt to track back along the more trampled route from where the ConFoes had hiked and see if she could find a body—a ConFoe body lying somewhere next to Joshua.

Tracking, tracking was the key to gaining the information needed. And tracking was tough, tedious work, even under the best of circumstances. It hadn't been the best of circumstances for a long, long time and things didn't seem to be getting any better.

Chapter 6

Derek's speed increased somewhat once he found a gravel roadway. True, he had shied away from the highway as too visible, too dangerous. But trudging his bruised and battered body cross-country with a hundred pounds of cumbersome equipment was no way to make progress toward anything but an eventual heart attack. It was tricky and dangerous in the dark; in the light, it was hot and agonizingly slow.

At midmorning he rested in the shade alongside a rivulet of clear, cold water that meandered through an idyllic meadow in a flat vale. He took a swig of water and examined his map fragment. After some effort, he knew where he was. The problem was, Derek had no real idea where he should go.

The com unit contained in the scanning equipment was short-range only; the long-range laser hook-up was with A.K. in the truck and had been completely fried. Without decent communications gear, he only really had two choices, neither of them good.

The first alternative was to locate a useable vehicle and return to the ConFoe's southwestern base in Arizona—hundreds of miles away. Maybe he would get lucky and meet up with a ConFoe patrol on the way. Then again, in an unauthorized vehicle with no identifying beacon, he might get unlucky and be targeted at range by A.K.'s cousins in arms.

Second, he could find an open spot, set up camp, and start a campfire, then wait to be spotted by the ConFoe satellites. Of course, that could take some time, given the spreading wildfire that his very team had ignited to the southwest. It would also make him quite visible to the mals, if any were about. And, again, even if the ConFoes spotted him first and sent a team, they would likely take him for a mal or a deserter and shoot first and ask questions later . . . over his dead body.

Transportation was his best bet in a rigged game. Cars meant roads, so he calculated a vector to the nearest backwoods road and hefted back on the pack and took to his task.

Duty is most easily accomplished when you are too tired to think.

As he mindlessly put one foot in front of the other, Derek's mind wandered back to the recruiting vid years before.

"One family, one volunteer. The Conversion Forces need you to make sure your family is safe for their conversion and beyond. Don't let the rabble-rousers, the cultists, the gangs, and the lunatics take eternity away from your loved ones or from you. Help yourself and your family while helping both mankind and the few remaining and misguided malcontents by enforcing the next, mandatory phase of man's evolution. We are looking for enthusiastic outdoor types as well as technically proficient altruists, so don't worry. We have a spot for you in this world and the next. Transferable conversion preferences and credits awarded based on qualifications and length of service guaranty. One family, one volunteer, one tour. An infinite future for you and yours."

The insipid jingle and patriotic music still resonated in his head now four, no five, years later. He hated the music, hated the jingle, hated the Conversion Forces. The only redeeming thing about the whole debacle was that they had been true to their word about the credits. As soon as he had completed boot camp, they had issued the credits based on his training scores and his overly enthusiastic six-year commitment. He had immediately transferred them to his mom for Katy, so her conversion would be appropriately modified.

Just a bit longer and he would see her on Alpha Two, smiling and running up to greet him. Just another year. For now, though, it was another step. And another, and another, and another into his infinite future.

That's when he saw the cabin.

Maria did not sleep well.

Her mind returned again and again to the tracks she had found as twilight fell—tracks leading away from her faux triumph over the ConFoes.

She saw the maniacal ConFoe butcher heading to a high spot, calling in to his evil brethren, and leading a force of man-apes, swarming over the crags and charcoal deadfalls of her once peaceful, living vale into the halls of Sanctuary itself. The hideous primates chittered and screamed in ghoulish delight as they ran down the men and women of her home and ate the babies. The man-apes jumped up and down on the chests of the defeated and pulled off their arms until the Believers begged for conversion.

Then, pale goblinesque creatures in white coats strapped down the tortured souls and attached sensors and electrodes to them and turned on their hideous computers and equipment. The Believers screamed in terror and pain and shame as their immortal souls were sucked out of their bodies and placed into small, but secure, stainless steel canisters.

The goblins gave the man-apes the soul-filled canisters and the beasts shook them violently and placed them in a pit of charcoal and napalm. They lit the petroleum jelly and danced and howled as the flames licked greedily at the sides of the canisters, searing them with white-hot intensity forever.

And between the howls of the man-apes and the queer

whizzing of the goblins' soul-sucking machines, she could hear the cries of anguish of the Believers, deep inside the sterile, stainless steel hell they had chosen in their weakness. Some cried her name, accusing her. "Maria, she's the one," they'd say, "Sanctuary fell because of her."

Above all else, though, she heard the cries of the children. They would not be ignored. They would not be silenced. "Mommy, Mommy," cried one tiny, terrified voice, "why did she lead them here? Why did she let them get away? Why do I burn and burn and burn?"

The dreams echoed in Maria's mind as she awoke. The cries of the Believers stayed with her as she returned to the trail she had found and started on her way. With no one to assist her, no one to give orders to or take orders from, no one to talk with her, she knew the voices would not fade until she banished them by action or by death.

She was no expert, but it seemed that her quarry was heavily laden and moving slowly. Although she probably moved not much faster, given the need to track, his pace was the only thing that gave her hope.

It gave her hope, but it didn't banish the screams.

Derek hadn't expected to see any structures at all along this weed-infested stretch of gravel roadway. The single, un-improved lane had meandered higher and higher toward a saddle-pass between two towering snow-capped peaks. The saddle itself was just above the tree line, probably something just short of 11,000 feet at this latitude. The cabin was several hundred feet below the top edge of the trees. The slope fell off sharply, leaving the cabin's front clearly visible from the south despite the somewhat stunted piney growth on all sides. It had to be situated well over 10,000 feet above sea level.

Great view, but a hell of an inconvenient place to live. Socked in by snow a good bit of the year, subject to sudden fierce storms even in the good season, and damn scarce of oxygen. Of course, those same things would also mean that no one would bother you much way up here. Hell, even the ConFoe satellites didn't regularly search for infrared sources at this altitude.

But there it was, a picturesque little cabin perched most of the way up a mountain. Oh, it wasn't pretty like those log cabin kit places that the contractors hereabouts used to push to the summer tourists, but it was square and true, with a genuine birch rocker on the porch, and a real glass window on the south side. Derek hadn't seen a non-military building with unbroken ground-level windows for years. A path wound around the cabin from the east side of the porch to a small lake in a well-rounded depression on a brief plateau to that side.

The apparent good repair of the cabin and the fact that the path to the lake was visible from a distance surprised Derek and put him on guard. Someone had taken care of this place; someone had been here on a regular basis and not that long ago. He looked closer, inspecting every detail, then cursed himself for his oblivious stupidity when he noticed it. A faint wisp of smoke was rising from the natural stone chimney.

Danger, perhaps, but also an opportunity to get what he needed. He slipped off to the side of the poor excuse for a road where he could sit and think, but still keep an eye on the place. It was still a bit of a hike to the cabin, all uphill and much of it exposed to that big picture window view.

Just because he was tired and hungry and longed for shelter, a hot meal, and a speedy ride out of the wilderness was no reason to go off half-cocked. Survival and duty were the only things left to him now.

★ ★ ★ ★ ★

Despite her merely serviceable tracking ability, Maria had only two really major delays in her belated following of the seventh ConFoe. The first came when the fellow had suddenly and inexplicably changed directions three-quarters of the way across an alpine valley.

She was surprised and dismayed when she suddenly realized there were no more tracks in the direction she and supposedly her foe had been heading. She lost time while she backtracked to find out when the guy had changed course, searching slowly to either side of his earlier vector looking for the minute signs of human passage through the wilderness. She lost even more time as she pondered the course change.

Had he received some communication? Had he seen something? Did he know he was being pursued?

He didn't appear to be hunting for game or hiding. The tracks along the new vector showed no more signs of stealth or attempts to take cover than had those she had followed earlier. It was like the fellow had one of those GPS navigational systems they used to put in personal cars and that annoyed everyone by mouthing off, "Turn left in seventy-five meters, turn left in fifty meters, turn now, continue for four point three kilometers," until their owners turned them off or replaced them with a screen that gave constant stock market updates as they drove along.

The second major delay was when she tracked her quarry onto one of those scenic roads that traversed the back passes and wandered aimlessly, though spectacularly, through the old national forests. It was not that the gravel route provided no way for her to continue to track the ConFoe scum. The occasional scuff in the gravel or trampled weed continued to provide solid, if infrequent, confirmation that she was still on target. In places, there was even enough dusting from the yellow pollen of the Ponderosa pines to make out a boot-print. But even the meager width of the roadway made it difficult to easily scan to either side to determine if number seven had gotten new traffic instructions and careened off unexpectedly somewhere on a new tangent. For a while, her pace slowed considerably as she veered from one side of the right-of-way to the other, searching the shoulders for signs of passage into the trees beyond.

Finally, she decided to stop trying and rely on the fact that the guy had decided to follow this overgrown and underused four-wheel drive roadway. If she didn't see any confirming telltales of his passage for a mile or so, she could always come back and look more carefully.

Number seven wasn't Superman. As long as she made reasonably good time and put in what she imagined was a longer day than he, she would catch up to him. Tomorrow or the day after, at worst. Then, then he would face her and die.

Chapter 7

Derek sucked unenthusiastically on the packaging from his last MRE. It was best to build up his energy for whatever lay ahead. By morning he would either have new stores of food from the cabin or he would be dead and in the process of being turned into beef-jerky by some crazed lunatic that had taken refuge up here during the riots and gang wars that had plagued the cities after mandatory conversion had taken effect. Either way, MREs were not in his immediate future and he was grateful for that at least.

He tossed the foil container casually aside with no more respect for nature than A.K. habitually had shown.

He would wait for nightfall, then move up the road, past the winding and overgrown driveway that once serviced the cabin. Once well beyond and up-slope of the cabin, he would stash his non-combat supplies and come back down-slope upon the cabin from the rear. A quick reconnoiter and he would slip in and surprise the sleeping occupant. He hoped whatever deranged coot lived here was not quite so crazy that he set a nightly spring-gun trap on the doorway. There was no way to tell and it would considerably mess up his plan, not to mention his filthy uniform, if the discharge from a sawed-off shotgun mangled his face and chest into steak tartare.

Best to keep low as he went in the door, just in case.

He napped fitfully 'til midnight, thankfully without dreaming, then set about his plan in the pale moonlight. The trek up-slope took longer than he anticipated; distances can be deceiving in the mountains. He took special care as he passed the long driveway that curved up toward the cabin, but he sensed nothing but the squeak and sway of a faded sign hung on a wooden post at the end of the drive. *For Sale. Coldwell Banker. Agent Ken Ritchart.*

That had to be pretty old. Who would pay good money for something as completely useless as land?

He refocused his efforts and moved on up the road a quarter mile toward the pass, dropped off his heavy pack of scanning equipment, then turned right into the brush and doubled back toward his target. The sparse and scraggly trees above the cabin provided little effective cover as he made his way back down, attempting to be stealthy as he gingerly picked his way down the steep, rocky slope. Fortunately, the cabin had no windows on the north side—sensible from an architectural standpoint given the shade and the pressure from uphill snowpack during the winter—so he felt relatively safe in his approach.

He reached the rear wall of the cabin and carefully pressed against it, straining to discern any sound through the minute chinks that might exist in the filler between the thick, sturdy wood, but there was none. It could be a sign that all was still and quiet within or merely a sign of competent construction and good maintenance—there was no telling which.

Derek took a few minutes to catch his breath from both the tension and the physical exertion of his approach, then moved around the side of the structure away from the road and slipped to the edge of the front porch. He ducked under the smooth, de-barked pine railing onto the worn planks of the porch, itself. Crouching so as to stay beneath the unblinking glare of the picture window, he shifted his weight slowly from one foot to the other as he pressed toward the door, mindful of the need for silence.

He stared at the door and at the porch immediately in

front of it for a full minute. Somehow, something was wrong; his combat senses tingled with warning. But try as he might, he couldn't discern the problem. The door was plain enough, rough-cut hardwood timbers banded by three black iron strips, with a simple latch to match. No tripwires or triggers were visible, at least not in the light that the night afforded him. The boards on the porch were worn in a gentle arc outside the door, the obvious result of ten thousand steps or more having trod in a familiar pattern over the years gone by. No, there was not even a peephole through which he might be being watched.

Suddenly, he realized what his eyes had registered earlier, but his mind had ignored. He looked up with a start to his left.

Where the hell was the fucking rocking chair?

"Nice evening for a sit along the lake, doncha' think?" The raspy old voice came from a scrub of trees thirty-five feet away, even with the front of the cabin, but toward the lake. Derek turned rapidly toward the sound, cursing his incompetence; the whole time he had been circling around that side of the cabin, his senses had been focused inward, toward the structure itself, ignoring the full field of battle.

"Slowly there, fella. I'd just as sure blow you in half from this distance, but it would leave a heckuva stain on the porch and I'd have to clean it real good, so'n it wouldn't attract any critters. Besides, a piece of shot might take out my nice, purty window and I reckon you ain't worth a window."

Derek instinctively slowed his movement and spread his arms away from his body, his right hand still clutching his automatic weapon. Never disagree with someone who has the drop on you, at least not until you can assess the situation and come up with a plan.

As he turned, he saw the old codger, leaning forward in his

rocker, elbows on the arms of the chair as he casually waved the gun at Derek's midsection. White hair spilled out beneath a John Deere Construction Equipment baseball cap, topping a wrinkled, weather-beaten face framed by an unruly white and gray beard. The old man sported a plaid, long-sleeved shirt with several dark stains; sturdy, but worn, jeans; and heavy hiking boots.

He was old, but neither feeble nor palsied. The gun was steady in his hands. Derek could probably take him in a fair fight—even with the bruises and stiffness that still assaulted his midsection—but he saw no way to get into such a situation. Rushing the gent would be sure to get him blown away. Even bringing his weapon and its rubber bullets to bear would take enough time for the codger to make a decision to fire, picture window be damned. Derek stalled for time.

"Uh, sorry. You startled me." He made a show of slowly lowering his weapon to the planks of the porch. "Just for protection, you know. I was . . . I was about to knock and see if anybody was living here and, you know, maybe take refuge inside for the night."

The old man snorted in disgust and derision. "Hellfire, boy. Don't lie to me. Here I come all the way out here to live, so'n I don't get lied to by the politicians and the salesmen and all the rest o' what passes for civilization, then you have to go and come all the way up here just to lie to me straight off. Tain't no way to start a respectable conversation."

There was no reason to lie, but the instinct of a prisoner is always to do so, not so much to deprive the enemy of information, but as a way of attempting to assert some control over a situation where, in fact, none exists.

"Sorry, I . . . uh . . . just came over the pass . . ."

"Hell's bells, you did," interrupted his captor. "Ya came straight up the old scenic ridge road, stopped mid-afternoon, then snuck about for more'n an hour, huffin' and puffin' and gruntin' your way uphill, then crashin' and slippin' your way back down the hill." The coot squinted slightly and looked him up and down. "Stashed somethin' uphill, too, by the looks of it."

There was no use pretending anymore. Besides, Derek didn't really want an enemy. He wanted food, shelter, and some transportation back to what passed for a life on this godforsaken world. He exhaled deeply and made a conscious decision to relax.

"For somebody in the middle of nowhere, you keep a pretty good eye out for intruders."

The old guy snorted again, but relaxed sufficiently to actually rock slightly in his chair.

"You get dropped on your head a lot when you were young?" He paused momentarily, but didn't really wait for a response to his question. " 'Cause, you sure ain't that bright, boy. Look over your right shoulder, back south and west. Whaddya see?"

Derek strained his neck back and to the right, his tense muscles creaking with the unaccustomed stretching. South and west, an orange glow still glimmered behind the dark profiles of intervening mountains and ridgelines.

"Started up a few days ago," noted his captor. "Kinda hard to miss, especially before the wind shifted."

Derek felt stupid, but he again felt he was on top of the situation. He had come from where the fire was, so its lingering presence was natural to him. No doubt it had scared this old mountain man. He turned back, with a knowing smile. "So, you were watching the fire, in case you had to . . ." He almost said "head for the hills" before he thought better of it, ". . . uh . . . evacuate."

The old man stopped rocking and shook his head. "Tarnation, boy. You apparently got dropped on the head up until you was full-growed." He stood up. "Fire's a good piece away and the breeze has been away from here more'n a day now, so it ain't headed hereabouts. 'Sides, there's a good stretch of burnt timber between it and here, even if'n the wind were to shift back. Things are quiet here, but not so quiet that watching a dull orange glow darn near thirty miles away passes for entertainment." The hermit shifted his hips left and right and shrugged his shoulders to work out the stiffness and kinks from having sat motionless for such a long time.

Derek waited for him to explain.

"Y'see, there weren't no weather the day the fire started. It weren't no lightning strike. These days, a fire startin' where there ain't been lightning means one of two things. The most likely is people—either stupid people not mindin' their camp-fire or stupider ones yet, tossin' their lit cancer-sticks into the brush, less'n, o' course, they just be pyromaniacs startin' fires for jollies or some sick gratification or somesuch. And people, well people almost always mean trouble. That's why I moved out here."

Derek was right. The old coot was a hermit. No telling how long he had been out here.

"What's the second?" Derek asked politely.

"Huh?"

"You said fire without a storm meant one of two things. What's the second?"

"Not too bright, but you do pay attention. Coal seams."

Now it was Derek's turn to say, "Huh?"

"Sometimes you get fires in the mountains, underground fires in the seams of coal. They burn away slow and quiet like, cause there ain't much oxygen under the ground. Every once in a while, they reach the surface or the rocks shift and the fire gets exposed to the air and they flare up."

81

Derek had never heard of, had never imagined, such a thing.

"What starts them in the first place?"

"Hell, if I know. Some of 'em, they be goin' fer thirty, forty, a hunnert years or more. Back when the rich folk all took to buildin' places in the mountains, you know, down at the lower elevations, they'd just build whole developments right on top of some coal seam fire, then act all surprised and outraged when sudden-like there would be this big fire all around 'em. People are stupid."

"That's the truth," agreed Derek.

"Stupid and mean," continued the old man. He gestured with his shotgun, bringing the wandering aim back on target as a way of getting back on subject. "Time to prove you're smart and nice. No more fibs. I'm an old guy and I don't take too kindly to wastin' any time I got, even if I don't get much by the way of conversation lately."

Derek collected his thoughts for a moment. Aside from the macho bullshit banter and insults of the squad, Derek hadn't really had a conversation himself—not a real conversation—for a long, long time. Not only that, but he was still on a mission. He did still have a duty and maybe, just maybe, he would get a chance to perform it without interference from A.K.'s brutality and Manning's delight in terror. And if he was going to be stuck in this world and finish out his service in the Conversion Forces, he'd best be thinking about what he was supposed to be doing here.

So Derek began at the very beginning, with an introduction. "My name is Derek, Derek Williger."

The old man looked at him for a moment before responding without lowering his weapon. "Kyle Patterson."

"You're not going to believe this, I expect, Mr. Patterson, but I'm from the government and I'm here to help."

★ ★ ★ ★ ★

If he'd been alone when she found him, it would have been easy to kill him. Aside from his one abrupt change in direction, there had been nothing to indicate that he was concerned about being followed, about being tracked like they had tracked and hunted her. It probably would have been easy to sweep down on him unawares, even perhaps while he slept, with her weapon blazing and cries of victory and vengeance for Joshua, for Sanctuary, frothing on her lips.

Maria gazed through the night-scope on her weapon up at the vignette taking place in front of the mountainside hideaway. Given the dim light, the distance, and the fact that the dusty lens was old and scratched from use by others less careful with equipment than she, the scene was difficult to make out with precision. Her ConFoe prey was on the porch, apparently without a weapon, talking to a man on the ground, off toward the small lake to the right of the cabin. The other man had a cap on, but was largely obscured by an intervening bush. She could not tell if the two were friends or foes, only that there was nothing in their gestures—no arm-waving or clenched fists—to indicate that they were arguing.

The ambiguity was problematic. For all she knew, this was a ConFoe safe-house or supply station; the cabin was in a remote area too far away from Sanctuary for her to have any knowledge of it—they focused their patrols on the area nearby and along the main routes to the plains from there. Maybe the ConFoes had secured the lesser-used passes as a way to close off an area they were sweeping. For all she knew, her target could be about to communicate his squad's activities to ConFoe HQ via a transmitter hidden away out of her sight in the cabin. Perhaps he already had.

The thought of such possibilities caused her adrenaline to surge and bile to rise to her throat. She wanted nothing more than to firebomb the place and sort through the ashes for clues later, like she had on the highway.

On the other hand, it troubled her somewhat that her bloodlust was so strong and so quick to stir. That was what the leaders back at Sanctuary always accused the ConFoes of—an animalistic desire for destruction. Then, too, the other man could be a mal, maybe even a Believer. Even though the mals were made up of wildly divergent, even belligerent and contradictory, groups and factions, she could not kill someone who was not a ConFoe out of hand. It would be wrong; it would be a sin. If he were a Believer, living alone in freedom in this world, he would be safe in the next world, but it was not her choice to send him there. If he were a mal, but not a Believer, her duty was to offer him the opportunity to choose to believe, the one choice never offered by the ConFoes.

Maria wasn't naïve. She lived in the real world, the only real world. She couldn't merely walk up defenseless and inquire. That was a good way to die.

No, the choice was not what Jesus would do. Jesus would get blown away in a hail of gunfire.

These days, Believers were not so trusting, not so pure. The contradiction between her ideals and her situation was troubling, but every religious organization with a military or security force had long-since been faced with the same quandary. She chose not to try to answer questions that had puzzled mankind for millennia. She was not so egotistical to believe that she would find the solution, the perfect answer that they had missed. She had learned to merely forge ahead and let God's will manifest itself.

She needed more information before she could do anything.

She left the easily watched roadway and headed overland

to circle toward the cabin from behind the small lake. She reckoned she could be within earshot in an hour, maybe two.

She forced her adrenaline down. She put aside her vengeance. She swore to her God, to the God, that she would let their words determine their fate.

Chapter 8

"Don't have to pay no taxes if'n I don't make any money," grumbled the old man, an edge to his voice. The mention of government had apparently riled Kyle, not that Derek had really expected anything different. "Done my service for my country, too. Besides, don't put no stock in all those damn foolish wars they was always gettin' into back b'fore Henrietta and I came up here."

Derek glanced around, trying to determine where Henrietta stood silently in the darkness, with yet another weapon trained on him.

"Don't you fret none about her. She ain't . . . here no more, may she rest in peace." Kyle suddenly looked even older in the dim light.

"How long?"

"Henrietta, she's been gone six years now, seven come October. Died peaceful-like, in her sleep. I think she just didn't have another winter in her—winters are a might tough up here."

"No, how long have you been up here?"

"Oh, hell, we moved up here damn near thirty-five years ago. Didn't like the crowdin' y'know. All them yuppies movin' into the hills and puttin' Pizza Huts and athletic clubs and all sorts of other damn fool nonsense everywhere. Told the nice, young feller at the real estate place we wanted some place secluded, with a nice view, and he did all right by us. Never did come pick up his sign afterwards, though. Guess it was a bit of a drive."

"You mean, you've been alone up here for thirty-five years?"

"Not even close. Zack, he used to deliver supplies now and then up until, I dunno, about ten years ago. We ordered less and less. Guess it stopped being worth his while finally, 'specially since we only paid with meat."

The mere word caused Derek to salivate. "Meat?"

"Elk, mostly. Big old herd moves through the pass every spring and fall. I take a few, no more than I can use, that's fer sure. You should see those big ol' boys when they's bugling for mates during ruttin' season. Fine, strappin' elk, there, and the honeys, they come a runnin' for a good bugler."

The old man paused, then seemed to push his mind back to the subject at hand. "Anyhow, ain't seen nobody since b'fore Henrietta passed."

"A lot's happened in the world since you've been up here, Kyle. A lot. I'm here to give you a choice as to what to do about it, but first I have to explain it all to you."

"Then you're not here to collect taxes or throw me outta my place?"

"I'm here to give you something, if you choose to take it," replied Derek smoothly, as he had been trained. He immediately, however, felt a pang of guilt for his lie by omission.

"Well then, bucko, let's not stand out here in the dark. If'n you promise to behave, we'll go in and I'll rustle up some stew and you can tell me all about whatever damn foolishness the government is pushin' on unsuspectin' folk these days."

Derek smiled at the thought of the stew and began to bend to retrieve his weapon. A motion from Kyle halted the effort.

"Leave it be there fer now. Ain't nobody gonna take it, but it ain't never too wise to trust the government too much and, right now, that's you."

Derek didn't really mind. The old fellow seemed friendly

enough. Besides, Derek gladly would have traded his weapon—heck, he would have traded his left testicle (which still ached like a son-of-a-bitch)—for a bowl of Kyle's elk stew.

Kyle casually snatched up Derek's weapon as he went by and the two men went inside. Not friends, not yet. But not still enemies. Derek was happy to leave it at that for now. There was time yet to be enemies after they had become friends, after he had explained everything, after Kyle made his choice.

But, most importantly, after they ate.

Maria could not always keep the cabin in view as she moved in a wide arc toward the lake beside it, but that was probably best. She did not wish to be seen. At some point, however, she glimpsed the cabin again and noted that the two men were no longer in sight, but that smoke was rising vigorously from the chimney, plainly visible against the clear sky, its haze joining the shimmering swath of the Milky Way in the dark firmament above her.

The door remained open, she noted. It would assist the draw of air by the fire and help alleviate the heat produced by the flames. She hoped they were cooking.

She feared that they were sending a signal to the ConFoe satellites that hide among the points of light heavenward . . . no . . . in the night sky. Not heavenward, never heavenward. For all their promises, nothing produced by the ConFoes had anything to do with heaven.

She quickened her pace.

The cabin was one large room, with planked wooden flooring, like the porch, and rough-hewn pine walls, unfinished, just like the outside. On the left a Franklin-style stove sat off to the one side of the fireplace, its round exhaust piping disappearing into the maw of the massive fireplace at that end of the cabin. Near the front of the cabin on that side was a stainless steel sink and some cupboards. A massive pine bed was in the back-left corner, along with a matching dresser. A wooden table with two chairs sat in the midst of the cabin, while a rectangle of a trapdoor suggested a root cellar below. A slipcovered couch sat facing the large picture window on the right side of the cabin. Stores and equipment of various types lay scattered behind it in the back-right of the cabin.

The flowered pattern on the slipcover and the block-patterned quilt atop the made bed suggested a woman's touch at some point in the history of the cabin, but one that was long past. The savory flavor of Kyle's elk stew also suggested some domesticity, but, then, it was hard for Derek to judge. Too long he had eaten nothing but MREs and the bland fare at the mess at ConFoe's regional headquarters.

Derek had started to try to explain the situation, but Kyle was banging pots and clearing space on the table for an extra person at first. Once food had been served, Derek's mouth was too full of meat and broth and chunks of potato to permit clear communication.

Kyle stifled Derek's futile efforts with a wave of his hand. "I'm not in a hurry, less'n you are," he noted.

Derek was grateful for the opportunity to shut up and eat. Kyle ladled up seconds without being asked and leaned back in a second rocker, this one by the foot of the bed, while Derek finished his meal. As soon as he realized that there truly was no rush, Derek stopped shoveling the food in his face and took the time to enjoy it.

An hour or so after they came in, Derek was finally ready to talk. It was late, but both men were keyed up by the night's activities. It was time for Derek to explain.

It was always hard to know exactly where to start a mal's orientation, especially when the individual had been isolated from society for some time. Derek needed to fix on what Kyle knew—more importantly, what he thought he knew, since misinformation and fear and rumors were some of the ways that the mals attempted to hold sway outside of the urban regions. Inside the cities they just used brute force and intimidation, at least until the cities had been fully "pacified." Now, of course, no one went there.

Derek decided to start with a few questions.

"What do you know about the Mandatory Conversion Act?"

"You mean that metric crap? Hell, boy, I'm too old to start measurin' everythin' in units different from the ones I learned. Government must not got much to do, if'n they be sendin' fellows like you out to force people into that stuff and nonsense."

"No, no, not metric conversion. Conversion of people."

"You mean like the Spanish Inquisition?" The old man smiled broadly. "Nobody expects the Spanish Inquisition!" He looked wildly about the room with his eyes. "Where's the comfy chair?" The old hermit guffawed until he coughed, then slapped his knee.

Derek didn't get the joke or maybe too much time alone had sent the old coot completely over the edge. Best get down to basics.

"What about computers? Certainly you know about computers."

"Sure, I know about computers. Don't got much use for them, 'ceptin' they say my SolarFord has a chip or something controlling the automatic transmission. 'Course, I ain't used nothin' but second gear for years now, so I don't 'spect it does anything."

A shot of adrenaline coursed through Derek's veins. "You have a truck?"

"Never mind about that. What about computers? All I know is that everybody spent a lot of time cooped up typin' crap to each other on the internet, which as far as I could tell was full of nothin' much but perverts, porn sites, and people trying to sell you insurance."

"What about medical technology? Ever have a doctor give you an MRI or a CAT scan?"

Kyle Patterson bristled noticeably as soon as Derek mentioned the word "doctor." "Damn quacks! Yeah, they gave Henrietta one of them CAT scans—she said it felt like being in a coffin, real claustrophobic like. Then they'd said she gots the cancer and I'm just a dumb son-of-a-bitch, I don't know any better, so I lets them cut her up to get it. Then they blast her with radiation 'til her beautiful hair all falls out. They tell her she ain't got hardly no time to live, so we decided to get away from all the people and the shovin' and the salesmen and the doctors and come up here."

Derek did not interrupt Kyle's pain.

"But she did, you know, she lived twenty-odd more years. 'Course, we couldn't have no kids, 'cause of what them doctors had done, but we had a right nice life in our cabin, just the two of us, without all that crap."

Derek let the man settle a bit before continuing. "Do you know what an avatar is?"

Kyle screwed up his face for a moment, looking as if the government had seen fit to send Derek off to give the citizenry a basic skills test and that it was somehow important that he pass or at least try.

"Some Hindu crap of some kind, ain't it?"

Derek smiled. The old crackpot had some education before he came to the wilderness. Of course, they were in the mountains southwest of Boulder, Colorado, where Hinduism had mixed and flourished for some time during the New Age days from which Kyle dated. "Actually, it originally was a Hindu word for the human vessel that a god took when visiting earth. But I'm talking about computer avatars."

Kyle seemed disappointed that he had missed the question. "Guess I dunno, then."

"What about Moore's law?"

"Is that the Mandatory Conversion Act?" asked Kyle expectantly.

"No. I'll explain in just a minute."

Derek thought about his approach. The man understood about computers and medical scans, but that was about it. He would need to do a full-scale orientation.

Outside, Maria lay beneath the porch and listened.

A world away from the small cabin, two technicians settled in for the graveyard shift and began their own, more cosmic, observations. Their moves were relaxed and unhurried, their conversation a mix of efficient, technical jargon and casual small talk. They had done this before and they would do it again. They knew the drill and were comfortable with the routine. Finally, they finished the preliminaries and settled in to watch.

Chapter 9

"Did you ever watch the Weather Channel, Kyle?"

Kyle looked perplexed by the change of subject. "Yeah, sure, back when we was just regular folk."

"Do you remember when they would give the computer forecast for the next five days?"

Kyle nodded uncertainly.

"Computers are good at that kind of stuff. Basically, they can do two things. They can store a lot of information in a very small amount of physical space. Second, they can process that information—run calculations on the information, compare it to other information, change variables, and compare the variations to one another."

"Yeah, they're big ol' calculators. Less'n that's what folks used to say."

"More than that, they can translate the numbers and the formulas and the variations into pictures and sounds—that's how you can see things on the computer screen."

"Like them darn video games kids was always wastin' their time on."

Derek thought back on his history. "Yeah, but that was a long time ago. Things have gotten a lot more sophisticated since then. See, back in the late twentieth century, a guy named Moore noticed that the processing speed of computers was doubling about every eighteen months. That's Moore's Law. Another guy noticed, similarly, that practical computer storage capacity was doubling about every two years."

"So, you got big, fast computers, is that what you're saying?" The grandfatherly man gave Derek the kind of indulgent smile usually reserved for people who spend too much time talking about their job or their kids.

"Actually, you have very small, but powerful and fast, computers."

Now Kyle began to look noticeably perturbed. His eyes sparked and his bearded chin jutted out defiantly. "Look, mister, whatever you're sellin', I ain't interested, hear? I gots no use for no teeny-tiny computer predictin' the weather or somesuch. I look out the window and I can tell whether it's snowin' or gonna snow soon. That's 'bout all I need to know. Besides, I ain't got no money or credit or whatever the tarnation people use these days."

"Calm down, Mr. Patterson. I'm not here to sell you a computer, at least not in the way you think. I'm just trying to build off of examples that you know."

Derek decided he had better move to the meat of it, before he irritated or confused his subject further.

"Now take those CAT scans we talked about a few minutes ago. They've gotten a lot more sophisticated, too. If you take that technology, along with the old-fashioned stuff like x-rays and newer stuff like MRIs, basically magnetic scanning, and the ability to read your genetic structure at a cellular level and apply something like Moore's law to it, you end up with pretty powerful technology."

"So, now you gots teeny computers that take really good pictures of the insides of stuff." The old codger rolled his eyes. "I tell you what, you go call Polaroid and I'll call Kodak. Hoody-hoo!" For somebody who had spent the last six or so years all alone, the guy hadn't lost his ability to wax sarcastic.

It was time for a new tack.

"Did you ever hear the story of the invention of chess?"

That shut the coot up, but only for a second.

"You gonna tell me how the computers can play chess now? Everybody knows that."

"No, the story of how chess was invented for some prince or other muckety-muck in India or some place like that."

Kyle tilted his head down and squinted up at the babbling government representative. "Yessirree, sounds like you got the details down on that story."

Derek brusquely ignored the insult. "The important part is that the prince decided to reward the inventor by giving him one grain of rice for the first square of the eight-by-eight checkerboard, two for the second, four for the third, eight for the fourth, sixteen for the fifth, and so on, doubling for each one."

"So the inventor got a bag full of rice? What's that got to do with anythin'?"

"More than a bag full—if you double something sixty-three times it becomes an enormous number, more grains of rice than existed in India to give the inventor. When the prince realized he could not give what he promised, he killed the inventor to avoid any embarrassment."

"That's government alright."

"Maybe, but the point is that just such doubling has been occurring in both computing and scanning technology for decades now. For all practical purposes, mankind now possesses infinite computing power and storage with minimal space or power requirements—it's all molecular based these days with self-replicating nano-machines."

"Nano? You mean like the crazy space guy on TV from Ork?"

Derek wished he had paid more attention in training to historical pop culture references. He could do nothing but wave off the question. "Uh, no, I don't think so. Machines that grow more of their own kind, like algae." Kyle's silence clearly indicated to Derek that he had once again confused his subject. Maybe the late night was getting to one or both of them. He again circled back to something he knew the old man understood.

"Let's talk about video games. The computer showed you a game world and you could do things in that world, like race cars or shoot alien invaders or whatever. And the representation of the person playing the game in the game world was known as an avatar—a computer manifestation of a real person in the virtual world of the game."

The lights came back on in the old man's mind. He nodded energetically. "Yeah, I played once with one of the neighbor kids, way back when Henrietta had to take his mom into see some lawyer about her son-of-a-bitch drunk, wife-beatin' husband."

Derek steered Kyle back on track. "Well, people would use avatars on the computer for more than games. They would use them in chat rooms, where they could communicate with other people who were on the internet."

"Them places where all the perverts used to hang out and talk dirty."

Derek hesitated briefly. The official histories always glossed over the considerable impact that the porn industry had in developing virtual worlds, avatars, and bio-sensing and feedback devices during the early stages of developing full conversion technology.

"Among other things," he temporized. "The advances in computing power and storage and scanning also affected the games and virtual worlds until it got to a point where the technology was so advanced that you could scan a person, a real person, in minute detail—down to their individual molecules and the neural pathways of their brain—and you could store that massive amount of information in a computer, and the computer could process it so fast that the person could actually consciously exist in a virtual world in a computer. When you really sit down and think about how technology advances, you realize that it was inevitable that people would eventually be able to live inside a computer."

Kyle Patterson was clearly appalled. His mouth dropped open and his eyes screwed up in disbelief. "Live inside a computer?!? With a bunch of perverts?!? Who the hell would want to do that?"

"Well, at first," admitted Derek, "no one much did, especially since the scanning process at that level of detail is . . . destructive to the subject being scanned."

Kyle furrowed his brow only briefly. "You mean, it kills them."

This was always the tricky part. "Let's just say that a person's consciousness can't exist in this world and a virtual world at the same time."

" 'Cause they're dead in the real world . . .''

"Well, in a manner of speaking. That's why, except for a few techno-geeks, the first to choose conversion to a virtual world were the terminally ill and those in great pain. They would leave this world and exist in the virtual world. Since the physical body of the scanned subject is no longer capable of functioning, once you go virtual, you stay there. It actually avoids all sorts of messy complications, like people moving back and forth between virtual worlds and the real world or the same consciousness existing in two places at the same time."

"Like a Xerox machine spittin' copies out all over the place."

"Yes, in a way. Replication could lead the power-hungry to dominate the virtual worlds and would stifle diversity and, most importantly, fundamentally alter the nature of those worlds in a way that would make them alien to life on the real world."

"But if the virtual world is just like the real world, what's the point? Won't those people be in pain and die there, just like they would here?"

"Sure, except for the fact that digital individuals are able to be processed so as to eliminate pain and repair physical damage in ways which we can't in the real world. It's tedious and was, at first, an incredibly expensive process, but, like most technological developments, it became somewhat affordable to the masses over the years."

Derek swallowed hard in an attempt to clear the lump in his throat and stared fixedly at a corner of the cabin in an effort to keep his eyes from misting. He hoped Kyle would think he was just giving the fellow a chance to digest what he'd been told. In reality, Derek could not help but think of Katy. His service had paid for her modification and now, on Alpha Two, Katy was walking and running and had been doing so for close to five years. She would be almost grown up now, but he did not doubt for a moment that he would recognize her when he converted in and that she would come running up to hug her big brother in that better world when all of this was over.

The old man interrupted Derek's reverie. "That's a right interestin' story, boy, but I ain't in no pain, other than missin' my missus, and I ain't dyin', leastwise no faster'n everybody's dyin' at any given time. So I thank you kindly for the somewhat bizarre offer, but I'll give it a pass." Kyle got up from his rocking chair. "You can stay the night and be about your business in the mornin'."

Suddenly, Derek was too weary to continue. It had to be past three in the morning and the adrenaline and duty that had kept him going for the last several days had long since subsided. The cozy cabin, his full belly, and the lack of any perceived danger were lulling him into a warm comfort that did not exist anywhere in his Conversion Forces experience. There was no reason to rush the old man—Derek couldn't even convert him if he wanted to until he retrieved the equipment from up the pass.

"I agree it's time to rest and I appreciate the hospitality— you don't really see that much in my line of work. You sleep on what I told you. There's a bit more to come before you decline the offer I have yet to make."

The old man muttered something about salesmen never taking no for an answer as he gestured Derek toward the couch and toddled off to the outhouse, taking both guns with him. He returned a few minutes later weaponless and headed straight to his bed. Derek took a moment to remove the slipcover from the ancient couch and fold the worn and faded cloth neatly, before hitting the john himself, then sacking out. He didn't see where the old man had stashed both their guns and he didn't bother to look.

No doubt his host could slit his throat as he slept, but then he had been at risk of death since he met the fellow. Though he had not intended it in such a way at the time, he also knew that telling Kyle that he had more to say in the morning was practically a guaranty of safety. It wasn't just that the guy probably craved company after all these years, it was inherent in humans to be curious.

Derek's information was assuredly a puzzle to the hermit. A puzzle that came with a potential payoff. Even if he might not want the payoff, Kyle could no more smother Derek in his sleep than someone could attend a reading of a will and not ask, "How much?"

None of what Derek had said was news to Maria. She had

not been entirely isolated from the real world while these developments had occurred. Some of them even predated her. Of course, he had skimmed over the rise of the virtual pleasure palaces of the porn purveyors that were precursors of the development of true virtual worlds and full-bore conversion technology. More importantly, he had said nothing about the theological implications of conversion. And, of course, he hadn't really gotten to the punch-line yet, that the old man was about to face a terrible, unforgivable choice.

On the other hand, she was impressed with the manner in which he had spoken to the hermit. Maybe it was because the ConFoe had apparently been captured by the old guy, but there was none of the ego, none of the swagger of the ConFoes she had previously encountered. There was no spewing of vulgarities, no threat of violence or torture, no hurrying the victim along to the doom of his soul, just a slightly-sanitized version of the history of conversion technology.

When she had silently sworn to let their words determine their fate, she had been thinking of the second man—the one that she had feared might be a ConFoe contact. But number seven—his name was apparently Derek Williger—had done nothing tonight to deserve death. More importantly, she still might gather some useful intelligence for Sanctuary before she did what she eventually would have to do. She lay quietly as the men wandered out separately to use the facilities and returned to the comfy cabin, with Derek shutting the cabin door firmly behind him on his return.

There would be time enough tomorrow. At some point she knew she would have to intervene, to save the old man from the predation of his government, but now she too would rest. She slid carefully out from beneath the porch and made her way to a thicket at the far edge of the small lake. She silently ate a charred MRE and lay back to fall asleep, the stars twinkling silently far above her.

Far, far away to the southwest, hundreds of miles from Maria, someone else stared at the twinkling stars and cursed their silence. Time was running out for Hank and Ali and for their research. The equipment was failing and was irreplaceable. And still no answer came. Only a few had not abandoned the cause, but Hank and Ali would stay 'til the end.

Hank coughed, the cool, dry air irritating his throat as he inhaled, causing him to hack again, harder. He, too, was failing and was irreplaceable. And, once he and Ali stopped listening, mankind would never know.

Hank looked at the input again. It was fuzzy and unreliable. And it kept getting worse, despite his and Ali's technical expertise and considerable diagnostic efforts.

"There's nothin' to do, but reconfigure," he said to Ali. "We've gotten everything we're gonna get from this one."

Ali's shoulders slumped. "Are you quite certain? A reconfiguration will be a substantial effort. It is not like we can just press a button."

"Hell, Ali," said Hank amiably, "you and me, we passed on the easy path a long time ago. Ain't nothin' worthwhile, you don't gotta work for."

Ali nodded. "This is undoubtedly the situation." He got up from his chair. "We had best commence, then."

"Ain't nobody gonna do it for us," drawled Hank, as he pushed back his swivel chair and rose to help.

Chapter 10

It had to be Saturday. His nose and his ears confirmed it while his eyes were still closed, his mind still half-asleep. The sizzle and pop of Mom cooking up breakfast in a big ol' iron skillet— the heavy scent of frying fat in the air—guaranteed it.

Mom always cooked up a big, hot breakfast on Saturday morning, even when bacon and eggs began to get expensive. A bacon and egg sandwich on buttered wheat toast was Katy's favorite meal and, given all that she was denied, Mom could not help but give Katy her favorite meal once a week. She was similarly generous to Derek, allowing him to eat nothing but a big bowl of heavily buttered popcorn for the Sunday evening meal.

Derek's eyes fluttered open, but Mom was nowhere in sight. Instead, a grizzled old hermit whistled softly to himself while he fried up a mess of potatoes and elk fat. The visage of the old man and the aches in Derek's painfully adult body quickly reminded him of where he was and what he was about. Sadly, he realized that he had most assuredly already experienced the best moment of the day. He looked around the room, daylight streaming in the picture window and the open door—too high and too dry to worry about mosquitoes up here. Kyle caught the small movement of Derek's head and stopped fiddling with the frying potatoes long enough to walk a steaming mug over and set it on the end table next to the couch.

"Coffee?" croaked Derek, incredulously. Where would this hermit get coffee? Not even the ConFoes had coffee anymore, though they had plenty of beverages with a morning kick to them—caffeine or otherwise.

"Hmmmph," grunted Kyle. "Mountain tea. This ain't the Ritz, y'know."

Derek pulled the cup towards him and gave it an expectant sniff. "What's in it?"

"Roots, wild-rose petals . . . hell, don't get too fixed on what's in tea, boy. It's all just dried weeds in a bag." The hermit scraped his fixings onto two plates and plunked them down at the table. "Best get up and eat while things are hot. Then you can finish your sales pitch and we can both get about our business."

Derek scrambled up and over to the heavy wooden table. Not even stiff muscles and a full body ache could slow him from sitting down to a hot meal laden with grease and carbohydrates. As he ate, he made an effort not to think of the quaint domesticity of the old mountain man. It wouldn't do to think of him as some kind of folksy grandfather or, worse yet, as a good friend. It could make things difficult when the geezer made his choice and Derek did what he had to do.

Instead, he hunkered down and focused on his food and what he still had to say and what he would do, what he was duty bound to do, when the time came.

The smell of food cooking was almost more than Maria could bear. Ensconced again in her hiding place under the wood plank porch, she, too, focused on figuring out what she would do next.

Kyle finally prompted the discussion as Derek sat back from his cleaned plate. "Is this an age thing?"

"Huh?" said Derek, wiping the grease from his mouth with the sleeve of his uniform.

103

"Y'said folks can convert to livin' in computers and y'said somethin' 'bout mandatory conversion. Well, God knows the HMOs and the insurance companies, they was always complainin' 'bout the high cost of keepin' old folks alive 'past their time,' whatever the hell that means. So I figured that maybe they make old folks convert as a means of getting rid of 'em, so'n they can save money and all. Hell, the governor of Colorado said some darn foolishness 'bout a 'duty to die' once, even."

Derek smiled. The old coot was pretty sharp, but then he supposed you couldn't be too stupid and eke out an existence for years on your own in this place.

"You're kind of right, but it's got nothing to do with age or insurance companies."

Kyle waited silently for him to continue.

"You moved out here partly to get away from the press of civilization, but you have no idea how pressing civilization got after you moved on. The fundamentalists in most countries got their way and outlawed abortion and most types of birth control, but did nothing to stem the promiscuity that had arisen when those things were both legal and common. Population surged—there were more than three billion Chinese alone and almost two billion Indians—the Hindu kind—even after the nuclear exchange with Pakistan. There simply wasn't enough food, certainly not enough clean water, to support twelve billion people on earth and counting."

Kyle scratched his beard and frowned as he contemplated Derek's words. "Zack, he was always complainin' about them damn Californicators, as he called 'em, stealing all of Colorado's water. And he did say somethin' about some riots in Denver one of the last times he came by." The geezer somehow seemed even older as he thought about the world's woes.

"Lots of the big cities had riots, and riots meant fires and destruction. Of course, destroying the infrastructure of commerce didn't do much to help an already bad situation."

"So, you're sayin' folks, they thought they would have a better life in the computer, in a virtual world?"

"Sure. Think about it Kyle. In a virtual world, you don't really use up any resources. There is an unlimited supply of virtual water and the crop yields can be programmed to be anything you want them to be . . . because nothing is real. It just seems real."

"So folks . . . desperate folks . . . would convert so they could provide for their family . . . or at least seem to . . ."

"So their kids could have a better life than they did. It's the age-old motivating force of every generation, Kyle. Virtual reality made it attainable for everyone."

"And the government, they went along with this?"

"They encouraged it, Kyle. Every year it cost tens of thousands of dollars and a heap of taxes and resources to keep a family going in the real world. For less than a year's worth of those same resources, the family could be converted over into one of the virtual worlds and never cost the government a dime again."

"S'long as the family agreed to kill themselves and their kids to do it." Kyle spat into the stoked ashes of the fireplace with undisguised disgust. The globule evaporated instantaneously as it hit—the tangible liquid converting into an ephemeral gas that dissipated up the chimney. "Sounds like every cult I ever heard of."

"You're not dead when you're in the computer, Kyle. Your consciousness just resides in a different place, forever. And instead of a desert of sand and starvation, you have a silicon chip of plenty and immortality."

"And people, they do this?"

"Almost everybody has."

Kyle's hands fluttered, as if to wave off Derek's implied offer. "Like I said last night. No sale. T'aint crowded here and I don't want to go no place where it is, even if'n I got all the food and water and 'resources' I could ever want. 'Sides, with most everyone else gone, things will be just right for me here." He stood, obviously finished with the conversation. "I 'spect you best be on your way."

Derek made no move to stand. "You remember, Kyle, I said there was a Mandatory Conversion Act?"

Now the old man was clearly riled. Kyle's face grew beet red and his gnarled hands curled into tight fists. He strode abruptly up to his still-sitting guest, bending down to meet Derek's impassive gaze face-to-face. "You go to hell, boy! You go to some damn virtual hell! I ain't on no welfare and I ain't usin' anybody else's resources or costin' the damn government a single, solitary damn dime. So you just git off my mountain and tell them I ain't interested." He spun around with amazing alacrity for his age and marched over to the partially open door. He grabbed the inside latch and pulled the door fully open, stepping back and to the side as he did, turning back so as to face his no longer welcome guest, his movements as much a demand for departure as his angry words.

Derek had half closed his eyes during the exchange to keep out the spittle flying from the old man's mouth as he shouted. He began to speak as he turned toward his angry host. "Everyone has to make a choice . . ." His words suddenly faltered mid-sentence. He was no more ready for the sight that greeted him at the door than was the irate old man.

Silhouetted by the bright sunlight was a lithe woman in a gray jumpsuit cradling an automatic weapon. Her brown hair fluttered in the breeze, revealing a small scar along her jawline that made her pale features look somehow less delicate without ruining her stern beauty. She stepped slightly forward and put her left foot down so that her boot would block any attempt to shut the door on her. She trained her weapon on the stupefied ConFoe and turned her head slightly toward the startled cabin-dweller around the edge of the door. "Mr. Williger was about to explain that you have to choose between immediate conversion and immediate death. I'd like to discuss expanding your menu of alternatives."

The old man glared angrily at Derek, his steely gray eyes boring into his erstwhile guest with venom.

"That right? You were going to kill me, if'n I didn't agree to your godforsaken conversion?"

Derek hesitated to reply. This was not how orientation was supposed to go, according to the ConFoe training manual. Of course, it wasn't supposed to be interrupted by a gun-toting mal getting the drop on you, either. He considered his words carefully—lying would be sure to alienate his subject and aggravate his undoubtedly self-righteous, armed opponent. "I was just beginning to explain that mandatory conversion was not . . . limited to welfare recipients when we were . . . interrupted."

Kyle gave Derek a grudging grunt of acknowledgment. "Anything else you hadn't gotten to yet?"

"In his haste," the mal intoned sarcastically, "Mr. Williger has glossed over a number of salient points. Religious persecution. Torture. Murder. Genocide."

Derek nodded his head slightly. "That's what it has come to," he agreed to his enemy's obvious astonishment. He struggled to find the words that would justify what the Conversion Forces had become, but his courses in orientation had never contemplated a true debate—just a unilateral explanation and responses to frequently asked questions and protests that would ease the subject to accept conversion, hopefully without ever getting to the subject of the unpleasant alternative. With a shake of his head, he cleared the rote explanations out of his mind and pared all that he knew of ConFoe's existence down to its bare essentials. "It's really just a matter of self-defense," he said simply.

That was a mistake.

The mal soldier's finger tensed on the trigger of her weapon. The look of revulsion and disgust on her face was so intense that Derek could almost taste the bile rising in her throat himself. She did not shoot, but her words slammed at him like a burst of automatic weapon fire. "You hunt down peaceful citizens and kill them in self-defense? You torture them until they deny their religion in self-defense? You poison the crops and burn down the forests in self-defense?" Her eyes flamed with anger and disbelief—her gun remained tightly focused on Derek's center of mass.

There was no advantage to lying, even if the truth cost Derek his life. It saddened him that Katy might never see him again, but the truth saddened him even more. "Yes. At least the killing . . . the genocide is in self-defense. The torture is an unfortunate byproduct of the process which I loathe as much as you."

The woman started slightly at Derek's reply. She seemed at a loss for words.

Kyle wanted nothing more than to have been left in peace, to know nothing of the conflict between these people, nothing of the bizarre and grisly politics of the civilization that he had long ago left behind, but it had intruded itself upon him. Now, his mind churned. All the options seemed to have as a prerequisite the death of someone in his cabin. This earnest and angry young woman would kill Derek and leave. Or Derek would kill her and, if Kyle refused his invitation of conversion, then kill him. Or Kyle would be forced to kill them both. Not that he was in control, at least not yet, but none of those choices appealed to him. Moreover, now that he was infected with partial knowledge, the puzzle of it all would likely drive him mad if the two of them were to die in the obviously coming fight. Suddenly, he was glad that Henrietta never had to see what the world had come to. He also realized that, much as he instinctively sought to live, some permutations of how things might play out would bring him to her—and maybe that wasn't so bad.

He intervened by instinct. "Seems to me, if'n I have to make a choice that's eternal, I oughta hear both sides first."

"That's fine by me," said the woman curtly. "Some of us believe in informed consent." Her grip on the assault weapon remained tight, however, and her aim did not waiver from her ConFoe opponent.

Derek spoke. "It seems to me that full and frank discussion is rarely . . . facilitated by the threat of summary execution implicit in being at the wrong end of an AK-47."

The mal soldier continued to glare at her ConFoe opponent.

Kyle spoke up. "Man's got a point, missy. My house. My risk. What say, I take your gun and stash it with the others and we talk it all out? 'Twouldn't be fair otherwise."

Fairness.

Now there was a concept that Maria thought had long ago left the world. But if it lived, it would have to live in the hearts of the Believers and in old-timers like Kyle. Just thinking about it calmed her slightly. Her finger relaxed on the trigger.

The idea of vengeance for the fire in Sanctuary's valley

still compelled Maria, but this ConFoe was different, odd. He was still dangerous, but not in the same way as those apes that had pursued her and set the fire. And deep down, she could only distinguish her military acts from those of her foe because she believed herself to be a freedom fighter. This ancient mountain man deserved a choice . . . a real choice . . . an informed choice. She would be fair to Kyle. She would even be fair to her ConFoe enemy.

Besides, the ConFoe was weaponless and seemed pretty beat-up. She calculated she could take him if she had to, gun or no.

She slowly lowered her weapon and let the old man take it. Derek continued to sit at the table calmly.

"Thanks, missy," said the old gent.

"The name's Maria."

"Thank you kindly, Maria. Now if you two can avoid killin' each other for a few minutes, I'll be back in a jiffy."

Kyle headed out the door, shutting it behind him.

Maria looked at Derek without expression. "I killed your friends, you know."

He looked back at her without passion. "They weren't my friends. They were just . . . my squad."

His uncaring attitude confused and somewhat disturbed her. Her right eyebrow unconsciously arched slightly.

"They killed your friends, I think," he continued.

"Don't you know?" she said flippantly. "You were there, weren't you?"

"I meant . . . I think they were your friends. I know they killed them." He hesitated before continuing, undoubtedly thankful that her finger was no longer coiled around a hair trigger. "I was there. I . . . tried to give the one we were chasing a chance to be converted . . . but he was . . . killed."

That was it, then. Joshua was dead and this man had seen

him die. Maria looked at him with distaste. "Better dead, than damned for eternity," she spat as Kyle returned to the cabin.

"Them's fine friendly words to come home to," he muttered as he looked from one to the other. "Maybe we should sit a spell." He gestured toward the table and Maria made her way warily to the opposite end from Derek. Kyle casually set a fork and the skillet with the leftovers from breakfast down in front of the girl, then pulled the rocking chair towards the table betwixt the two and settled in.

"Maybe I should tell you what this feller here 'splained to me, to get us all on an even keel and all."

Maria paused between forkfuls of cold, greasy potatoes. "Don't bother. I heard."

"Well, I mean last night . . ." continued the old man by way of explanation.

Maria stopped shoveling food for another moment. "Yeah, I know. I heard that, too." She started to eat again, then stopped. "Thanks for the food. The smell was driving me crazy all night."

Derek watched Maria eat.

If Derek had thought his tensions had eased when Kyle talked Maria out of her weapon, he was even more relieved by what she had just revealed. He almost chuckled, thinking back, about his lack of worry as to whether the hermit would off him during the night. No doubt this woman could have killed him during the night, but she had not.

She was apparently a soldier with principles.

He strove to be a soldier with principles.

Maybe there was some common ground. Maybe he could convert them both. "Kyle is one hell of a cook," he said lightly to ease the mood and his task.

111

"There's no reason to blaspheme," replied Maria icily.

Crap. They didn't teach you how to deal with this in orientation training class. And he used to think that exams had been hard.

Chapter 11

Kyle shushed them and Maria finished eating in peace. Then the old man cleared the table.

"So, Maria, jus' what do you think Derek left out of his explanation?"

Maria shrugged her shoulders briefly and tilted her head slightly to her right, her dark hair falling somewhat away from her face, thinking about how to begin without unduly antagonizing either of her listeners and without sugarcoating the hideous truth. Finally she spoke: "All the rough edges the victors always leave out of the history books—the blind alleys and failures along the way to their 'victory,' the power plays and petty rivalries that shape policy, the thoughtless misery their policies generate, the suffering and violence used to implement their will, and the fact that government policy is the ultimate embodiment of collective ego, that, like all governments from time out of mind, they know what is better for the people than the people do themselves."

Derek visibly bristled. "Mandatory conversion was adopted as a policy by both democratic and undemocratic forms of government—it is the only sensible solution to the continuation of life on earth," he interrupted.

"Hush, now boy. You got a long spell to speak, now give the little lady her turn," cautioned Kyle with a stern look toward the ConFoe. "Explain what you mean, honey."

Somehow men would never learn that no military officer in any army liked to be referred to as "honey," but Maria let it slide. The geezer was ancient; he probably hadn't even seen a woman, except for pictures in thumb-worn old copies of *National Geographic*, for years. Maybe not even that—he seemed bothered earlier by the references to the influence of the adult industry on the net. Perhaps that would provide an opening in which she could drive the wedge of truth.

"Well," she began, "he slid right past how this whole sick business of conversion began with the smut-mongers in the porn business."

The old man's right eyebrow arched markedly. "And how's that?"

"At first, the porn sites on the internet just depicted . . ." She hesitated, embarrassed by her faith from getting too graphic in her discussion. ". . . the usual disgusting things they used to show in dirty magazines." Having moved over the delicate part, she pushed on. "Later, the men would type what they wanted the women to do and watch. But soon after, the technicians in the industry developed virtual reality goggles and avatars and bio-sensing feedback mechanisms that monitored the pleasure senses and altered the scenario being experienced to maximize sensory satisfaction. Gloves and suits for the users began to enable them to feel like they were touching and feeling things that weren't really there, things that were only in the virtual world of the computer, and they did sick things, things they could never get away with in the real world."

"Damn perverts," muttered the old man. "Pardon my French," he quickly nodded to Maria. She continued, a slight look of puzzlement flitting quickly over her face, then disappearing.

"There was a lot of money in that form of 'entertainment,' so the smut-mongers funded a lot of the new bio-feedback research and development and implemented a lot of the cutting-edge equipment for their seamy, disgusting businesses, purposes for which the equipment had never been intended by the scientists. A lot of techs first became familiar with the cutting-edge equipment and science by working for the porn companies."

Maria continued her explanation. "When scanning technology began to catch up with the ability to craft virtual worlds, the first areas of the brain to be scanned were the pleasure centers and the first subjects to be scanned voluntarily were the sickest of the sickos—creeps that wanted to live forever in pleasure palaces and dungeons where everyone bent to their will."

As Maria paused momentarily to gather her thoughts, Derek seized the opportunity to interject. He wanted to keep some control over the conversation, but he didn't want to piss off his potential convert. "I don't deny that the adult entertainment industry had an impact on furthering the technical developments that make conversion possible. But it was inevitable, you know. They just rushed it along. None of the officially sanctioned virtual worlds are anything like what you describe."

She looked at him haughtily. "Still, the mark of the devil permeates the process."

"Maybe God just works in mysterious ways," he responded. It was the catch-all response that the ConFoe training manual recommended whenever a religiously-inclined mal made an objection or comment you didn't have a ready answer for.

"You have no business talking to anyone about God," she shot back.

"Then I guess you have no business talking to anyone about porn." His smart-alecky response felt good as he said it, but he immediately regretted it. It was tacky and sophomoric.

"Stop bickering," warned the old man. "I un'erstand the point that the technical aspects of the process had less than savory beginnings. So does makin' soap, but it's the use something is put to that matters, not where it comes from. Why don't we jus' move along? Where'd things go from this . . . uh . . . shady start?"

"What he said," she began, inclining her head toward Derek, "about the science stuff is pretty accurate. The capabilities of the equipment advanced fast, really fast, and all the guys in white coats couldn't wait to play God, to create their own little utopias and populate them with real people—or at least the data they derived from real people. The technical types—the really nerdy ones that didn't have much of a real life—started opting in. Then, the rich and famous with a technical bent—y'know, the ones that always had the latest and best sound systems and vid-screens—they followed the faddish trend like the mindless consumer lemmings they have always been."

Again, Derek tried to nudge the conversation toward more favorable ground. He doubted the hermit was fond of conspicuous consumption. "You're forgetting about the other early adopters, the people who were dying or in pain that were helped by conversion."

"Helped?" Maria scoffed. "Instead of living and dying as God intended, the medical establishment just kept on hooking people to more and more machines—monitors and insulin pumps and implanted dialysis units and fake arms and bones and eyes and hearts, until the people's souls just became another part of the machinery. Don't worry. I won't forget to mention that. It's what started the whole slide into oblivion."

Derek attempted to clarify before Maria could start off on another rant. "Terminal patients, people in chronic, persistent pain, quadriplegics . . . they could all be altered and move into a virtual world where they could live and be whole." This part of Derek's orientation pitch—at least the passion of it—did not come from his training, it came from his heart, it came from his own personal experience. "It was expensive, especially at first, but it gave true hope to the hopeless—a place where they could go and live without pain. It also wiped out the quacks and the fakers in the world of treatment. Why go to Mexico for untested medicine or to India for 'spiritual surgery,' when you could go to a better world? Your family, or at least most of them, could even go with you."

The sincerity in the words gushing forth from the ConFoe took Maria aback. There were practically tears in the guy's eyes. Finally, it made sense. "You're one of them aren't you? Brother or sister . . ." She looked him over to estimate his age, ". . . maybe a child with a problem." She considered for a moment. "Not terminal probably . . ."

She noticed the puzzlement on Kyle face and explained. "It was, like he said, expensive at first. All the big charities got into it. It started with the wish foundations. Why send a dying kid off to see DisneyWorld when, for a bit more money, they could send the kid to a virtual world forever? The support group charities would even fund sending the parents along for the ride. Soon after, the disease charities—you know, the ones for heart disease and AIDS and cancer—they realized that it was cheaper to convert people, than to figure out how to cure them here on earth. The tobacco people started settling all their lawsuits that way, too—you could even collect frequent buyer points on each pack of cigarettes and purchase a conversion with them once the emphysema or cancer struck."

The old man twitched at the word "cancer," but said nothing.

"It solved a lot of problems," asserted Derek.

"It solved problems like suicide solves problems," Maria retorted, "but with more cost to the human soul."

Kyle again stepped in to stop the bickering. "I 'spect we'll git to the theology soon enough. Let's make real sure I un'erstand the history first off." He nodded curtly at Maria and she took up her explanation once again.

"Saving money, that was the wide and well-traveled path straight to perdition. You see, Kyle, it saved money for the government, too. Resources were scarce, tax-cheats in ample supply, and population increasing all the time. I mean, why take care of sick and homeless people when you could euthanize them legally?"

"When you could eliminate their misery in a cost-effective manner," interjected Derek as a kind of simultaneous translation.

"That's when the coercion began," said Maria with a shiver. "Suddenly, Medicare and Social Security and the socialized medical programs overseas, they wouldn't pay for operations or medicine, not when they could just convert the patient cheaply and eliminate the drain on their resources. Same kind of thing on the medical research side. Why pay for research to cure something, when you could just convert the victims? Of course, the lack of government and charitable funding for real medical solutions meant that the pharmaceutical conglomerates weren't making money finding cures or getting new drugs approved anymore. There was no percentage in that. Instead they put their R&D money into software enhancements for the conversion process. A constantly increasing supply of sick and miserable people meant a growth industry for them."

Maria make a sick face as she thought of what had occurred. "Misery was a good thing for the bottom line.
Spreading AIDS guaranteed favorable demand. Suddenly it
didn't make sense to be careful about anything. Cigarette
companies went back to adding the deadly doses of nicotine
their clients craved. Vegetarians and health eaters were
laughed at, even more than before. Sexually transmitted dis-
eases ran rampant. Risky behavior knew no bounds. If anything bad happened, short of death, the hospital or the
government would solve it by conversion of the individual
who had made the bad choice. It was a panacea for everything."

"Panaceas are only bad if they are false. What's wrong
with an ultimate solution, a final solution to a host of ills?"

Kyle looked sternly at the ConFoe. "I wouldn't use that
phrase, if'n I were you."

Derek shook his head in bewilderment. "Huh?"

"Final solution. That's what the Nazis called it when they
tried to wipe out the gypsies and the Jews and the Poles.
Damn near succeeded, too." Again, he nodded toward
Maria. "Pardon my French."

Maria let the comment pass again. She didn't know
French, but he hadn't said anything that sounded foreign,
just rude. Maybe the French were rude people back in his
day; she had no idea.

Derek hesitated. Kyle's reference to Nazis confused him.
Some mals called the ConFoes Nazis. Derek knew it was a
bad thing, without really knowing why. He had never paid
that much attention in history class during his school days.
He just knew that the Nazis were always the bad guys in old
movies. "Point taken," he conceded without really understanding. He wasn't stupid. He could adapt to his audience's

sensibilities without really caring why they had them.

"This particular solution," intoned Maria, taking up her lecture once again, "was applied on a sweeping scale, even at the level of international conflicts. No more refugee camps, just U.N. conversion facilities. No more starving kids in Africa, just send in the Mobile Expeditionary Conversion Forces."

"No more conflict in the Middle East," declaimed Derek proudly—the training manual always recited this as a stellar example of the successes of conversion.

True to the word of Derek's trainer, Kyle's eyes widened and he rocked slightly back in his chair. "Really? Gotta say, that is one impressive feat. How'd that work?"

Maria waved her hand dismissively and took back control of the conversation. "It didn't solve the Mideast situation. It sidestepped it. One virtual world where the Jews control Jerusalem and all their neighbors stay clear of their claimed territory and one where the Arabs control Jerusalem and the Jews are nowhere to be found."

Kyle smiled and shook his head in bemused amazement. "That would be the one thing that would do it, sure 'nuf."

"The U.N. solved all the ethnic wars and border conflicts the same way. Taiwan, Northern Ireland, Kashmir . . . you name it," said Derek proudly.

"That makes for a lot of these here computer worlds, doesn't it?" asked Kyle, once again rubbing his beard in apparent contemplation.

"Yeah. Some are not quite as fully realized as the main worlds. Alpha One, which replicates reality as closely as possible, and Alpha Two, which does the same, but eliminates pain, disease, injury, and the like, are the two biggest. Like I said before, though, computer power and storage capacity are infinite for all practical purposes, so it really doesn't matter how many there are. I have a full menu with my equipment uphill, when it comes time for you to choose."

The last set Maria off like an exploding Ponderosa pine. "You keep using that word, 'choose.' Like you give anybody a real choice, a true choice. I hated it when the proponents of this sick scheme called themselves 'pro-choice.' The only thing about it that is right is the connection to the historical antecedents in the abortion struggle. Except here, you want to abort humanity as a whole—not just one life at a time." Her eyes were fiercely intent and the scowl on her face stole any prettiness that she had once seemed to have.

Kyle held up his hands to try to stop them, but the two debaters paid him no heed.

"We're not killing anybody, we're converting them!" shouted Derek. His voice conveyed a quivering vehemence that was not dictated by the training manuals. Life in the ConFoes was bad enough. He would not . . . could not . . . be able to tolerate it if he thought of himself as a mass murderer.

"And just what do you think happens to the souls of these people you 'convert' when you're finished and walk away, leaving their corpses to rot?"

"Conversion has absolutely nothing to do with religion! You . . . you cults just think it does. Look, the government even created special virtual worlds for the major religious sects, so you don't feel threatened by the process."

Maria glared at him with genuine venom. "You mean, so maybe we won't fight back. Most of the religious authorities refused to cooperate with the creation of those worlds or even sanction them after the fact."

Finally there was a pause long enough for Kyle to get a word in edgewise. "What's wrong with havin' your very own world?" he asked. "Don't think it's fer me, but what's the harm?"

"Don't you see?" pleaded Maria. "There's only two possibilities for what happens to your soul when you are converted. Either your soul leaves your body when you die from the scanning process—and that makes conversion murder . . . genocide—or your soul stays with your consciousness and gets converted into the virtual world with you . . ."

"Of course it does," concluded Derek, emphatically.

". . . in which case, it stays with you there forever, because everyone's immortal in virtual worlds, aren't they Derek?"

"Well, sure. Why would anyone want to die? Of course, every world has an escape hatch . . ." Kyle looked at him quizzically. Derek had to remember that his main effort here was to orient and convert Kyle, not win an argument with this religious fanatic. ". . . Just in case the virtual world is somehow intolerable, there is always a place where you can go to leave it."

"You mean you can change worlds?"

"No. That's not permitted. The virtual worlds are kept entirely separate from one another. It's a failsafe to prevent any problem in one world from spreading to the rest—a kind of anti-virus protection, if you will. So, you can't leave one virtual world for another, but your avatar can be deleted."

"And there's the problem. There's no room for God in any of this. If your soul goes with you and you stay in the virtual world for eternity, you never leave this world and go to be with God. You spend an eternity cut off from him—that's what hell is, Derek, an eternity without reuniting with God."

"Then leave when you choose," Derek stated matter-of-factly. He had the typical male tendency to problem-solve during arguments. Somehow women always hated it and he had never understood why.

"By your definition and mine, that's suicide. Despite the garbage they teach you in ConFoe training, religious groups aren't suicide cults. We don't have stashes of cyanide-laced Flavor-Aide sitting in our storerooms. Suicide is a mortal sin. You would just move from a man-made hell to satanic one. Not even that really, they are both born of Satan."

"Now, just hold on there, kids," interjected Kyle. "I don't know much 'bout hell, but things are sure 'nuf getting a tad too hot right here right now. This here cabin is comfy enough, but it sure ain't big enough for a religious war." He looked at each of them in turn, before continuing. "I think I get the point that some of the more holy types, they didn't like this conversion thing. Y'mean everybody else is all gone off to Neverneverland, 'ceptin' the . . . devout ones?"

Derek spoke up first. "No, there are other mals. There were more in the early days, after the act took effect."

"Mals?"

"Malcontents," explained Derek. "The term used to refer to . . . resistors . . . of mandatory conversion. Some were anti-government survivalists, others were religious types. Some were just isolated from civilization and liked their simple, agrarian ways and just didn't have the education to understand what was going on, even if things were explained to them. Worst were the warlords."

"You mean like in China and Afghanistan?"

"No," responded Maria icily. "Like in Chicago and New York and Moscow . . . gangs that filled the vacuum caused by the retreat of civilization into their infernal computers. Thugs that looted the cities and terrorized those not yet converted: raping, pillaging, killing for sport."

"Until the ConFoes came in and defeated them," noted Derek with a semblance of quiet pride for the past glories of his organization.

Maria shrugged briefly and snorted quietly—not a becoming gesture. "Until the ConFoes became the biggest, baddest gang of all and took all the raping and pillaging and killing for sport unto itself."

Derek wanted to retort, but he knew she had a point. Somehow repeating "God works in mysterious ways" didn't seem like it would be effective in this particular instance. There was a long pause before he said, quietly, "We do what we have to do. I wish we could do it with less . . . force. I really do. But it has to be done."

Kyle stood up and began to pace back and forth in front of the picture window in anxious consternation, like a sheet-metal duck in a target-pistol carnival booth from days gone by. "Y'see. That's the part I'm still not gettin', there, Derek. I understan' the two of you don't see eye to eye on things and, well, that's the nature of the world sometimes." He gestured widely at the vista outside the window without looking at it. "Sure don't seem that you're usin' the real estate for nothin' else. Why not just leave these folks peaceful-like and do your thing in the computers while they do theirs in this here world?"

Maria spoke up before Derek could. "Every government that ever was thinks it knows better than its citizens what's good for 'em. Don't you see, Kyle? They're imposing their will upon us. It's the Crusades again, except the earth is Jerusalem and the Holy Warriors are the heathens on this go-around."

"Bullshit," remarked Derek simply.

"You're the government representative here, ConFoe. Kyle's been here for decades without anybody from Sanctuary . . ." She shut her mouth, wincing hard momentarily as if she had bit her tongue. ". . . er . . . we call our religion, Sanctuary . . ." she clearly lied quickly before continuing, ". . . without anybody marching up to demand he convert to our belief or be summarily executed."

Could it be that Maria had never heard the standard ConFoe spiel on the justifications of mandatory conversion?

"I already told you. It's self-defense."

Maria looked at him in disbelief, as if trying to decide if he was brainwashed or simply incredibly stupid.

"I travel on foot with an aging automatic weapon, with a dwindling supply of ammunition," she noted, "while you roam the earth in armored personnel carriers with some pretty heavy-duty weaponry and spy satellites up in the sky to help you coordinate your movements."

She looked him up and down. "Except in a fair fight, one on one, exactly how do I threaten the ConFoes? And if I do scare you, little boy, and all your heathen, apish friends, then why don't you just run away to your computer and leave us in fuckin' peace?"

A bit crude, but Kyle had to admit it was a damn fine question.

He paused momentarily in his pacing to look at Derek. The ConFoe's hands were tented in front of his face, the fingers spread wide, with the nearest resting lightly on his bottom lip. Derek's eyes were looking up and to the left, no doubt reflecting his mind deep in thought for exactly how to proceed.

Derek looked up to see the old man staring at him. Derek hated revealing this part. The military man in him always said that it was unwise to admit to any weaknesses, but the PsyOps people had long ago decided that it was the single most effective explanation in getting the mals to understand the need for mandatory conversion, probably because it was true. So they had decided to reveal it as a matter of policy in the last stages of orientation, if necessary. After all, the individual being oriented was destined to be converted or destroyed, so there seemed to be little risk. Of course, all of that had been determined as policy early on, back before the resistance to mandatory conversion had become organized and increasingly militant—an event which had itself been brought about by the ConFoes' increasingly brutal and violent nature.

He looked at Kyle.

"Think it through. You know the facts. All, or at least almost all of humanity now resides in virtual worlds maintained by super-powerful and self-maintaining computers at some unknown safe place. We all agree that the nature of those virtual worlds is such that the consciousnesses that reside within them are immortal and eternal. There is no reliable evidence that any intelligent life exists elsewhere in the universe. So, short of the sun going supernova—and maybe even not then, for all I know—there is no threat to the existence of humanity *forever* 'til the end of time, *except* the threat posed by anyone left behind or, I guess, any aliens out there in the universe attracted here because intelligent life appears to exist on this planet."

Maria objected, "But how are a few Believers any threat to your computers?"

"Maybe you're not, not yet. Then again, maybe some of the religious cults out there seek redemption . . . you know, to redeem the misguided members of their . . . flock . . . who chose conversion."

Redemption.

Suddenly some things that Maria had heard discussed in whispers in Sanctuary, but had not understood, made sense. She sat mute as Derek continued.

"Populations have a way of growing. Science and technology are more easily rediscovered and re-implemented than discovered in the first place. How many years would it be . . . could it be before those left behind do something to destroy . . . by accident or design . . . the billions of consciousnesses, of souls by your measure, that exist in those virtual universes? Would you trust the future of your universe, of your existence, to your enemies? Or even random chance?"

Kyle visibly shuddered as Derek ended the debate. The life seemed to go out of the old man as he contemplated the life and death decision that he would soon face at the hands of the ConFoe.

Derek continued, putting the issue starkly before the hermit. "Everyone must convert or be destroyed. There is no other way to assure the future of my family and billions of other families, of mankind itself. There can be no survivors."

A chill crept down Maria's spine.

A tear fell from Kyle's eye.

Then the picture window exploded into a million lethal, glittering fragments as automatic weapon fire propelled Kyle forcibly back and down, his lifeless, bullet-pummeled body bowling over the rocking chair and crashing into the sturdy crossbar beneath his handmade table, his shattered body and unconverted mind racing his single tear to the floor.

Chapter 12

Both Derek and Maria instinctively dove down and back, unintentionally acting in concert to reach up and throw the heavy table over as a protective barrier from the death that lay outside the window.

Derek's mind accelerated into overdrive, adrenaline coursing through his veins and invigorating him in ways that mere blood and oxygen never could.

Where are the fucking guns?

Where are the fucking guns?

The mantra raced through his mind, speeding faster and faster as no answer responded to its screams.

Where are the fucking guns?

Maria's mind also seethed with adrenaline, creating a rush that neither sugar nor drugs could ever duplicate, but she had no time for questions which had no answer. The guns she knew, wherever they might be hidden, were outside. They were, therefore, out of reach and useless to her now. And now was what mattered. She gave them no more thought. The hermit, though, he had to have more than one weapon. Kyle Patterson was a good man, but he was also a smart man, a mountain man. There had to be other weapons, weapons that were in this room. If she were him, where would she keep them?

A second burst of automatic weapon fire riddled the facing side of their makeshift bunker as if to prompt her thoughts and actions. Her eyes darted quickly around the single, cluttered room, the terror and violence of the moment contrasting with the homey, quilted pattern of the bedspread as Kyle's bright red blood flowed quickly, spreading across the plank floor in a pool reaching toward her.

The mattress. Guys always hid crap under their mattress.

Maria sprang in a low crouch toward the bed as Derek threw his body into the underside of the table, forcing it toward the window and up onto the aging, slipcovered couch, the precarious placement expanding the table's effective protective coverage of the room. That accomplished, Derek darted right to bar the door.

Another spray of bullets thudded into the heavy table, dislodging it from its lopsided perch atop the couch and sending it thundering back down onto the floor, as Derek wedged a triangular shiv into the bottom crack of the door. It was really only a doorstop, there was no actual bar or bolt to lock the cabin door effectively. Kyle probably had not locked his door for decades. Why should he have? No one wanted to hurt the old man, except the ConFoes, and he had not even known of their existence.

The hermit's blithe lack of concern would be Derek's undoing. The doorstop would never prevent a heavy-booted thug from kicking in the door and now, again, the window was unblocked, allowing dum-dum bullets to slam into the interior of the cabin, shredding and destroying all that they touched. It was only a matter of moments before they touched him or the master of the dum-dums stormed into the cabin itself. He searched desperately for some way out of his predicament.

Maria was holed up behind the bed, a hunting rifle steadied against the bedpost at the foot of the feather mattress. Where had she gotten that? Not that it was any match for the automatic weapon, and who knows what else, they faced. Were there other weapons in the cabin?

Kyle did not answer, could never answer, his eyes staring wide at the beams he and Henrietta had carved so many years ago. His lifeblood pooled beneath him, spreading until it reached the crack for the trapdoor down to the root cellar. Derek's eyes continued to frantically search the room. He lunged for a kitchen knife as he heard heavy footsteps on the porch, followed by a sniggering voice.

"C'mon, baby. Let's not play hard to get. Let's just play. After all, I've been tracking you . . . stalking you for quite a ways now and the decrepit old mal geezer you came to visit seems to be . . . resting at the moment. Resting in pieces." The speaker sniffed exaggeratedly in mock sorrow. "He won't be watching . . . unless you want him to." Derek didn't have to wait for the sick, drooling wet giggle that inevitably followed to know the identity of their pursuer, of Kyle's cold-blooded murderer.

That twisted little ferret, Manning, had somehow escaped the explosions back at Interstate 70 and had tracked Maria up to the pass. He had undoubtedly witnessed her conversing with Kyle through the picture window and had quickly re-acted to eliminate any competition for, or, more accurately, any potential protection from, his leering, psychotic "affec-tions." Looking back at Maria, tensed behind the bed, Derek could see that although she had never met the loathsome ferret-boy, she instinctively understood what she was facing.

Suddenly, another thought surged to the surface of Derek's adrenaline-soaked mind. The ferret-boy apparently didn't realize his former comrade was here. That could be the advantage he needed to thwart the prick's undoubtedly twisted plans for Maria. As the footsteps continued on the porch and Manning made exaggerated smacking sounds with his lips as some kind of perverted foreplay, Derek clutched his kitchen knife tighter, turned toward Maria, and put one finger to his lips, then pointed toward the trapdoor in the floor. As a solid thud against the front door of the cabin sent the wooden shiv skittering across the floor, Derek dove for the trapdoor, opened it, and dropped through.

Maria understood and provided cover, doing her best to delay Manning's entrance. "Anybody who comes through that door will be singing soprano for the rest of their life."

Manning smacked his lips exaggeratedly again. "Oh, baby. I love it when you focus your attention on my balls."

Who was this guy? She thought she had gotten all of the ConFoes besides Derek. Had he shown up later at the scene of the explosion? She continued her bravado delaying tactics as Derek clambered quietly down the ladder under the trapdoor and closed it behind him.

"I killed your seven friends and I'll kill you, too, you dumb son-of-a-bitch. You don't scare me."

"The time will come when I do scare you, lover. And you should learn to count." He counted for her, punctuating his litany with bursts of gunfire.

"A.K. in the forward truck." Frrrpppt.

"Pancek, Digger, and Sandoval between the two vehicles." Frrrpppt. Frrrpppt. Frrrpppt.

"And Wires in the ditch." Frrrpppt.

"Maybe you got Derek, before or after your little fireworks. All I know is that he wasn't there for the show. We'll just give him a single shot." Blam!

"But, at best, that makes six. I think I'll do you once for each of them. How about it, sweetheart?" Again, the slurping, high-pitched giggle emanated from her stalker.

She used one hand to quickly toss the quilted bedspread

131

from the bed to flutter down across the bloodied floor, covering the outline of the now closed trapdoor, then resumed her grip upon the ancient hunting rifle.

"I guess Derek must have been the grease-spot under the second vehicle," she suggested, eager to lull him into a false sense of security. "Nothing left of him but a blood-soaked jacket. A shame it wasn't you."

Manning laughed convulsively. "Fuckin' raccoon stole my jacket and hid under the truck." She could almost sense him reaching for the latch as he told his tale. "So I chased after the bastard. And you know what I saw when I looked at the trucks?"

"No," she lied.

"A wire hanging down from a broken tail-light, looping down into an open fuel tank."

"You should take better care of your equipment," she said as she noticed the latch on the door moving slightly. She brazenly egged him on, hoping to distract him as he came through the door. "How many days after the explosion did it take you to figure out what caused it?"

The latch stopped moving. "I wouldn't insult me if I were you, bitch." The door eased inward a fraction of an inch. "I understood it like *that*," Manning said, but instead of the snap of fingers, she heard the snap of a fresh magazine being loaded. "Clear as day. I knew the frickin' score when I saw the flash of the brake lights come on in the front truck and I ran like hell, straight down the highway while A.K. and the boys, they were fryin' up like bacon. But me, I'm pretty quick; didn't even get singed."

"I've no doubt you're fast."

Suddenly, the door flew completely open and a burst of automatic weapon fire exploded randomly across the interior of the cabin from somewhere still unseen on the porch.

"You'll wish that was true when I'm killing you," growled Manning angrily. Though still out of sight, Maria somehow correctly imagined the smarmy leer on her tormentor's face.

"Well, little boy, a real man would have taken me out at the scene. What's the matter, were you hiding up a tree along the road, two miles downhill, crying for mommy?"

She knew most ConFoes had no respect for women and hated mals. She prayed that goading him would make him do something stupid.

It worked. She had guessed correctly and nothing, she knew, could piss off some guys more than a woman being right. With a guttural roar and yet another burst of untargeted fire, he rushed into the room.

Maria saw a small, vicious ConFoe charge through the open doorway, his weapon firing randomly, uncontrollably. His dark, beady eyes quickly located her and he flung himself pell-mell toward her, screaming like the lunatic he surely was. She only got off one shot before the ConFoe killer was upon her. She was sure that it hit him square in the chest, but he only faltered for a moment, then kept on coming.

Whatever it was, it wasn't a root cellar.

He should have guessed that, of course. The soil depth up in the mountains really wasn't that great, especially on a slope this steep. As his eyes adjusted to the gloom, he realized that he was on the heavily angled hillside that fell away under the level cabin, in a protected area where Kyle Patterson had stored everything from his tools to broken furniture—anything he didn't want to have cluttering the cabin, but didn't want to throw away completely. The cabin walls extended down to the ground on the north, east, and west unbroken. The south wall had a wooden panel which, he realized as he got his bearings, must open up under the porch.

As he listened to Manning and Maria exchange insults between random bursts from Manning's assault rifle, he scanned the darkened area for better weapons, tucking a hammer in his belt and grabbing a coiled ring-saw—a serrated wire with finger rings on either end, used for woodworking in tight spaces—with his left hand.

As Manning charged in above him, Derek flung aside the panel to the area beneath the porch and made his way out as quickly as he could. He would have more surprise and a better ability to move coming at Manning from outside the cabin.

Suddenly, he heard the boom of the old man's rifle and the sounds of a scuffle in the cabin above. He frantically pushed his way through the random junk hidden beneath the porch and out one of the open ends, slowing only long enough to peer over the edge of the porch before pulling himself up onto it as quickly and quietly as he could.

As they rolled along the floor struggling, arms and legs flailing maniacally at one another, Maria did her best to punch and press as much weight as she could into her attacker's chest. Even with the blasted Kevlar vest she found he was wearing, there was a good chance that her shot had knocked the wind out of the maniac, maybe even broken a rib or two. It was a slim advantage in a brawl for her life, but she would grab at any straw, no matter how thin. She gouged and scratched and pounded with an apocalyptic fury she had only once before experienced, for she knew that Derek could not save her.

Even if he wanted to, even if he were willing to kill his comrade-in-arms, Derek was trapped in the cellar. Manning's initial grab and throw had landed them square atop the blood-soaked quilt covering the trapdoor. The slick wetness of Kyle Patterson's lifeblood coated them hideously as they struggled for purchase and advantage in their wrestling match.

Fortunately for her, at least in terms of survival, the ConFoe was trying harder to subdue and paw her, than to kill her. His blood-covered hands felt her up crudely, rather than pummeling her. He tried to pin her, not to kill her, not yet. He smiled maniacally, with obvious sexual arousal, as his red-smeared face lunged toward hers.

Unfortunately, the Kevlar vest protected the ConFoe's torso from any punches she could provide and the two of them were too closely intertwined for her to knee him effectively in the crotch. Too small a target, anyhow, she thought as she butted him hard in the nose with her forehead. More blood, his blood, spurted out upon the two of them as they struggled.

Suddenly, a hammer glinted in the air above them, swinging down toward the back of her tormenter's maniacal, crimson head. But somehow, Manning heard or sensed the attack. Maybe the widening of Maria's eyes as she glimpsed the hammer of her salvation tipped him off. She would never know.

All she knew was that Manning threw himself hard to his left and the hammer hit a glancing blow off the back of his Kevlar vest and flew from what she now saw was somehow Derek's hand and skittered away across the floor.

Manning abandoned her like a pit bull abandons its rubber bone when a fresh steak is tossed into its cage, charging up and into Derek's bent-over body. The two of them crashed about, scattering the homey contents of the cabin helter-skelter in their violent frenzy. A knife flew through the air and was lost amongst the debris of battle. Then, somehow, each of the ConFoes gained purchase with both hands on the other's throat and squeezed, beginning a race towards death by asphyxiation.

She looked about frantically for the ConFoe's weapon but it was not in sight, lost somewhere in the commotion. She froze for just a moment in panic and indecision while the two squad-mates pressed the life from one another, their eyes locked in a death-grip stronger than that exerted by their hands. Suddenly, Derek broke off the staring contest and looked at her and then at the blood-stained floor beside him. A coiled wire with finger rings on either end lay there. Where it had come from, she had no idea. He looked at it and then back at his opponent.

Manning had gotten the upper hand in their battle of oxygen starvation. He straddled Derek, sitting heavily on his chest while he strove to choke what little air remained out of the traitor. Derek's grip began to loosen as his body screamed for oxygen.

Maria understood Derek's eyes and before Manning could comprehend what was happening, she looped the bladed wire around their crazed attacker's head. Derek flung his hands down and out of the way as the razor-edged noose tightened above Manning's Adam's apple. The astonished ferret-boy let go of Derek as his fingers sought for purchase between the saw and the tender flesh of his neck, but it was too late. Maria had grabbed a nearby wooden spoon and thrust the handle into the finger rings as soon as she had looped it around her sleazy, perverted enemy, twisting the handle around and around and around in a frenzy of retribution until the struggling stopped and the blood came gushing, spurting forth. She continued to tighten the wire until the spurting stopped and the wire met bone.

Derek, now standing above her, panting, finally put his hand on her shoulder. "It's all over," he told her simply as she continued to maintain the pressure on her makeshift garrote, her eyes wide and unblinking.

"It's all over."

"It is all over, Hank," said Ali with a sigh. "Now number eight will not move, not one bit. The main drive is completely frozen. Cracked bearings, I would surmise."

"Can't you fix it?" replied Hank, looking up wearily. He was slumped in a worn, armless chair, his stained lab coat trailing down onto the floor, threatening to get caught in the casters as he pivoted and pushed back from the flickering row of computer screens in front of him. He surveyed Ali, the messenger of bad tidings. His assistant's gray sweatshirt was stained with grease, grains of sand trapped in the thick, black splotches. "We're between configurations. Our amplification and resolution will be shot to hell."

"I do not think that number eight, she will ever move again. Our only alternative is to work around it. Could we not use a smaller array?" He wiped a gob of lubricant from the side of his thumb onto his denim jeans. "We must be grateful for what we have. We are, after all, most fortunate that the cells are still providing power. Without power, we will not be able to search at all, no matter what configuration is set."

Moisture welled up in Hank's eyes, but his anger and determination overcame the depression of this latest defeat. "We're the only ones looking, Ali. You know I'll never stop. The math can't be wrong."

Ali smiled, his white teeth contrasting with his dark skin. "You are preaching to the choir, boss. You know that I am a true believer."

Hank turned back to the terminals and took up his task once again. "I don't want to believe. I want to know," he said softly, quoting his hero.

Outside, the flat desert warmed in the sun. Tonight it would cool under the twinkling of thousands of stars—the Milky Way cutting a swath high in the sky. The stars would speak to Hank again tonight. Their energetic hum would fill the sky, but, as always, they would say nothing.

Hank believed in the math, but he knew he would never really know. It was all over.

Chapter 13

She swam toward the shore of the mountain lake, then stood and strode to him, clean, fresh, and pure. Rivulets of bright water flashed and sparkled as they tumbled down her firm body. She made no effort to cover her nakedness and gave no disapproving look as he surveyed it. Instead she smiled and ruffled her hair with one hand to help it dry, laughing gaily in the rosy hues of the setting sun. A mischievous wink greeted him from her perfect face.

Derek smiled back and stood from the rocker to embrace her, his arms engulfing her and his clean plaid shirt soaking up the residual moisture from her swim. After a long, deep kiss, they sauntered arm in arm toward their cozy alpine retreat, isolated and safe from everyone and everything. There, they would make love on the big pine bed and, afterwards, she would whisper his name as they snuggled on the couch, looking out the big picture window at the moonlit valleys below.

"Derek."

He smiled with contentment.

"Derek." Her voice was harsher and louder than should be.

"Derek. Hey, ConFoe!"

Derek awoke on the rocking chair. His body ached. His clothes were covered with dirt and caked with dry blood. His neck was purple with bruises from his recent battle with the ferret-boy. Maria stood over him in clean, practical clothes scavenged from the cabin after the battle. The hermit's cabin loomed unpleasantly behind her, the doorjamb splintered, a gaping maw ringed with sharp talons of glass where the picture window once was, and bloody boot-prints tracked across the boards of the once-pretty porch.

He blinked twice, but the grim harshness of reality would not blink away. The soft focus and golden hue of a few moments before would not return. He had been dreaming. He rubbed his face with his hands. At least it had been a pleasant dream, much more pleasant than he had dreamt in a long, long time. Even his dreams were shitty since he became a ConFoe.

He looked up at Maria, his eyes squinting in the morning light.

"Your turn," she said, gesturing with her head toward the lake, out of sight to the side of the cabin. A few scrapes and bruises had joined the older scar on her face, but the new badges of battle were clean and none looked to leave any permanent mark. She continued, "You might want to scrounge whatever you want before you wash up. Me, I'm never going into that charnel house again." She strode away to a stack of food, clothing, and other supplies she had gathered before her bath and began loading them into a backpack that used to belong to Kyle.

And there it was. Another moment that decided his fate without any real input from him at all. All dreams of leaving the troubles of both the real and virtual worlds behind and taking up with Maria to live in Kyle's and Henrietta's cabin safe from the ConFoes and the mals vanished in the blink of an eye, like a magician's flash paper. As he shuffled his aching body back into the chaos and stench of the cabin battleground and started picking through it, looking for useful items to salvage for whatever lay ahead, he realized that his life, such that it was, was merely a series of unhappy journeys from one random nexus to another, all set in motion by that damnable recruitment vid and its incessantly annoying jingle. Induction, training, assignment—all within the control of the ConFoes and their nameless leaders. Mission after mission after horrific mission—all within the control of A.K. and his testosterone-charged, macho-bullshit sadism.

This mission was a microcosm of it all: a surprise ambush; a painful chase; a second, more destructive ambush which failed to kill him only because he lagged behind from weariness and a desire to escape the vulgar banter of his squadmates; and a series of unexpected meetings, each one fraught with the specter of death. Now, fate—no Maria—had snatched his dream of a life happily-ever-after and he was gearing up for yet another trek into the unknown.

Mankind had found a way to control the universe—to control all universes.

Derek couldn't even control his own life.

He was trapped in a box, the kind they apparently put mimes in. He couldn't see it, but he felt it all around him every time he reached out for happiness. Duty. Contract. Circumstance. Cowardice. Inertia. The choices of others. They closed in upon him, until he was afraid to reach out for joy, or even comfort, lest he find out the box defining his existence had shrunk even smaller.

He shook off his despair as best he could, comforting himself with the belief that he had, at least, made Katy happier by joining the ConFoes, that every misery he suffered was matched by an equal and opposite measure of joy in her life. But thinking of Katy was also painful; he couldn't yet share her joy and he feared that something he did might still take it from her. So, instead, he turned his thoughts to the minor tasks that faced him immediately, small things within the confines of his box, things he could still control. He snagged some clothes, found a cache of elk-jerky, and grabbed some other useful items, dumping them near his knapsack before heading to the lake to wash up. He brought some of the salvaged clothes with him—his ConFoe uniform was in sorry shape. Still, he washed the uniform out as best he could, figuring to fold it up and bring it along after it dried, just in case he might need it in his unknown future.

Neither Derek nor Maria ever found their weapons, dangling on a thin rope hooked under the seat in the privy, but they had the old man's rifle and Manning's weapon, along with three full magazines of ammunition and several grenades. It would have to do.

When Derek had dressed and returned to the front of the cabin, he saw that Maria had stowed his gear for him and laid out a couple of metal plates with potatoes and jerky. He sat cross-legged and started to chow down without waiting for any benediction by his mal compatriot. He tore off a piece of the leathery elk meat and began to chew. It didn't have the savory taste of Kyle's stew, but it was still light-years ahead of the now depleted MREs.

Maria chewed on her jerky, avoiding Derek's gaze. Neither spoke for quite a while, focusing instead on Kyle's last batch of jerky. Occasionally, Maria would glance furtively at Derek, her eyes quickly moving away and narrowing. Her muscles were taut as she ate, chewing with an almost military cadence.

Derek's dream of living happily-ever-after with Maria had been just that, a dream, but he couldn't help but feel the tension and it sure wasn't the good kind of first-date tension. It smelled of fear; perhaps the day's events had been more traumatic on the girl than he had thought.

Finally, Derek could stand the silence no longer.

"Look, I'm not going to hurt you."

Maria looked at him, her eyes softening a bit, but fear and uncertainty still shining through. "I . . . I guess I know that. I mean, after all you saved me. You attacked your own squadmate." Her eyes searched his face for answers to questions yet unspoken. "I . . . I should thank you . . . I do thank you . . . for that. I just don't . . . well I don't know . . . why." She hesitated, staring at Derek intently.

"Look, Maria," Derek replied. "The guy was a sick, vindictive psychopath. You saved me at the end, you know, and I thank you for that."

He waited for her to acknowledge his thanks or agree that Manning was a monster, but she obviously still had something on her mind.

"I just don't know what your expectations . . ." Her voice quavered and trailed off into silence.

Derek started in realization. Did she really think that little of him after all of this? Was it the legacy of the ConFoe uniform? He cringed inwardly as he thought of the stories of terror and rape that the mals undoubtedly indoctrinated into their women, not without some truth, to steel their resolve for the battles ahead. Whatever fantasies he might have, he would never do that.

"I'm . . . not Manning. He was a vicious little ferret. I . . . won't . . ." He stopped exasperatedly, then gathered his thoughts. "Your . . . virtue . . . is safe with me." He continued in a rush of words, "I only wish you'd killed the bastard on the highway. It would have saved us both the trouble and kept him from trashing a perfectly nice cabin."

She nodded as he spoke, a certain amount of relief apparent in her eyes, but the uncertainty still lingered in her manner and her voice. She looked past him toward the silhouetted cabin, once again looking peaceful and innocent in the growing darkness.

"But, it wouldn't have saved Kyle, would it?" she said, her voice hardening near the end.

This girl, this mal, was made of sterner stuff than he had imagined. She did not fear for her body; she feared only for her soul. She did not fear him, at least not in that brute way; she feared only his scanning equipment. At the same time, he realized, she could have escaped her fear at any time. She could have killed him as he dreamt of her naked body. She could have shot him as he strode, defenseless, from the lake. She could have left in the gathering gloom and returned to the Believers, her people, and left him behind.

But she had not.

Derek's ego and his still-aching gonads longed to believe that it was because she was attracted to him, but his brain told him that it was either because she was too moral . . . too good and too polite . . . to kill him or to suddenly abandon him after they had mutually aided one another . . . or that, like him, she had duties she had not yet fulfilled and didn't know how to fulfill in the current situation.

His reverie was prolonged by the fact that he didn't really know how to answer her question.

"As I said . . . before . . . to Kyle. My training teaches me that a member of the Conversion Forces can leave no mal survivors."

Maria looked at him with an expression of mixed sadness and resolve. "My training also teaches me that the ConFoes leave no survivors."

He quickly interjected to forestall her from any precipitous action or conclusion. "But I will not kill you or forcibly convert you."

She almost smiled. "And I will not kill you, but cannot leave you free here to return to the ConFoes."

"I would never . . ."

"Not willingly. But you know them. You know they could make you tell . . ."

"Which leaves us where?"

She reached over and tossed him a blanket. "Which leaves us sleeping under the stars. God does work in mysterious ways, you know. We can decide in the morning."

Derek was content to push off the decision for the morrow. Too much had happened already today. A good night's sleep would allow his subconscious to make sense of it all and find a plan.

"May God watch over *us* and keep us safe through the night," Maria prayed aloud.

Not "me," "us."

As a member of the Conversion Forces, Derek should have been insulted, even outraged, by this mal effort to undermine his world view. But he was not. If, indeed, he had no control over his life, he kind of liked the idea that someone, somewhere was watching over it—maybe even making sense of the whole sorry mess. He stared at the starry lights in the heavens and wondered if that could truly be.

Unnoticed by Derek, or even Maria, one of the lights in the night sky above flared minutely and then blinked out, like many of its brothers had before it. It would never watch or speak or listen again.

Hank and Ali noticed the passing of the light, but neither one commented on it to the other. They had seen other such lights disappear, as if by the flick of a switch, before. They knew that they would see it again. The world was returning to a dark age and there was nothing that they could do to stop it.

Still, they scurried in the increasing darkness, gathering what they could before things progressed to the point that no more could be gathered. They continued to work, silent as the remaining stars.

Maria slept well.

It was the same cold ground she had slept on many a night and the same cruel world greeted her in the morning when she awoke, but, somehow, knowing that she was safe—even if just for one night—deepened her sleep and allowed her pleasant dreams.

She awoke with the sun shining in her face, but with a pleasant breeze cooling it and playing lazily with loose strands of hair. A cup of cool water and a plate of small potatoes scrounged from Kyle's cabin was set near her for breakfast. She stretched and rolled from her side to her back and saw Derek sitting on the other side of her sipping his own cup of water. An empty plate sat on the ground near him.

"You have to shoot me," he said.

That certainly took the sheen off the morning. Her mind reeled in confusion.

"Excuse me?"

"I've been thinking it through. Neither one of us wants to kill the other. I won't convert you and you can't risk leaving me alive. That leaves very few choices."

She turned her conscious mind to the task. "I don't understand why that means I should shoot you." She hesitated to go on . . . to suggest what had occurred to her in her musings as she fell asleep the night before, because to her it would be anathema—a mortal sin, perhaps worse. But she was not him and she had to respect his beliefs—or his non-beliefs—as long as he didn't try to impose them on her, so she made the suggestion. "Couldn't you just convert yourself?"

He shook his head. "There's two problems with that. They say that techs at the conversion processing facilities have a way to check as to whether a ConFoe conversion that is submitted is an unauthorized voluntary conversion. I don't know how they do it—whether the process checks for body damage to repair or they implanted something during training or what. But they threaten to flush any canister with a voluntary ConFoe conversion that occurs before the end of the grunt's tour."

"I couldn't . . . wouldn't . . . ask you to risk that."

"You know, as bad as life has become in the ConFoes, I might even risk it, but there's more. They also threaten to reverse your sign-in bonus."

She looked at him curiously; her nose wrinkling and her brow furrowing as she cocked her head slightly to one side like a puppy. "You'd risk your immortal soul, but not your paycheck?"

Derek smiled broadly and let out a sudden exhale that was almost a laugh. "The enlistment bonus consists of credits used to make physical alterations during the conversion process."

So she had been right in her assumption the previous day. She didn't know what to say. She looked him over. Less than handsome and showing a bit of wear and tear, but overall not a bad specimen. He noticed her appraisal and blushed slightly.

"Does your family have shortcomings . . ." He blushed even brighter. ". . . er . . . physical deformities of which I am unaware?" she asked.

Derek shook his head, still smiling, but his eyes betraying a wistfulness she had not seen before. "Nothing like that. They used them for Katy, my sister. She is . . . was . . . paraplegic. No matter what happens to me, I wouldn't want her to be . . . crippled . . . again."

"Oh." Suddenly, the world was once more a sad and dangerous place, devoid of innocence. "They would do that?" It seemed unbelievably cruel, but then the ConFoes had refined cruelty to unfathomable depths.

"I don't know. They might. Whether I live to see her on Alpha Two or not, I . . . well, I just need to know that she is and always will be . . . whole . . . there."

Maria understood his meaning, even if she could never understand how someone could hope to be whole while denying the existence of the soul, but she stood mute on that theological point for now.

"There's also a practical problem. If I were to convert here, my canister might not ever make it to the processing facility. I could be between worlds forever."

"In limbo."

"In what?"

"Limbo." Her voice took on just a slight professorial tone. "It's what we call the place between worlds, between life on earth and heaven. It's a sad place—no one wants to be there for long."

"So, really, when you were talking to Kyle before about the virtual worlds—that's what they are to you, limbo."

She had never thought of it that way, but Derek had a point. She nodded slightly. "No one wants to be there for long."

Now Derek shook his head, smiling. "Certainly not for eternity." He gave a small grunt. "And eternity is our biggest selling point."

Maria chewed a potato and thought a bit.

Derek again watched her eat, distracted from his plans for a moment by the simple pleasure of her presence. But the moment passed and reality intruded once again.

"So, how does my shooting you help this in any way?" she asked.

"I don't want you to shoot me now, not here," Derek said, pointing to himself, then realizing that he was pointing to his own chest. "Er . . . or any place vital."

"Then where?"

"A leg, my leg would be okay." Derek had lived with a paraplegic in the real world. He could handle being crippled in this world or the next if he had to.

"Yeah, yeah, I figured that part out already. You said not now, not here. I suspect you originally meant not this geographic location. So where, when?"

Derek's military training kicked in. He liked Maria. He trusted her with his life, but he would not trust her with the lives of others. After all, she was the enemy. She was a mal.

"I can't tell you that, you understand. Not yet. Let's just say far from here, where I can be 'rescued,' but you can still be safe."

He could tell from her expression that Maria was unhappy with his response, but understood. He suspected she especially liked the part about far from here. If something went wrong—if he died or she died or they ran into others of his kind, they would not associate them with this geography. And her duty to her home—he guessed from her earlier clearly regretted comment that they called it Sanctuary—was to move him far away from this place.

Maria began to gather up her things and tuck them into the backpack nearby. "Then I guess we're going on a road trip."

Derek grimaced. "More like a very, very long walk."

She stopped, puzzled. "We're not taking Kyle's truck?"

"I looked around a bit, while you were still sleeping. I couldn't find Kyle's truck."

Maria snorted in mock derision. "Silly boy. It's obviously on the other side of the pass."

Derek looked at her incredulously. "How could you possibly know that?"

"Look around. Sure, there's not any deadfall among the trees—he's cleaned that up pretty regular—but there's plenty of these scrawny, twisted little trees and nary a stump in sight."

Derek's look had morphed from incredulity to utter confusion.

She continued. "The man's been living here decades, but hasn't cut any firewood here. Probably cuts it on the other side of the pass. It maintains the pristine view, after all. Then, he loads it up in the truck and hauls it home whenever the load is full."

"Why not just drive it home every day?"

"The thing's undoubtedly ancient. Probably doesn't want to wear it out any faster than he has to. May take quite a while to charge up on the solar panels at this point, too." Maria stood and shouldered on her backpack.

Derek did the same. As he did, his eye caught sight of the wrecked cabin in the background.

"Should we, you know, bury the bodies?"

Maria frowned. "Like I said, I'm not going back in there." She looked about at the surroundings for a moment. "Besides, it would be a lot of work and there's no real reason to. If anyone finds them before the animals get 'em, they'll just think your squad took out the old man in a fight and go on about their business. I doubt they'll be able to tell if all this occurred before or after the other . . . incident . . . on the highway."

Derek concurred. "That works for me."

Maria started to walk, then turned back to Derek. "I would like to say a few words for Kyle." She paused. "But I'd like to wait until we can look back at the cabin, from a distance."

Derek understood. The personalized violence of the place still troubled her. It was better to put some distance between them and it. "Sure."

Maria paused again, looking at the ground, rather than turning back to her walking. Finally she spoke. "I don't plan to say any words for . . . him." She gestured with her head toward the cabin. "You know, Manning." Derek had told her the ConFoe's name when they had talked last night before they fell asleep exhausted. Somehow it had been important to her to know his name.

Derek snorted. "Fine by me. The only reason I could even dream of to say words over that bastard is that it would piss off the little prick."

Maria gave a nod and headed out the driveway and up the forgotten road to the top of the pass.

As they walked, Derek could see that Maria had been right. The ill-kept road did show signs of some vehicular traffic uphill from the driveway, where it had shown none on the stretch he had walked as he approached the cabin. He hadn't noticed the difference when he passed this way a couple nights before, when he had trekked uphill before circling back on the cabin, but it had been dark and he hadn't been looking.

They picked up Wires' bulky scanner where Derek had ditched it partway up the hill. Maria looked at the equipment with undisguised contempt and Derek had to admit that the scanner was a bother to carry. But there was the promise of a truck over the saddle of the pass and Derek had carried . . . was carrying . . . heavier burdens than this.

After all, the ConFoe training manual told him that every ConFoe soldier carried the fate of the world, all worlds.

It was a lot to carry.

Chapter 14

Hiking with Maria was a whole lot more pleasant for Derek than any mission with the ConFoes had ever been. Even struggling through the steeper sections of the climb was more pleasurable with Maria's derriere as his focal point than strolling through a flat, shaded meadow behind his squad-mates' sorry asses.

He thought, too, that it was more than the fact that he hadn't seen a woman—certainly not a desirable woman—in some time. Maria was an impressive woman. Certainly she was an excellent soldier. It was no wonder that she had managed to track him to Kyle's. And her smile, that was genuine, more genuine than anything you ever saw in the "adult" virtual reality programs, back when he had still had access to them during training. Such things weren't allowed on missions.

It wasn't that the pornographic vids were too much of a distraction, so much as the Conversion Forces liked to have the men testosterone laden and frustrated when out on patrol. It put them on edge. It revved them up and made them more effective.

Derek's musings were interrupted by a loose rock skittering into his chest as it bounded from the scree Maria was moving through above him.

She heard his "oomph" of surprise and turned back to him.

"If you kept your eyes on something besides my ass, you might have seen that coming," she said jokingly.

"If I kept my eyes on something else, I might have

minded the pain when it hit."

They continued on, enjoying the hike, their minds churning in an attempt to imagine a world where they would not be enemies.

They crested the pass in the late morning, surrounded by banks of melting snow amidst the rocks. Maria proved her skills yet again by locating Kyle's refrigerator, a cache of elk meat stowed in the hollow of a massive chunk of dense snow and ice.

"How is it that the bears haven't gotten this?" wondered Derek aloud as they built a small fire and feasted on the find.

"They're probably at lower elevations by the time he stashes this stuff away in the late spring," replied the wilderness-savvy Maria. "Besides, not that many bears left. Even with the 'decline' in human population, they haven't come back much. The ConFoe patrols kill 'em for sport when they see them, don't they?"

She was right, of course. The ConFoes killed everything that moved if they had a weapon handy. All that pent-up testosterone. Manning had even used an armor piercing shell on one black bear, Derek remembered sickly—almost losing the taste for his delicious lunch, if not the lunch itself.

"Yeah, they . . . we do."

She looked at him sternly. "They do. I'll bet you never did."

Derek smiled weakly, his appetite returning. She was right, again, of course. "Thanks. Thanks for . . . knowing that."

Maria also turned back to her meal with vigor. "If we can, we'll stop back here and pack a bit of meat and ice into the truck. At least we'll have meals for a few days of our journey."

"Yep."

"Wherever we're going."

It still wasn't time to tell her, even though he wanted to trust her and knew she was fishing for information.

"It'll be at least that long," was all he would say for now.

Maria had also been right about Kyle's forestry habits. Many of the scrubby trees on this side of the pass had clearly been harvested, some recently, others some time ago. Small ones were replacing those cut, but it would be years before the new growth would be worth cutting. The old man had avoided clear-cutting, probably because of good forestry management habits, rather than a desire to mask his presence from foes he had never imagined, so it took a bit of time to locate the truck near his latest cuttings, but eventually they did.

The truck was big old SolarFord two-ton, two-seater pickup from before ConFoe times. Accordingly, instead of guzzling scarce, dirty fuel, like the ConFoe vehicles now did, it was covered with dull black photovoltaic cells that soaked up the sunlight and charged up a bank of batteries located in an internal compartment between the cab and the bed of the truck. The tires were oversized snow tires, beginning to show wear, but still capable of throwing mud and gravel up behind. The bed was partially filled with cut firewood, which was covered by a black tarp to keep the wood dry.

Derek dropped the tailgate and clambered into the bed. "I'll unload the wood."

"Keep the tarp and leave some of the wood."

"The extra weight will cut down on our range," Derek replied.

"I don't know how far we need to go," countered Maria innocently.

"We'll need some range," said Derek simply.

Maria sighed softly with exasperation. "Then whether we

take some wood depends on how sunny you expect it to be where we're going and whether you want someplace to hide your 'equipment' in case someone takes a peek under the tarp," she said, gesturing toward Wire's scanner with obvious distaste.

Derek thought about it for a minute. "I'll leave enough wood to hide the scanner." With that, he set about his work.

In the meantime, Maria checked out the cab of the truck. The glove compartment actually contained gloves, of all things: a pair of leather work gloves, well-worn, especially where the finger joints fit into the handle of the ripsaw she found behind the seats. She also found wrenches, pliers, and fuses that could be used to repair the truck if needed. Finally, the glove box contained several road maps: one for Colorado; one for the western United States; one for hiking trails in the eastern Rockies; and, strangely, one for Wisconsin. Maybe Kyle or Henrietta was from there and used to visit at some point in the distant past. She pocketed the trail map—it might be useful to the Believers if . . . when . . . she returned to them. The others she left alone.

The driver's seat was in pretty bad shape—well worn and stained with dirt and sweat from years and years of use. The stuffing poked out from the seat and front edge of the cushion. The passenger seat, on the other hand, was in much better condition. But then, it hadn't seen a passenger in a long time.

Maria left the cab and checked under the hood. Mechanical things weren't really her specialty, but the old solar equipment was prized among the Believers, so she knew a bit. As far as she could tell, everything was in order.

Finally, she shut the hood and came around back to the growing pile of wood off the end of the bed. Without a word, she began picking up logs and chucking them various directions into the scrub and trees.

Derek stopped his methodical transfer of logs from the truck to the ground.

"What are you doing that for?" he asked her.

"A pile of wood tends to get noticed, even from a distance. Logs strewn about the weeds and trees don't."

He looked at her with agreement, but without understanding.

"You haven't been chased . . . hunted . . . ever, have you?" she said matter-of-factly, without the acid, bitter accusation that he knew could have tinged her voice.

"No, I haven't," he replied softly, as he took to hefting the logs into the woods from the truck bed. "I've only hunted," he whispered to himself as he completed his work and secured the scanner beneath the remaining logs. "And I've never even liked that."

The ancient SolarFord started up surprisingly well and the two of them decided that it had sufficient charge to make the brief trip back uphill to fetch some meat. Maria worked on packing the meat and snow while Derek studied the maps from the glove compartment. When she got back into the cab, he handed the maps to her.

"I can't navigate, if I don't know where we're going," she said, taking the maps.

He hesitated a moment before replying. "South, but back east first, so we're traveling on the plains as much as possible. It will extend our range."

Maria glanced at the map. "So, south to I-70, then into Denver and south on I-25?"

He pursed his lips and shook his head. "No, I-70 might

not be safe from either of our factions. We'll move east along the back roads, through Nederlander and towards Boulder, then south on 93, for now."

He was probably right about I-70. The Believers would certainly kill or imprison Derek if they had the chance. Yet she couldn't help but feel that Derek was somehow testing her, using her suggestions and replies to gauge her knowledge or her trustworthiness. It perturbed her. Sure, she was keeping secrets. She would never reveal the location of Sanctuary. But, confound it, so was he. They both knew that. But he couldn't let it be. Why did he pick at the scab of distrust between them by his conversation, rather than letting it heal?

"You're driving," she replied simply. Derek re-started the truck and they were off on their journey into the unknown.

The door to Sanctuary opened up onto the badlands of hell. Drifted soot and ash gathered in the lees of charcoaled logs, harboring the still-hot embers from the firestorm against the now-cool breeze blowing across the devastated valley. Here and there, clumps of forest fuel still burned even days after the main conflagration had passed. No chirping bird or buzzing insect intruded upon the tableau of emptiness and destruction.

General Antonio Fontana surveyed the depressing scene with a methodical, steely gaze. No tear moistened his cheek as he made a slow, 360-degree assessment of their military and survival situation. When the door had first been opened, he had quickly detailed several patrols to search for Maria, but he had no real hope that she had survived the fire. It had been pure foolishness that had driven her to scoot out the door at the last second and she had assuredly paid for her lack of judgment with her life, but, blessedly, not with her soul.

Whether they found her burnt body or not, there would be

157

a brief service and prayers for her in the morning.

The service would have to be brief, because Fontana didn't like what he saw, not in the least. The entire valley had been consumed, leaving no vegetation shielding the mine entrance, no cover for the trails used by Believers as they came and went from their refuge, and no food or game to support the population hidden away beneath the mountainside. The vista on the other side of the ridge, where their air-holes and secondary and emergency exits were located, was reported to be no different. Their hideaway lay naked and exposed to the photographic and infrared equipment of the blasted ConFoe satellites.

In some ways he was surprised that the ConFoes had not already fallen upon them in force. The squad that had set this blaze had had plenty of time to report in and the cool air exhaled from the mine's air vents as part of the underground warren's natural "breathing" process would show up like brightly colored balloons against a clear blue sky on a tasked satellite's output scans.

Worse yet, nature, itself, posed an even greater threat than their heathen enemies. The first serious rain would wash a thick, hideous slurry of mud and water and ash down the denuded mountainsides in a torrent. Half-burned logs would clog the waterways and the frustrated liquid would permeate any avenue it could find in its gravity-induced search for a lower resting place.

Sanctuary could be well-sealed against ConFoe invaders, but it was far from watertight. The floodwaters would empty into the mine, rushing toward the safe-places for the women and children, destroying their hope for the future. The sky was clear at the moment, but that would not last indefinitely. They did not have long.

He started to think to himself that they had been lucky so

far, but he knew that luck had nothing to do with it. God was watching out for them, protecting the Believers, but giving them a sign that hiding from their tormentors was no longer His will.

Circumstance and desire conspired to reveal God's will. It was time to implement the Plan.

The Plan had been conceived during the long, dark times deep in the bowels of Sanctuary when the military and religious leaders pondered the issues of the survival of the Believers and their place in this final battle between the forces of good and evil. It was, of course, holy writ that the forces of evil, the ConFoes, could not, would not, be victorious in the end over the forces of the righteous. But the Believers' teachings also warned that there would be terrible, dark times before the final victory and that the final victory would not come from a miraculous, heavenly bolt from God's right hand, but from the pain and death and misery of a final battle between the Believers and the ConFoes.

Accordingly, they had thought long and hard about that eventuality in their secret Sanctuary—not only about the tactics of the situation and the training of recruits, but about what event, what circumstance could possibly be the final, strategic showdown between the warring forces left on this world.

Clearly, the battle would need to be one that raged over ultimate objectives of the warring factions, not subsidiary matters or tactical targets. That made it simple.

What was the ultimate objective, the unholy purpose of the ConFoes? Not the elimination of all of mankind—that was merely a means to an end. The ConFoes existed to protect the computer universes from intentional or unintentional destruction by mankind.

Eliminate the computers and you eliminate the purpose for the ConFoes' foul existence. As an added bonus, the annihilation of the computers and the multitude of foul, unholy, and artificial virtual worlds they contained, would free billions of souls from limbo and send them back to God where they belonged.

And so, deep in their carved-out caverns, the leaders of Sanctuary had pondered long and hard on the same questions that had faced the leaders of the world's governments many years before. Where could the computers that housed mankind be hidden and how would they be protected from destruction? There was a scientific logic to answering that question, a scientific logic that had been investigated *publicly* in the United States years before, when the government was trying to determine where to store safely the nuclear waste it had accumulated over the decades.

The location had to be geologically stable—not prone to earthquake or volcanic activity. It had to be dry—flowing and dripping water are difficult to contain and predict and can be terribly destructive. It had to be remote—too many people nearby caused too many variables, too many witnesses to construction, and increased risks. And, finally and most importantly, it had to be defensible, from terrorists . . . or holy warriors.

A variety of salt domes in Utah and Texas fit the criteria and had been investigated thoroughly by the government. In the end, they had not been used because the government decided that the heat generated by the nuclear waste was better contained inside the barren mesa of Yucca Mountain in Nevada. After more than a decade of lawsuits and wrangling and a few more years for structural modifications and enhancements, the special trucks and railcars carrying impregnable stainless steel canisters of all sorts of nuclear waste had trundled ceaselessly out into the desert and into the confines of that place.

That left the various salt mines available for the computers. It was only a question of figuring out which one and coming up with a tactical plan to take it with a light infantry force.

The Believers had not been alone in their planning. Their intermittent contacts with other mals revealed that at least the more organized and militant among them had gone through the same thought process. Most of those other mals, of course, did not share the religious rescue aspects of the benefits of the Plan, but many had indicated that, if the time came that it was clear the ConFoes could not otherwise be defeated, they would join in on a last-ditch effort to save what remained of humanity.

The Believers did not bother to attempt to bring the warlords and gangs that dominated the urban areas into the circle of allies. Their reputation for violence and chaos was unparalleled even by the ConFoes; they could not be trusted. The Believers interacted with them only through individual envoys that disguised their affiliation and traveled to the cities in search of rare equipment or replacement parts to scavenge or obtain by trade.

Tonight, Fontana would go deep within Sanctuary and urge that the Army of the Believers march on the most likely of the salt-dome repositories, while the women and children sought refuge in other less desirable, but now less dangerous and exposed, mines elsewhere in the Colorado Rockies.

His panoramic survey of the area and his thought process both complete, Fontana turned back into the coolness of the mine. He quickly dispatched messengers to those clusters of other mals that shared the Plan and could be trusted, setting up a meeting in a safe, neutral location where the forest still stood for the following night. He also sent an operative into Denver to glean whatever intelligence or equipment she could in the next few days.

The spy, Kelly Joy Lanigan, was quick, confident, and apparently able to fast-talk her way into and out of any situation. She hadn't been to Denver now for many, many months, but she had done an admirable job on prior missions. She set off at once on a salvaged mountain bike, promising to return within forty-eight hours with whatever she could find.

Fontana went to his "room" in the mine and pulled out his worn copy of the Bible, the gilt-edged pages gleaming dully in the dim light. He fingered it open to the back, to the chapter of Revelations. Deep in his soul, he knew that it described the battle that lay ahead for his forces.

He just had to figure out what it meant in terms of his battle plan.

Hank shut the thick operating manual with resignation. His battle was over; he could do nothing more meaningful with the equipment and manpower he had left. He and Ali would begin to mothball what was left, so it would be preserved against that future day when the search was once again taken up.

He had failed. His life, his work, had come to naught. But the scientist in him stubbornly continued to catalogue what he had done, what he had attempted, and to see to it that the equipment was left in proper order for the next to come.

The search for truth never ended when it came to science. It was just delayed, put off by society for awhile. These impediments to the march of knowledge alternated from time to time. Sometimes it was the ignorant, other times the fundamentalists, the bean-counters, the apathetic, or the narcissistic. None of them felt that science was truly important and, when they held sway, the world would enter another dark age of stagnation and superstition, from which it would eventually emerge in a renaissance of activity and growth and insight.

The world had entered a dark age. The last candle had been put out and now he was cursing the darkness.

Hank had no guaranty that the world would ever emerge from this dark age, darker than any night the world had ever known, but he had to act as though it would, else his depression would surely overwhelm him.

As he worked methodically, he imagined some band of future explorers or scientists coming upon his treasure trove of information, like an Away Team from the quaint old *Star Trek* vids. They would remark to one another about how advanced the civilization had been and how the data would benefit all benevolent and peaceful peoples.

"Live long and prosper, my friends," he murmured as he continued to format the last run he and Ali had processed.

"Live long and prosper."

Chapter 15

Maria shivered in the warm truck as it hummed efficiently down Route 93 south of Boulder toward Golden.

Conversation had lapsed as the routine of travel set in for them and the sunny day progressed. Parts of the trip had been breathtakingly beautiful, but now they were down on the plain, hugging too closely to the eastern edge of the first foothills to have any view of the mountains themselves, with nothing but dusty flats and dirty brown scrub plants and weeds between the scattered remnants of what was once civilization.

"I can roll up the window if you're cold," volunteered Derek, confused by Maria's shiver.

"It's not that," replied Maria, opening her window a tad more to alleviate the heat from the sunlight streaming into the cab through the south-facing windshield. She nodded to her left. "That place just gives me the creeps."

Derek looked over toward the dilapidated wooden sign that had once identified the Rocky Flats facility—the place where the military had constructed nuclear weapons triggers many years ago, when nations had actually fought over real estate and resources and ideology.

He shrugged his shoulders as he continued driving, his left hand on the wheel with his left elbow resting on the frame of the open window and his right arm outstretched, resting on the back of the passenger seat.

"It's perfectly safe. They cleaned it up years ago. Sent the high-level radioactive waste out to Yucca Mountain."

Maria stared sullenly at the sign, apparently unconvinced. She couldn't tell him of her fear of radiation. She couldn't tell him how, living in a mine, the Believers constantly tested for levels of radon exposure—natural radiation in the ground that could be quite damaging in poorly ventilated areas. The radon could be lethal and needed to be guarded against, lest the Believers unwittingly accomplish the ConFoe's genocidal task for them.

"Look," said Derek, reassuringly, "you'll see in a minute. They built big, nice houses almost up to the edge of the property. They wouldn't do that if it was dangerous."

She looked at him, incredulous.

"What kind of training did they give you?"

"Huh?"

"Are you brainwashed?"

"Huh?" repeated Derek.

"You actually seem to believe that the government would never lie to you, that they wouldn't do anything that wasn't in your best interest."

"Why would they?"

"Government is just people. Imperfect, selfish, ignorant, greedy, and power-hungry people. How can you have spent . . . What is it, years? . . . with the ConFoes and believe that government is beneficent?"

Derek was stung by the vehemence of her question and ashamed of what he knew of ConFoe atrocities. He drove on in silence for a few moments.

"Look, the ConFoes . . . well, they have done some pretty horrible things, I won't deny that. But I told you what the reason was and you can't deny that it makes sense. Change . . . change is always messy . . ."

"Messy?" Maria interrupted forcefully. "Messy? You

think genocide is messy?" She glared at him. "You probably just wash your hands before you sit down to dinner."

Derek didn't get the reference, but he understood the meaning of her remarks.

"Okay, violent and . . . sometimes terrible, but mankind is evolving, not just to a better reality, but to a different mindset."

Maria's brow furrowed and her eyebrows tilted inward. "How . . . you tell me how mankind's mindset is improved by forcing people to live an artificial existence separated from God."

Derek folded in his right arm and put both hands on the steering wheel, slightly opening his palms to gesture as he responded. "Look, I'm not going to argue theology with you. All I know is that in a world where resources are unlimited and nobody can get hurt or killed and everybody can be happy without bothering everybody else, I just don't see how power and money and government and all that are necessary anymore, or at least significant motivators of human activity."

Maria's delay in responding suggested she realized he had a point, but was not willing to concede. Finally, she shrugged. "I don't know. Selfishness has no bounds. Besides, inertia is a powerful force, even when it comes to mindset."

Derek nodded, pleased to note that their discussion was becoming less heated. "I mean, sure, you're right. There will be some inertia, but eventually when the unlimited potential of the virtual world sinks in, everyone will just gravitate to doing their own thing—thinking great thoughts, creating great art, living an idyllic life." He let his enthusiasm run away with him without thinking. "It'll be heaven."

The barrier between them slammed shut again, as Maria turned to look out the right window at the sun peeking at them from the crest of the first foothills. "No," she said, sadly. "It will never be heaven."

Kelly finally rested a moment in relief when she reached the eastern edge of the burned-out area and was once more under cover of the trees for her journey. But after a quick sip of water from her ancient sports bottle, she pedaled rapidly on. It was a long trek into the city and back out. She didn't have much time and she needed to spend as much of it as possible actually in the city to accomplish anything.

She mostly avoided the old roads, sticking to the hiking trails and bike paths that meandered through the foothills northwest of Denver. She had an old pair of birding binoculars and decided to ride to the crest of Lookout Mountain to reconnoiter. The hill—the first foothill west of the city when you headed out into the mountains on the interstate—had a good view of the city and the surrounding plains. She wanted to take a quick look while it was still light, before heading in.

She passed by a bevy of ancient television and radio transmission towers, the first harbingers of the coming of virtual worlds, now rusting and silent. There was a small lake on the flat near the towers and she took the opportunity to refill her sports bottle. Then, she remounted and pedaled into a nearby parking lot. The sign at the entrance indicated the lot was for Buffalo Bill's grave, whoever that was—she hadn't ever bothered to break into the ancient cabin, snack shop, museum, and information center next to it to find out. Whoever he was, his final resting place had a great view.

She avoided the obvious perch of the flat, concrete observation deck, with its vista of Golden, and, instead, followed the short path toward the black wrought-iron fence surrounding a gravestone made of chunks of white quartz. To the southeast of the silent grave, there was a viewpoint nestled in the trees. Here she could look past the television towers and beyond the dome of the Jefferson County courthouse toward downtown Denver. The wide lanes of 6th Avenue pointed straight away from her position, vectoring toward the tall buildings of the city.

The sun warmed her back as she looked out over the plains for any sign of her enemies, just as the natives had many, many years before.

Derek pulled into a park of some sort near a big, domed building on the southwestern edge of Golden, making sure to leave the truck parked in a patch where the sun still peeked between two nearby hills, so it could soak up solar energy during their break. After more than three decades, the photovoltaic cells were nowhere near as efficient as they had once been.

High on the hillside above them, a huge letter "M" made of crushed, white rock stood out from the dark vegetation, even in the shadows of the dwindling day. Derek knew from his briefings on the area that it had been constructed long ago by students of the nearby Colorado School of Mines as a manifestation of school pride, but it always said something else to him as he passed it on his travels with the squad. It was a sign of possession, a monogram of ownership of the very hills themselves. This, the giant mark taunted, is the realm of the "Mals," with a capital "M," a people of pride and dignity and worth. A people that deserves the respect of a proper noun, not the dismissive disrespect of being referenced by a lower-case contraction.

Despite the many years since the letter's construction, no weed intruded on the uniform whiteness of the stones forming the giant mark. The edges of the letter were straight and true, apparently undisturbed by erosion or gravity. No doubt the mark was maintained by the mals, much as it had been maintained by decades of students at the school. On moonless nights they would pull the emerging weeds and straighten the loose rocks along the edges of the line.

Pride never died.

Only soldiers died.

Soldiers like Derek and Maria.

All too often they died for pride. Pride was easier to drill into a recruit than understanding and, thus, the basis of more killing than any cause or belief, itself.

Apparently, Derek had not been drilled enough. Here he was, traveling with the enemy, just trying to find away to get along . . . and understand. Maria, he hoped, was doing the same.

The two companions stretched their legs a bit and used the restroom facilities, which to their surprise, still had running water, apparently fed by a lake or cistern of some type up in the foothills and, therefore, not dependent on electricity or pumps for water pressure.

Derek wet a kerchief and began to wipe the dust from the dull black solar panels to increase their efficiency. Maria took his cue and did the same, concentrating on the passenger's side, while he worked on the driver's side. It took a while, but they got the job done.

Having finished their task, Maria started to open the passenger door to climb back in to continue their journey.

Derek waved her off. "Hold up, there."

Maria stopped, her hand still on the latch for the door. "What, you want me to drive?"

"Nah," replied Derek. "I just want to let it sit in the sun as long as we can, before we head out. The route hugs the hills pretty tight, so we won't be getting much power, even though it will be twilight for quite a while."

"We could stay here for the night. After all, running water is not something we should let go to waste."

Derek shook his head. "Not safe."

"Too near the city? It's been quiet for quite a while; I think the gangs have moved on . . ." She stopped speaking mid-sentence, practically mid-word. She regretted her statement; it revealed too much about her and Sanctuary.

Derek seemed not to notice her counter-intelligence faux pas, wrinkling his nose a bit and shaking his head again.

"The gangs have . . . moved on. Nah, too near I-70; we'll be crossing it in just a couple miles."

"I suppose you want to go into the city, then," Maria said without enthusiasm. Even though there were a zillion houses on a zillion little side streets in which to hide, she knew she could never, ever feel safe in the city.

He looked at her with a sudden sharpness, his head snapping up to look her square in the eye. "Never, *never go into the city, any big city*. It's certain death." His tone backed off as he continued. "We'll skirt along the foothills until we get well south."

Nothing moved in the city as far as Kelly could tell. But as she brought the binoculars down, her eyes caught movement closer in, at the bottom of Lookout Mountain itself—two people in a patch of sunlight next to an old SolarFord pickup.

They might or might not have information. But a working SolarFord, that was a prize worth having by hook or, God forgive her, by crook.

She grabbed the mountain bike and started pedaling.

It was all downhill from here.

★ ★ ★ ★ ★

Maria looked at Derek, confused by both his information and his tone.

"I thought you agreed that the gangs had moved on."

"Actually," he said, sighing, "they're all dead."

Maria had no particular sympathy for the gangs. Before she had joined the Believers in Sanctuary, she had actually had a number of unpleasant and violent encounters with several of the urban gangs, particularly one led by a psychotic warlord that went by the name of Greco. But whenever her feelings about Derek, as a person, started to soften, something, usually something he said, would remind her that he was a professional killer—an obedient minion in the government's methodical genocide of all mankind.

"Killed them all?" she bristled. "Must have been quite a fight." She looked him straight in the eye. "What was your personal body count?" she sneered.

"I wasn't there . . . It wasn't a fight . . ." Derek stammered. His eyes showed shame.

"Then how did they all die?" she replied, uncertainly.

"Let's just say that if Rocky Flats bothers you, downtown Denver should fucking scare you to death . . . to absolute death."

Maria's mind raced. She let go of the truck's door latch and began to pace furiously back and forth while she worked through the ramifications of what she had heard, what a ConFoe had voluntarily revealed to a mal, a mal he knew was a member of a military force of some sort.

"You nuked Denver?" she finally blurted out.

Derek motioned toward the skyline of the now-empty city, the windows of the higher floors still gleaming, unbroken, reflecting the reddish hues of the sun low in the western sky.

"Does it look like we nuked Denver?"

171

"There's some kind of bomb that leaves the buildings standing, but kills the people."

"Yeah, neutron bombs, they call 'em. Some people say we did use some of those in the really big towns. New York, Mexico City, Beijing. I dunno. Maybe. Either they didn't have enough bombs or they didn't want to use them all. You see, a neutron bomb, that's temporary radiation. You use them when you want to kill a population, then move into the area with your own personnel later."

She stared at him, mouth agape. How could he be so non-chalant, so scientific about killing so many people?

Derek continued his clinical explanation of yet another incident of ConFoe atrocity.

"If you want to radiate somebody and you don't care if the territory is useful later, you just over-fly it with a crop-duster and let loose with a load of pulverized nuclear waste. That high-level stuff, that'll be hot forever. Fifty-thousand-year half-life or somesuch."

She looked at the skyline in shock, tears falling silently from her eyes. It wasn't enough that they wanted to abandon the world, the real world. It wasn't enough that they believed they had to take everyone with them. No, they had to poison the world for anyone that might escape their clutches and attempt to rebuild, to booby-trap the earth for anyone, man or animal, that might innocently wander into the spires of grandeur and progress that mankind had once erected.

Derek looked at her sheepishly. "I probably shouldn't have told you. It's against regulations . . . and, well, probably pretty awful from your perspective. From mine, well, it was a relatively clean way to deal with what for us was a pretty big problem—no muss, no friendly casualties, no house-to-house urban warfare. Just dump a load of garbage and move on."

Maria said nothing. Tears continued to flow as she paced, now more slowly in the fading sunlight.

"I'm told it's a pretty fast way to go." He shrugged slightly in embarrassment. "Not really painless, I know, but not . . . torture, either."

She hated what he was a part of, but knew that he was just an instrument of others. She wanted to stalk away, run away into the woods, and warn Sanctuary of this latest ConFoe treachery.

No wonder the ConFoes were more prevalent in the mountains in the last few months. The cities had been quelled. They were just mopping up the hinterlands before they won.

At the same time, she longed to redeem him and she knew that she could not safely leave him here. She owed that much to Sanctuary, if it still existed. More importantly, she was becoming reluctant to abandon what was proving to be a gold mine of intelligence data. Sure, he could be spreading misinformation intentionally, but what he said had the ring of sincerity and plausibility to it.

It smelled of truth—hideous, awful ConFoe truth.

Maria sat down on a concrete and wood park bench and cried, not just for the lost city-dwellers, but for the increasingly hopeless situation that Sanctuary faced—cut off now from scavenging the city and bearing the full force of the ConFoes' devastating attention.

She didn't know how long she sat sobbing, just that Derek let her, without rushing her or trying to comfort her—as if he instinctively knew that a ConFoe couldn't comfort her from this bleak pain. Finally she looked up in the dimming light and saw Derek unnecessarily wiping the solar panels again to keep his anxiousness to move out in check and to distract himself from the pain his organization had surely caused.

"It . . . wasn't your decision," she finally stammered. "J-just give me a few minutes." She motioned with her thumb back towards the cinder-block restrooms with the real running water.

"Don't take too long," said Derek, gazing southeast at the last rays of the sun bouncing off the buildings downtown. The delay had obviously made him antsy. "We've lost the light and should be heading out."

Maria gazed with him for a moment at the lost city, then turned to go and freshen up—to start again.

Kelly could have taken the hairpin turns of Lookout Mtn. Road down the hill for maximum speed, but the rapid movement of the bike on the exposed right-of-way would have given her presence away, even though the bike had been painted charcoal gray by the Believers to help hide it from their enemies. Instead, she dropped downhill, southward along the backside of the hill's ridge, to access the old hiking and riding trails. The Apex Trail, along the path of an old-time covered wagon track from the settler days according to a faded Forest Service sign, led down along the creases between the ridges of Lookout Mountain and behind an old cluster of touristy shops at the bottom to the edge of the park where she had seen the vehicle.

Kelly raced as fast and as heedlessly as she dared toward the location of the SolarFord. The downhill trek was at a bone-jarring pace that compressed her spine and left several cuts on her hands, face, and ankles from branches and vegetation that encroached upon the winding path.

She ditched the bike in the last of the bushes and tall buffalo grass at the edge of the park, as soon as she spotted the vehicle. She hunched down and approached as quickly and as quietly as she could, moving from cover to cover while the two individuals were both turned toward the fiery reflections from the tall buildings in Denver's central valley. Neither the truck nor the clothing of the individuals were typical for ConFoes, but, then, the bastards probably had mal spies and confederates. It would be best to listen in before she revealed herself.

Suddenly, the nearest individual, the woman, turned toward her and headed for some kind of nearby cinder-block building. Kelly had been trained to be still in such situations, in the professional military manner of all scouts. But the training was quite unnecessary in this instance. She froze in shock as she saw the woman's face.

It was Lieutenant Maria Casini.

As she strode toward the restroom, a slight motion caught Maria's eye. Without revealing her attention to Derek, who stood mere yards away, watching her retreating back, she fixed her eyes towards it as she moved deliberately toward the restrooms. Motionless, mostly covered behind a tree, was the shape of an individual. Maria's training in observation and her familiarity with her home quickly revealed the situation to her. It was a Believer scout of some sort dressed in the same type of gray jumpsuit she had been wearing earlier. A rubber band around the leg at the bottom of the exposed trouser leg clearly suggested to Maria that it was one of the mountain bike messengers and spies that they occasionally used for forays into the city or to communicate with other mal contingents.

She entered the restroom, winking in the direction of the agent, but unsure whether her signal had been seen. She couldn't converse with the operative, not with Derek so close by awaiting her quick return. She had ample information to convey, but no way to quickly do it. Worse yet, if she did nothing, the scout might go into the city and die of radiation poisoning.

What could she do? She had a map in her pocket, but no writing instrument and no time. Her gaze whirled around the room, frantic for some implement or some inspiration.

She grabbed up a small sharp stone, thinking she could scratch on the mirror or prick herself for some blood with which to write in some garish and grisly manner on the cluttered color map she held in her hand.

Outside, Derek called to her. "Hey, Maria. We need to get a move on."

Maria's gaze fell upon the map, ringed with advertisements and coupons from days long past. With a quick motion she ripped off a large coupon on the back, the sound of the tearing paper reverberating like gunfire in the small cement structure. She quickly stuck the coupon in the crack where the frame held the mirror. Taking her small stone she coughed as cover as she scratched a hurried arrow in the glass, pointing to the coupon.

Fearing that Derek would investigate or, worse yet, her compatriot would take some foolish pre-emptive action if left to her own imaginings for too long, she quickly strode out of the building, the torn map clutched visibly in her right hand—the hand toward the scout. She moved purposely and quickly toward the SolarFord, her index finger tapping deliberately on the obviously torn map in signal as she moved.

"Sorry," she said, more loudly than she really needed to, "they were out of toilet paper." She opened the door to the truck. "I know we've got a lot to talk about and a long way to go, but we'll get *there*."

Now what? Kelly was pretty sure that the Lieutenant had seen her before she entered the building, but she didn't dare move. The male—the Lieutenant's captor?—was pacing and staring toward the small building the Lieutenant was in, straight past the tree with which Kelly was desperately trying to meld.

Maybe she could rush him—he didn't appear to be holding a weapon, but it was hard to tell. The ancient SolarFord blocked her view. Maybe she could sneak forward and clamber under the black tarp in the bed of the truck before they left. Then again, maybe the Lieutenant was depending on her finding a way into the building, apparently a park restroom, to communicate.

A rip of paper and a sudden coughing convinced her that the latter was the case. The Lieutenant was signaling communication—paper—and impatience—coughing. She had just determined to chance moving back and around to the men's entrance to the same building when the Lieutenant suddenly strode out of the building and quickly into the SolarFord, talking and tapping on some kind of brochure or map in her hand. She did her best to memorize the Lieutenant's words exactly, so she could analyze the communication later. She got the gist of it immediately, though, and abandoned any hope of clambering under the tarp, as the truck fired up and headed off.

She had been left a message of destination in the restroom, she was sure. And she was expected to be there to receive further communication.

As soon as the truck was out of sight, Kelly rushed into the women's restroom, which was quickly darkening in the fading light. An arrow scratched hastily on the mirror pointed at a piece of paper.

She grabbed the paper and quickly turned it over, looking for any message, any writing.

There was none.

On the one side was a map segment, too fragmentary to identify quickly. On the other side was a coupon.

She turned the paper over and over again, rushing outside, into the last remains of twilight to see if she could discern something else dimly writ or scratched upon the paper's surface, but there was nothing.

She thought back. What side had been facing out when she had grabbed the paper from the mirror?

The coupon.

Shit. That was a long way to go. Especially if she was to be back at Sanctuary at first light the day after tomorrow. Especially after how far she had already come today through mountainous terrain.

She quickly turned on the water and refilled her bottle, then cupped her hands to drink deeply and splash her face. Then she rushed over to her ditched mountain bike and grabbed it up, pushing off and jumping onto it to commence her sixty or so mile trek to Larkspur.

Maria quickly lowered her visor to position the vanity mirror so she could see behind the truck, without being obvious. A ballpoint pen clipped to the visor taunted her silently. She casually took it against future need, as if the pen were blocking her beauty check.

She half-hoped to see her compatriot rushing towards the restroom to retrieve her message. She half-feared that Derek would spy the scout in the truck's side-view mirror.

She saw nothing and she was sure that Derek saw nothing. His eyes never veered to the rear or side-view mirrors.

Nobody worried about traffic too much these days.

The truck passed over I-70 silently. A flying ramp just south of the Jefferson County courthouse took the vehicle onto I-470, which circled the southwest side of the city at what Maria hoped was a safe distance. They traveled for a bit on the expressway, shielded from any view or radiation from the central city by the same slopes and ridges that had long-ago entombed dinosaurs, past an abandoned drag-strip, and along the eastern edge of a ridge known as the hogback, before leaving the wide expanse of the interstate. They headed south on state and county roads for a while before re-joining another interstate well south of the city.

She prayed that they would keep heading south and that she could follow through with her plan.

Otherwise, she had sent a poor bicycle messenger on a very, very long wild-goose chase.

Hank worked methodically compiling the data from the most recent searches. In many ways, the long years of work he and Ali had put into the project had been a wild-goose chase. Lots of effort; nothing to show for it, but empty hands and exhaustion.

In order to stave off depression and thoughts of a wasted life, he told himself not to focus on the past. That, he realized when he thought about it, was pretty amusing advice in itself. His life's work had consisted of nothing else but focusing on the past, attempting to discern a heavenly message emitted long, long ago.

The stars were countless as they whirled in the sky above, but Hank had attempted to listen to each one, the automatic drives and tracking software silently and relentlessly following each star in its turn.

At least in a wild-goose chase you knew there was a goose. All he had found was a goose egg.

Chapter 16

They drove without lights, the dim glow of the dashboard gauges and the dimmer starlight and moonlight providing the only respite from the blackness that engulfed them.

Maria glanced over at the gauges as the SolarFord continued quietly southward on the high plains of Colorado, hugging the fringe of the mountains.

"We'll have to stop in a bit."

"Yeah," replied Derek. "I don't want to run it down all the way. Pick out a house sometime in the next half-hour and we'll bunk down for the night."

"I . . . I couldn't do that," she lied quickly and reflexively. That didn't fit her plan. Besides he might be testing her again. Surely he knew that a fair number of the homes, especially those in the rural areas, had been booby-trapped by the former owners or the warlords or the ConFoes against pilferage, or maybe just for the sheer satisfaction of offing whoever might someday come by. She decided to side-step the testing issue. "We don't . . . I mean, I wouldn't feel right staying in somebody else's home, someone converted."

Derek shrugged his shoulders unconcernedly, the right side of his mouth curling up in a slight smile. "Yeah, and it wouldn't be safe either, would it?"

"No," admitted Maria, reciprocating that she too knew what he referred to, "it wouldn't be safe."

"See if you can find a park or something. Maybe we'll get lucky again and the water will work in the restrooms there, too."

Maria started to get out a map to inspect, but Derek extended his right hand and stopped her. "Just look for a sign or something," he said gently. "It's safer that way."

She didn't know if he was concerned that anything marked on the maps might be too well known to the mals that might still inhabit the area or just worried that if she flipped on an interior light to read the map it would make the SolarFord too visible from a distance. She didn't care. This would work to her advantage, as long as her rendezvous point had been as diligent about advertising along the roadways as it had been on the hiking trail map.

"I'll keep an eye out," she promised and looked out into the night as the SolarFord hummed steadily on.

Kelly's burning thighs kept on pumping steadily as she cruised along the center stripe of the southbound lanes on I-25. She had popped quickly onto I-470, skirting the city, and then turned south on the old highway, passing the shell of a huge shopping mall from the days of material excess on her left side at the intersection. As she headed south, her eyes strained to see as far ahead as possible at all times, mindful of roadblocks or lights or anything else that might hinder her progress or endanger her mission.

Taking the interstate was a definite risk. The gangs and the warlords controlled these roads, ambushing those who moved along them, stealing their goods and worse. But the gangs had been quiet now for some months and she had to risk it. It might add a few miles to her already long journey, but there was no danger of getting lost—there were even directions on the coupon as to how to get to her destination from the Larkspur exit—and the old highway made for a fine, smooth ride.

She nursed a small mouthful of water from her already seriously depleted plastic bottle, just enough to moisten her throat and keep the burn in her lungs from surpassing the burn in her legs. Castle Rock loomed over the highway ahead of her, the imposing rock formation blotting out the stars in a patch of the southern sky. Thank God the highway skirted around the edge of that—the flatness of the plain was the only thing that made her quest even possible.

She pondered the mysteries of her situation as she rode, not only in a vain attempt to answer them, but also to distract herself from the painful rigors of her pursuit of Lieutenant Casini and the black SolarFord. Was Casini the odd man's prisoner? If so, why hadn't she tried to escape into the nearby forest when they stopped? How had the Lieutenant even escaped the firestorm that had ravaged Sanctuary Vale? Did the driver of the SolarFord start the accursed blaze? Was the Lieutenant working with him? Was she even now drawing Kelly into some hideous trap? She couldn't believe that, but she had no rational explanation for any of this.

She lowered her head minutely, even further, to reduce the drag and sped methodically on to her appointed rendezvous. All would be made clear there, she prayed.

The mountain bike glided silently down the silver ribbon of highway, a messenger in search of a message.

Maria did her level best to keep her tone nonchalant. "How about there?" She pointed up ahead, to the right of the road, where the dim light of the crescent moon caught a small billboard advertisement, still peddling its product to a world that no longer cared.

Derek looked at the billboard in minor confusion, trying to make out its faded message. "Colorado Ren . . . something or other . . . What does it say?"

"Renaissance Festival."

"That some kind of park or fairground or something?"

"Yeah, renaissance faires and festivals were kind of private parks where people could go and pretend they were in ancient times, you know with horses and knights and antique shops and stuff."

"Why would anyone want to do that?"

"It was where people would go to play pretend before virtual worlds existed. They usually only ran a few weeks in the summer, so it should have shelter, but never had any permanent residents."

Derek looked skeptical, his eyes glancing down at the dim flickering of the charge gauge. It still showed more than forty minutes of running time.

"There was probably never anything modern there worth pilfering, so it should be pretty safe," interjected Maria before he could make a contrary decision, desperately trying not to sound as though she was attempting to close a sale.

Derek mulled it over. They were probably fifty or sixty miles south of the center of the city—more than a hundred miles from Kyle's cabin—a long ways for a mal to cover. Odds were Maria had never been to this place, that this was not some sort of trap, even if he believed Maria would do that. Most mals didn't stray far from their hiding places—it was difficult and dangerous. And, of course, he did trust Maria, had already trusted her.

That settled it. He was being paranoid.

"Sounds good. Tell me where to turn."

The fact that it could have been worse did not make Kelly any happier. She was losing time, time she didn't have.

The chain of the bicycle broke when she was south of Castle Rock. She knew she couldn't fix the chain, not in the dark, not without tools, not in time. She didn't bother to try, taking time only to grab her almost empty water bottle before abandoning the bike in the ditch on the side of the road.

Fortunately, she remembered there was a small subdivision only a couple miles back. She immediately started jogging north, before her legs could stiffen up too much. It was farther than she remembered, but finally she saw the development. It was less than a quarter mile off the road; neat rows of houses with attached garages. Some of the cookie-cutter houses had fences around their backyards. She scanned the fenced yards in the scant light from her vantage point on the mildly elevated roadway, looking for the telltale circular garden plot that would indicate an above-ground pool had once been in the backyard, but had been removed. That would be a house that once had kids, but kids that weren't too young when the house had been abandoned.

She was good at scavenging. She knew what she was doing. There was a good chance there would be a useable bike in the garage of such a house. There could be a bike elsewhere, of course, but she didn't have time to break into every garage until she found one. Besides, it was dangerous.

Finally, she spied what she was looking for on a cul-de-sac lot two blocks to her left. She sprinted for the location. Her legs were again trying to stiffen up. Besides, she was in a hurry.

Derek found the Renaissance Festival grounds curious and amusing and completely harmless. A circuit of the grounds from within the relative safety of the SolarFord revealed no inhabitants, nor any sign of recent activities, just a bunch of open wooden store fronts advertising odd items with even odder spelling. Pickle and roasted mushroom kiosks competed with shops labeled "Ye Olde Armourer" and

"Jeweled Snoods," whatever those were.

As a precaution, he parked the SolarFord not only so he wouldn't have to back it up to leave, but also so it would be in the sunlight first thing in the morning. A brief investigation of the open air stalls and storefronts, as well as a few nearby buildings, revealed a cot in the first aid station, along with some bandages which he pocketed for later need, and a big stone fireplace in the "Chainmail Emporium and Smithy."

He immediately set to starting a fire in the fireplace—a much less noticeable way to cook than an open campfire would have been—and, with Maria's assistance, roasted some of Kyle's elk meat on a couple sturdy sticks. Just to be safe, he quenched the fire as soon as the meat was done with some water from a rain barrel. He didn't know if there might be other mals hidden in this area. He didn't want to take chances, not any more than he already was.

He portioned out chunks of meat from the makeshift skewers. The two of them ate in amiable silence in the dark.

Finally, Maria broke the silence.

"You planning to use those bandages you took from the first aid station when I shoot you?"

"Yeah, maybe. I don't know. I haven't worked it all out yet."

"How much time do we have to figure it out?"

"Couple days, I guess."

Maria thought for a moment. "We'll be pretty far from here in a couple days."

He anticipated her concern. "Once, you know, once we set it up, you can have the truck to make it back to . . . up here . . . wherever you come from."

"And I'll just go about my life . . ."

"Yeah."

". . . until some other ConFoe squad comes by and takes

care of that . . . or I take care of them."

Derek stood suddenly and walked toward the open front of the smithy. He hated to be reminded of his treason. "Look, Maria. I . . . I'm just a grunt in a tight situation, trying to work it out as best I can. I can't solve the world's problems. I can't even solve . . . your problems. I'm just trying to give you a chance, without destroying my life."

"Or Katy's."

"Yeah. Especially Katy's." His burdens crushed down upon him. "I'm not proud enough of my life to care that much about it, but Katy, she didn't do . . . anything. I've got to do this in a way that protects her."

"I don't want her or you to get hurt."

He started to step outside, but turned back. "Thanks."

Maria left him alone with his thoughts for a bit. Finally, she joined him outside their shelter.

"So now what?"

"We're in unfamiliar territory. We should take watches."

Maria nodded in agreement.

"I'm . . . well, I'm awake right now. I have some things to figure out. Why don't you bed down and I'll wake you when I'm tired?"

Maria nodded again. It would be hours before the scout from Sanctuary could possibly arrive, if she even understood the message and could get so far so quickly. "Don't wait too long to wake me," she replied casually. "I can always sleep in the truck when we move on in the morning, unless, of course, you're willing to let me drive."

Derek smiled wearily. "Nah. I'll drive. It's a guy thing."

Maria bedded down on the cot, while Derek roamed about the Festival grounds, working on his plans and his demons.

Finally, he settled into some sort of hanging canvas contraption at a booth simply labeled "Sky Chairs," where he had a good view of the truck and the smithy. What these bizarre devices had to do with ancient times, he had no idea, but they sure were comfy.

Kelly had located a replacement bike on her second try, but the process had been time-consuming. She hadn't wanted to make too much noise breaking into the garages and she could barely see once she had gotten inside.

The first garage had been a nightmare of boxes and junk, with no recognizable pathways through the clutter. She tried to search, but finally abandoned it and, looking along the rear fence line, located another likely target in the next block. There, she repeated her routine, forcing the side door of the garage with minimal noise. She entered the black void of the mostly empty garage and tried to make sense of the dim shapes she could barely discern.

Finally, she felt her way along the wall until she literally bumped into the handle-bars of a mountain bike hanging upside-down from some space-saving bracket. She disentangled it from the mounting bracket and wheeled it out to the driveway. It was bright red, stiff, and in need of a good greasing, but the arid climate had kept it from rusting too badly as it had awaited her arrival.

She sneaked back out of the subdivision, over the subdivision's decorative fence, and onto the highway. Eventually, she was once again into her wearying rhythm, but her progress was slower. The old bike resisted the efforts of her aching legs. Still, she was back on track.

As the road signs marked down the miles to Larkspur, she glanced at the coupon again in the dim light afforded by the night sky. It clearly indicated that the place was not far off the highway, as well as declaring that she would get five dollars off general admission if the coupon hadn't expired more than twenty-five years ago. She followed the route instructions, taking Exit 173 onto Douglas County Route 53, gliding swiftly past the small buildings in what was obviously an old railroad town, then turning right across the tracks towards the Festival grounds themselves. A promontory loomed ahead to the southwest.

As soon as she saw the twin turrets of the main entrance of the Festival, she hid her new mountain bike in some bushes near a maroon and yellow "Welcome Participants" sign and took to her feet for the last mile. Her legs tightened up quickly again after alighting from the bike, but her rear was grateful for the change. She took a moment to stretch out, then started moving somewhat stiff-leggedly toward the antici-pated rendezvous point, relying on adrenaline to kick in if she needed to actually run.

She had barely started out when she circled back to re-trieve her plastic water bottle—emptied miles back—for re-filling at the first opportunity. Water was life. She was tired, but not quite so tired as to be stupid. She needed to refill the bottle.

She headed off again, past a green-enameled cattle gate toward the grounds, hoping for God's guidance as to what to do next. It was dark and slow going, but not nearly so dark as the garages had been. She thanked God for small favors.

The entrance was to the side of a series of ticket booths and information stalls, which had stacks of moldering maps in wooden holders next to the windows. Her eyes moved across the booths to the "Will Call" window at the far end. An unfolded map fluttered at an odd angle from the wooden box next to this window. The freshness of the creases and the unfaded patches of the map suggested that the map had not weathered in such unfolded state. She quickly moved toward the unfolded map.

A small line drawing of a fish symbol in ballpoint pen convinced her that she had interpreted the Lieutenant's message correctly and that her midnight ride had not been in vain. She looked at the map carefully and noticed another pen mark indicating the south side of the Festival's jousting field, as well as an arrow suggesting she move around the outside of the grounds to get there. Her rejuvenated spirits, as well as the fast-approaching end to the night, spurred her to the meeting point with relative alacrity. She took the map with her, not just for guidance, but to remove it from its place of understated prominence. The map and its markings clearly suggested to her that the Lieutenant was indeed a prisoner and it would not do for her evil captor to know that the Lieutenant had had assistance in making her escape.

Derek awoke before dawn.

Without bothering to look for Maria, he immediately shuffled off to the privies, then washed up with some rain-barrel water. Next, he set about cooking up the remains of the elk meat, which had been stashed in snow in the back of the SolarFord. It was more meat than they could possibly eat, but the packed snow had melted faster in the bed of the pick-up than they had imagined it would and he knew the truck would be in the bright sun all day. It was better to cook the meat before it spoiled.

He put his cares and plans aside and focused his mind on the fire and the grilling. He spent a few minutes gathering deadfall from the trees interspersed among the once brightly-colored shops and stalls, rather than using the concealing logs in the truck or tearing up any of the planking from the structures themselves. It wasn't that he cared about this place or these storefronts, it was just that wood used for building tended to be painted or treated and the tainted smoke would spoil the natural savor of the meat.

The fire started up quickly and he stoked it with thick, dead branches to efficiently raise the temperature and produce good coals for the grilling. While waiting for the coals to be just right, he took a knife he had gotten at Kyle's place and began to prepare the meat—butchering it on the smithy's huge, immovable iron anvil, which he first cleaned off with a bucket of rainwater and a little elbow grease. The first rays of the dawn assisted both his cleaning and his cutting efforts.

Roasting meat last night on hand-held sticks had been alright, but what he really needed was a decent grill to put over the fire.

"Yo," he called out toward the "Sky Chair" booth. He had recommended the chairs to Maria when he woke her for her watch. He could see several of the once vividly-colored canvas chairs swaying gently on the morning breeze. The canvas was fading and deteriorating from the elements, but the black plastic rope on which the fabric and wooden chairs hung was still shiny and unaffected by the elements.

The two most enduring things mankind had created were the computers that held their virtual future and plastic. And, although his job was to assure that the virtual future was eternal, if he had to bet, he would bet that all the mundane plastic crap that had been molded and extruded and mass-produced and that now blanketed the earth in the form of fast-food cups and Frisbees and lawn chairs and garbage cans and car bumpers would last longer. Plastic, that was surely eternal. He would fetch some of that rope before they left.

The lack of a response from Maria to his call broke through the trivial meanderings of his mind and brought his attention back to the moment, to the situation at hand.

"Hey, Maria," he called somewhat louder, looking up and down the wide, grassy aisle between the mock-medieval businesses.

Where could she be?

Kelly cursed, to her chagrin, when the first rays of light crept over the eastern plains to betray her stealthy approach to the jousting field. The nights were short in the summer and she had lost too much time replacing her bike and finding the message at the "Will Call" booth. She knew she was already late, but the revealing light forced her to move even more carefully, more slowly in approaching her target. Not only that, but the stupid tourist map of the park had no discernable scale, so she was a bit unsure how far to circumnavigate around the grounds, before cutting in to her critical rendezvous with the Lieutenant. Still, she could not be reckless—for all she knew this place was a ConFoe staging area. It would do no good for them both to be prisoners of these treacherous, unholy fiends.

Finally, she cut through a brushy thicket of bushes and trees toward the park, itself, surrounded by wooden stockade fence. She scuttled through a hole in the fence and looked about. The meager flutterings of a tattered banner tangled and twisted around a pole—a pale reflection of the gaily-colored pennants pictured on the map—caught her attention and verified her position. The jousting grounds lay below her in a shallow hollow, overgrown with weeds nourished by the natural fertilizer they had received long ago. She saw no movement, so moved somewhat more quickly toward the spot indicated on her map.

The rendezvous and escape would have to occur quickly— the sun was rising inexorably and the Lieutenant's captor might take her soon into firmer custody. She raced as quickly

as she dared toward the appointed spot and braved a loud
"pssssst" toward the nearby stables as she approached.

"I'm over here," said Maria quietly to her traveling companion, strolling from behind a post, one of the park maps
partially open in her hands. "I was just looking about a
bit."

"Yeah, well, breakfast is in the works," replied Derek with
an obvious tone of relief. "I think I remember the ticket
booths or whatever at the entrance having barred openings,
didn't they?"

"I guess," she replied, her mind racing to determine
whether this was yet another test, whether he knew she had
been to that place during the night. "What about it?"

"If you can get one off, they'd make a great grill for the
meat. See what you can do, will you? I'll finish cutting this
stuff up in the meantime."

"Sure," she said, turning down the lane towards the entrance with relief. She had dared not stay far from the smithy
and the SolarFord as dawn approached. She had almost been
away too long as it was. The bicycle scout had never arrived,
maybe never even received or understood her hurried message. She would probably never know. She headed back to
the entranceway, tucking a faire map and the pen hidden
within its folds back into her pocket.

No one answered Kelly's obvious signal. No one stepped
out of the shadows. She looked quickly about the place, her
eyes darting from one spot to another, confirming her location, checking for threats, searching desperately for the Lieutenant, and assessing each thing, each tiny item, to determine
whether it might be a clue, in case this might be some kind of
warped scavenger hunt or dangerous road rally—each clue

leading only to another clue, another place, another rendezvous.

There, there, leaning up against the center post for the
railing on this side of the jousting field was another park map,
one corner buried into the loose dirt to keep it from blowing
away. She dove for it in the now bright sunlight, her eyes
darting through its contents, seizing the information contained in it as quickly as she could.

The first thing Maria noticed as she arrived at the ticket
booths was that no map fluttered from the wooden box at the
"Will Call" booth. She walked casually toward the booth, as
if assessing whether this was the best set of bars to remove for
Derek's grill. She did not see the map she had left, even on
the ground nearby. She, however, did see tracks in the gravel
dust that coated the hard, bare earth which had been trampled and compressed by heavy traffic in the years gone by.
Her unknown contact was here and had received her message.

She looked up from the dirt and dust at the barred window
of the booth itself. The bars were hinged to swing open into
the booth. She reached between the bars to turn the latch, re-
leasing the left-hand side of the grate, then used a few upward
thrusts with a fist-sized rock to loose the hinge-pins on the
right-hand side. The barred grate of metal clanged noisily as
it fell inside the booth, but Maria quickly retrieved it by
kicking in the door on the side of the booth and grabbing the
grate off the worn wooden floor.

Emerging back into the sunlight, she headed toward the
SolarFord inside the Festival grounds, saying loudly, "Well,
I'd better hurry up and get this back to Derek. He's waiting
for it." She hoped it would sound as if she were talking to herself and it would dissuade her fellow Believer, who might well

be listening nearby, from contacting her recklessly.

But even as she spoke it, she realized it didn't at all sound like she was talking to herself. It sounded stilted and contrived and obvious.

Fortunately, no one was listening.

Unfortunately, no one was listening. For the first time in more than half a century, no one had listened. The dawn broke over the high desert plain, quickly outshining even the brightest stars, and silently bestowed upon the earth another helping of warmth and light and power. The magnitude of the sun's voice would, as always, drown out any siren song of the lesser lights, feeble and far, far away, but today it didn't matter, because mankind had stopped listening.

Hank and Ali finished their journals and their organizing the evening before and had spent the night sitting on a blanket, leaning up against the inert mechanism of their nemesis, number eight, and watching the night sky. Ali had brought an old iPod with a dual set of earpieces and they had listened this night to ancient MP3s of classical music while they counted shooting stars and each talked about where they would go from here.

The music was wondrous and melodic and inspiring, but it wasn't what they wanted to hear.

A reddish trickle flowed down the corner of Derek's smiling mouth; he liked his steak a bit rarer than Maria favored. The two gorged themselves to bursting, then wrapped up most of the cooked remains in one of the ubiquitous Festival maps. They would finish that off later in the day in the truck.

"Time to mount up and move out," said Derek after wiping his mouth with his sleeve. He leaned forward to push the leftovers they had not wrapped up—more than they could eat before it turned bad—into the coals of the fireplace.

Maria reached forward with her hand and stopped him. "Leave it," she said simply. He looked at her in mild confusion. "The animals will get it one place or the other," she continued smoothly. "Why dirty it up for them?"

Derek smiled broadly and shook his head in wonderment. Only a mal would worry about the quality of life of an unknown forest critter on a soon-to-be uninhabited planet. But, all the same, he stopped and leaned back instead.

"You're not one of them nature freaks, are you?" he said with a minor chuckle.

Maria looked at him, then looked down at the small pile of steak bones next to her. "I think even a ConFoe could figure out I'm not exactly a vegetarian."

Derek's brow creased momentarily. "So, you'll kill 'em and cook 'em, but you want them to have a nice time before you do?"

"God gave us dominion over the earth and its creatures. They exist for our benefit. It's just . . ." She stopped, embarrassed.

"Go on."

"It's just that if you have some respect for lower life forms, it makes it easier to respect your fellow man, even if you don't much care for him on a personal level."

Derek would never have thought of it that way on his own, but she had a point. The ConFoes had no respect for animal life or nature in general. They killed anything that moved, destroyed anything in their path, and burned houses and forests with pyromaniacal glee. Their treatment was much the same for mals, any mals. The ConFoes couldn't respect them and do what they had to do. That's why the instructors in training class always told you to move quickly and efficiently to orient and then kill or convert a captured mal. If you talked to them too long, if you became friends, if you began to respect them, you wouldn't be able to do what had to be done.

Isn't that what had happened to him?

He didn't want to think about, much less talk about it, any more. It would either confuse or depress him.

"Fine," he said, getting up and moving towards the truck with what little remained to be packed. "Leave it for whatever might be around."

"Don't be mad. I didn't mean to offend you."

Derek turned back to look at Maria, as she gathered her loose items to carry to the truck, her eyes avoiding him.

"I'm . . . I'm not mad. It's just that . . . whether you're nice or not nice to whatever critter comes along here next . . . it isn't going to make a bit of difference to what happens to either one of us in the end." He turned back toward the truck and walked slowly away, looking down and shaking his head slowly.

"God works in mysterious ways," Maria muttered to herself and she followed him and clambered aboard the SolarFord. The moment she slammed her door shut, the truck lurched forward and out of this place of olden times and values long past and barely half-remembered.

The slamming car door wrenched Kelly away from her reading.

Immediately upon finding a detailed message on the map near the jousting field, she had set about reading it, as any messenger would. First she scanned it quickly, both for any further instructions or clues as to a more comprehensive communication or rendezvous and for broad content. The quick scan was protection against the fear that at any moment the precious information would be, could be, taken from her and she would only have those nuggets of information she had been able to rapidly imprint upon her own mind.

The Lieutenant had obviously known what type of person would be reading this, had perhaps even once herself performed or been trained to perform the type of intelligence and messaging tasks that Kelly was now assigned. In writing, the Lieutenant had also protected against interruption, putting the most critical information in brief up front and only getting to the details and the less important later on in the missive as time allowed. The most important items were quite clear from the beginning of the surprisingly lengthy and detailed writings.

"NEVER GO INTO DENVER: RADIOACTIVE," it read. *"DO NOT ATTEMPT TO RESCUE ME OR ATTACK COMPANION."*

The rest of the paper contained the whole story—the death of the ConFoe squad, the confrontation at Kyle's cabin, the Lieutenant's efforts to glean intelligence and lure the remaining ConFoe far, far away before shooting him (although how the Lieutenant intended to manage that piece of military action, the message gave no clue), the ConFoe's justification for the use of lethal force, the permanent sterilization of the major urban centers with high-yield radioactive waste from Yucca Mountain, and the Lieutenant's ultimate plan to return alone with the SolarFord.

Kelly did not quite understand what else the Lieutenant hoped to find out from the ConFoe—the location of their regional base, perhaps?—and why she just hadn't killed him during the night. Obviously, the Lieutenant had not been tied up or anything—else she would not have been able to leave the clues and information she had. Kelly screwed up her face momentarily, perplexed by the whole situation. All that was for others to figure out. Her job was to get the information to Sanctuary.

She heard the crunch of the SolarFord's tires on gravel as it departed the Festival grounds, though it was out of sight from her here at the jousting field. She quickly decided to make her way back to the mountain bike by going through the Festival grounds and out the entrance, just in case the Lieutenant had left any further information for her.

When she came to the smithy, she found a platter full of cooked meat awaiting her. The sign of the fish scrawled in the dirt nearby persuaded her that it was not a trap, that the meat was safe to eat. There was also an arrow in the dirt pointing to a nearby rain barrel full of clean water.

Kelly prayed, then ate and drank, preparing herself for the long journey ahead. Before leaving she scuffed over the signs in the dirt and remembered to fill her plastic water bottle. But as she did all this, her mind reeled in wonder. How did the Lieutenant, a captive of the ConFoes, manage to leave her food and drink under the very nose of her enemy?

It was like manna from heaven.

"God works in mysterious ways," she said to herself as she gorged quickly on the still warm, red meat. Except for the time it took to eat and the few minutes she took to scratch with elk blood and a finely-sharpened stick on a clear spot on the map a brief report of her own activities, Kelly did not rest. Instead, she headed back to the mountain bike and doggedly pushed off for the long journey back to Sanctuary before it was emptied for the planned attack. Though she was no longer hungry or thirsty, she was tired and, this time, the last part of the trip would be all uphill.

Chapter 17

Given her long night and the surfeit of food, Maria fell asleep less than a half-hour outside of Larkspur, as the SolarFord hummed steadily onward, soaking up the sun's power as quickly as it expended it.

Derek cut to the east for a bit, ducking under I-25 and picking up the flat, straight ranching roads of the plains. He stuck to these side roads, methodically choosing to go south at every opportunity and, when that was denied him, heading east enough to avoid the mountains as they traveled. Cheyenne Mountain, in particular, down by Colorado Springs, had once hosted NORAD, the United States government's air defense command center, and he couldn't be sure that the nuclear-hardened facility didn't still sport a few ConFoes controlling satellites or ready to protect earth from alien invaders or somesuch. In any event, there was no reason to go closer than necessary to the place.

Other than that tactical decision, his route did not bear much thought and the road certainly did not require his full attention. He occupied his mind, instead, with the mechanics of his plan to fool the ConFoes into allowing him to convert before the end of his tour, while still giving Maria an opportunity to escape.

Right now they were headed towards the ConFoes' southwestern headquarters near Phoenix, Arizona. The high proportion of elderly residents in Phoenix had made it one of the earlier ghost towns in the early days of conversion. A sizeable ConFoe presence in those early days had also ensured that

199

the relatively modern facilities were not notably scarred by riots or looting. Sure, it was hotter than blazes during the summer, but the whole city had been an early adopter of solar technology, so the ConFoes had plenty of access to power for cooling the few buildings they actually used.

As soon as he was within laser communication range and they were sure the SolarFord had a good charge, Derek would assemble the scanner and its short-range laser communicator, then check in, claiming to have been shot by a mal ambush—a motorcycle gang would be a good, credible tale. That way he could say the mals took off at high speed to the west. As soon as the report was done, Maria would shoot him—seriously enough to be life threatening, but not so seriously that he wouldn't last the thirty or forty minutes 'til a ConFoe patrol could arrive.

This part of the plan would be difficult, as Maria would need to stand far enough away from him when shooting so as to ensure there were no powder burns that might suggest a self-inflicted wound. He hoped she was a good shot. After all, she had gotten Manning square in his Kevlar vest, but that had been at point-blank range.

Afterwards, Maria would take off to the east at full speed and head back to Colorado. She probably wouldn't be caught, although Derek would need to remember to say in his report that the attackers were guys, so she wouldn't be accused of the ambush if she were picked up—not that the treatment she would receive would be that different from the torture and death awaiting any mal who refused to convert. Even some who did not resist the process did not, he knew, fare well at the hands of his compatriots—especially the females.

It would be best if the patrol were to use the scanner to convert him as soon as they arrived—he could say he had set it up while awaiting them. But if the ConFoe patrol didn't show up promptly and he was beginning to feel woozy or, worse yet, they came too fast or his wound was not sufficiently life threatening, he would be forced to press the button to start the conversion and hope that he had not doomed himself and Katy for eternity. Once started, the conversion process could not be safely stopped.

Derek turned southward yet again, crossing into New Mexico, as Maria slept fitfully in the passenger seat—her eyes moving rapidly beneath her eyelids.

Even as he thought it through, Derek knew his plan wasn't a great one. It was filled with pain and danger and risk—both in this world and the next—and that was before the snafus that inevitably came up when you tried to put a plan into action in the real world.

It was a nightmare.

The trip back was a nightmare beyond comprehension for Kelly. Already exhausted from her race down to Larkspur during the previous night, she nevertheless maintained a steady pace back north and west toward Sanctuary—a testament to discipline as well as her physical conditioning. Having read the Lieutenant's missive, she gave Denver a wider berth than she had on the way down, skirting into the twisting, turning scenic drives of the foothills that were punctuated with bright yellow hairpin turns and six-percent-grade road-signs. Her legs screamed in agony on the uphill climbs, but the forest provided some shade from what was turning out to be a hot day. She also had several opportunities to refill her plastic water bottle—staving off for now the worst of the dehydration that this kind of prolonged exertion brought on.

She knew that the Lieutenant's message was important and could have a meaningful impact on the relocation and military plans that were being implemented when she had left Sanctuary, but she was too tired to think much about what that impact might be. Her mind, deprived of oxygenated blood by the altitude and the demands of her leg muscles, flitted from random thought to random thought. She tried to corral it, to bring her attention to bear on the consequences of her message and her future, but it was more elusive than the dappled shade patterns that flowed over her as she pedaled on and on and on. She eventually gave up on higher thought altogether and, instead, merely focused on the mechanics of her task—the pedals, the trail, her breathing, the number of miles yet to go. There was no future for her beyond the end of the trip.

Somewhere, unbidden, in her musings, she thought of the nameless runner of antiquity, the one that had delivered his message to Marathon. She was that runner. Today she was cycling the first sanctuary.

The steady rhythm of her pedaling became the focus of her existence.

One, two, three, four.

She would be released from her nightmare, but not before she arrived.

One, two, three, four.

Maria saw them first.

As they crested a small hill, Derek spied a fallen juniper tree blocking the road and hit the brakes hard. He cursed the antilock brakes that prevented him from skidding the truck sideways into the barrier. That alternative foreclosed by technology, he opted, instead, to steer for the more distant and, hopefully, less damaging left ditch, its reddish soil cut by veins of erosion. The front bumper of the SolarFord thumped softly, but solidly, into the opposite bank before the front wheels had even dropped fully into the ditch. The hit on the bumper caused the airbags to deploy with an explosive bang, followed by a cloud of whitish gas as they almost instantly deflated.

But in that instant—that slow-motion moment before the inevitable impact—Maria saw the gang members emerging from the scrub beyond the log, scurrying toward the vehicle.

In the startling clarity of that moment, she recognized the rightmost one—the one shouting orders she could not hear above the tumult of the impending crash—as Greco, the gang leader that had tortured and violated her before she had found Sanctuary, the inhuman monster that had ruined her chance of ever having children. As the bumper dug into the soft, red dirt and the airbag unfurled toward her, she wondered at how she was even able to recognize her nemesis. All of the gang members were grotesque, their faces hideously mutated by their encounter in the city with the radiation from Yucca Mountain. Somehow, the radiation made them even more frightening and loathsome, not because it made them more ugly, but because they had soaked up the nuclear death and it was leaking from them like phosphorescent fluid from a rusted barrel at Rocky Flats.

She screamed in fear and warning, but Derek never heard her above the sounds of his own cries of anguish and pain as the airbag snapped his right forearm and flung his hand with an audible thwack into his nose. Blood flowed as the white haze of the airbag gas enveloped her and a hand reached for her shoulder.

It was a nightmare.

Derek hit the brakes hard, thankful that the antilock brakes would slow the vehicle safely, preventing any skid even though he paid minimal attention to the steering wheel.

He reached over with his right arm and began to shake Maria awake as the SolarFord slowed to a stop in the parched, open land of northeastern New Mexico.

Maria screamed again and grabbed at his arm, then stopped screaming as her eyes opened, squinting and blinking in the bright midday sun streaming through the dusty, cracked windshield of Kyle's truck. She looked suddenly to her right and turned back to Derek more slowly, her face a picture of confusion.

"You fell asleep and had a nightmare," he said, even though he knew she would have figured it out for herself in a second or two.

She looked about with increasing understanding and concentration. "Where are we?"

"A bit north of Farley, New Mexico. The map says that there's a picnic ground on the next road, a few miles away. We'll take a stretch there, if you like."

"Yeah, sure," Maria replied softly.

Derek took his foot off the brake and the truck started rolling forward once again.

"You want to talk about it?"

"It was just a dream."

"They can seem real enough. You sure screamed like it was real."

Maria blushed. "Uh. Sorry."

Derek made a dismissive motion with his right hand, which, happily enough, had never broken and thwacked into his nose. "Not a problem."

Maria took a moment to compose herself, taking a drink of warm water from her canteen, before responding. Derek suspected she didn't like looking weak and girlish in front of him. He hoped she knew he was just trying to be a friend and did not want to discourage that.

Finally she spoke again. "It just seems . . . stupid to be afraid of something that's not real."

Derek shrugged his shoulders as the truck, now fully back up to speed, continued cruising southward. "But you think it's real. That's why it's scary."

He didn't understand her point. "It seems stupid to think it's real." She struggled to explain, her left hand gesturing minutely before her as if plucking her thoughts from the ether. "There are always clues in dreams—things that you realize after the fact make it obvious that it had to be a dream all along. I guess I beat myself up for not picking up on them sooner."

"Yeah, except just knowing that it is a dream doesn't always make it less scary."

"What do you mean?"

This time Derek blushed. "Well, for instance, I used to have this recurring dream that I was in bed and there was some evil, ominous presence in the room that was about to attack me and all I had to do was move before the knife thrust or whatever came down on me, but I was paralyzed. I couldn't move. And then, finally, I would move and that would wake me up." Derek gave Maria a sheepish, sidelong glance. "The scariest thing was that the room wasn't always the same identical, generic room. Instead, it always looked just like whatever room I was sleeping in looked when I went to bed the night before, so it was always like it was really happening."

"Sounds like a pretty typical nightmare, but I don't get what it has to do with your point."

Derek continued to drive, turning onto a somewhat wider roadway, heading west toward the promised rest area. "Eventually, I had the dream so much that I knew when I was having it that I was having a dream and all I had to do was move and I would wake up. But I was still paralyzed and I couldn't move and when I did wake up I was sweaty and thrashing about. I was still scared—not about being attacked, but about not being able to get out of the dream."

He saw a sign for the picnic grounds and nodded towards it as he continued. "Finally, I got to the point where I would have the dream and I would thrash about to wake myself up and I would wake up and the room would look just the same, just like it did when I fell asleep, but there would be this ominous presence in the room where I had just woken up and I had to move to escape it."

Maria pointed at the turn-off to the picnic grounds. "You mean you were still dreaming. In your dream, you woke up, but you were still actually in the dream."

"Yeah."

Maria looked at Derek as he turned off the truck. "And how many layers did this go? Did you awake from this second-level dream and find you were still in a dream?"

Derek shook his head as he gently brought the SolarFord to a halt in the sunlight and turned off the ignition. "Not that I remember. But, y'see, the scary thing was that once the second-level dream occurred, I could never wake up and know for sure that I was awake, that the dream didn't have more and more layers. The dream wasn't scary because it was real, it was scary because I never could know for sure that when I woke up that the world that I had awoken into was real." Derek hesitated, his eyes cast momentarily downward in embarrassment. "I would wake up every morning afraid."

Maria gazed out at some small butterflies flitting above the surface of a maroon-stained picnic table nestled amidst some scrawny pines. "No," she said softly as she watched the silent, colorful dance, "the really frightening thing is that you were not in control and that the layers might never stop, that you might be trapped in the dream forever with no escape."

He closed his eyes and looked up, letting the sun warm his eyes through the lids. "I never thought of it that way," he said simply. He opened the door to the sound of birds trilling in the bushes and trees nearby and headed toward the picnic table with the last of their elk leftovers. "I guess it wouldn't be so bad, being trapped in a dream forever, if you knew it would be like this . . ." He gestured about at the sun and the high fluffy clouds and the birds, ". . . you know, a nice dream."

Maria walked with him, soaking in the serenity and peace of the place. Still, she was overwhelmingly sad. She looked him in the eye as they set things out on the table.

"But if it was forever, would you ever go to sleep if you didn't know for sure, for absolute certain, that it was going to be a good dream?"

Derek shrugged. "Everyone has to sleep sometime. Most of my dreams are bad, but you get used to it, I guess. Besides, you're the one who just had the nightmare. Are you afraid to go to sleep?"

Maria shook her head, unconsciously reaching up to trace her scar with her thumb. "Not anymore, not all the time. I used to have nightmares a lot, but that was a long time ago." Suddenly, she realized what she was doing and dropped her hand back to her lap.

"It barely shows, but it is a scar," Derek said quietly. "Would it help to talk about it?"

Maria blushed, the rush of blood momentarily accentuating the light scar by contrast. "There's not really that much to tell. Back when . . . the gangs were in control of the cities, I was foraging for supplies in one of the outlying subdivisions. Unfortunately, the area was the turf of one of the feuding gangs, one led by a freak named Greco." She looked at the clouds lazing overhead, seeking to capture their peaceful serenity. "I . . . I was only looking for canned goods, but Greco thought I was a spy from a rival gang." Maria's hand flittered nervously, as she continued. "He went pretty much ape-shit when they brought me to him. He kept asking me questions about gangs and people I didn't even know. I . . . I had no information to give, but he wouldn't believe it."

"At first he just cut me a little," she said self-consciously as her fingers traced her scar, "to see if I would talk, but, then, well, he turned me over to his minions to see what they could get out of me." Her voice trailed off into nothingness. She looked away, her eyes wide to prevent the tears forming from escaping down her pale cheeks.

Derek yearned to reach out and comfort her, but he feared even a gentle hand on her shoulder would inadvertently bring back memories she was doing her best to force down. Instead, he spoke in quiet, soothing tones. "And they hurt you. You don't need to say more."

She looked back at him as he continued. "It does, however, make me even more glad that the gangs are gone."

Tears continued to well in Maria's eyes, but he could tell she still refused to let her emotions go. Instead, she merely nodded silently.

"More glad that Manning is gone, too," Derek added simply.

Maria nodded again, with just a flicker of a smile of gratitude registering on her tightly controlled countenance.

"How'd you get away, if you don't mind my asking?" asked Derek.

Maria shook her head slowly and her jaw relaxed somewhat as she apparently gained the upper hand on her emotions. "I don't really know. There was an attack or a battle of some sort. I heard a commotion outside of the house where they were keeping me and then yelling and the dull bark of weapons firing. I wanted to help whoever was shooting at Greco's people, but I didn't know what was going on, so I hid under the bed."

"Smart move," said Derek reassuringly. "For all you know, the guys shooting would have treated you even worse."

"No, not worse . . . maybe the same," said Maria quietly. She shrugged her shoulders. "It's really not much of a story. There was an explosion, I think, and I must have been knocked out. The next thing I remember, I was in . . . I was with the people I stay with now."

"Enough said," indicated Derek quickly. "I don't want to press for information you don't want to give and I really don't want to have."

She nodded and he knew that she was grateful for both his compassion and his understanding of her situation.

"Anyhow," Derek continued, "I'm glad for you that you got out of a bad situation, at least when you did. Try not to look back. Nothing ever changes there."

Hank and Ali slept the day away. They were used to being up nights and, so, that is when they did their compiling and final research entries. Besides, the days were hot and thirsty and they had nothing to do. Their dream was over and they no longer had a purpose in life.

General Fontana forced himself to sleep for at least a few hours. The relocation of the women and children was underway and well in hand. Now his only purpose was to lead the final march on the forces of evil. The march would depart at first light tomorrow. He knew he needed to take rest while he could today—he would be up most of the night with last-minute preparations—but his mind would not quiet. The names and locations of the major salt domes danced in his head.

Had he chosen the right one?

The march would be arduous and could not remain hidden from the ConFoes' eyes in the sky indefinitely. Even if he chose to attack nothing more than a vacant salt mine, the commitment of forces would come to the attention of the enemy. Except for the element of surprise, he had no weapons to match those of his formidable foe. There was no doubt that he was leading his forces into certain death. The only question was whether it was a march to the glory of the final battle or a march off a cliff to oblivion.

He prayed for a sign.

The sign read: "Bucksnort Tavern, 1 mile." The thought permeated the haze of pain and exhaustion of Kelly's mind, registering a few moments later as a realization that she knew where she was and how to get to Sanctuary from here, though there was still a long way to go. She pressed on, without slowing.

One, two, three, four. One, two, three, four.

Kelly was much too tired to smile at the realization that she was still on track. Smiling required energy. Smiling required happiness. Kelly knew neither of those. Besides, the thought that she was still on track flitted out of her mind almost immediately, replaced with random musings more akin to dreams than reality.

One, two, three, four. One, two, three, four.

On she pedaled, her pace a steady beat, her legs like the rhythmic pistons of an automaton—ever forward despite the throbbing ache of her back, the searing pain of her calves, and the ever more frequent cramps in her hands, feet, and thighs.

One, two, three, four. One, two, three, four.

Only the numbness of her seat and the delirium of her

mind permitted her to continue.

One, two, three, four. One, two, three, four.

She still had a long way to go, her befuddled brain told her, but she would make it, unless she died. That would be bad. She didn't have time to die. She could do that later.

One, two, three, four. One, two, three, four.

Right now, she had to press onward, a Christian soldier pedaling as to war.

One, two, three, four. One, two, three, four.

The setting sun hung low over the mountains, a beam of light bursting between peaks, pointing the way, beckoning her to Sanctuary, beckoning her as a Believer. Her legs thrust again and again with a fixed discipline that her meandering mind had long since abandoned.

One, two, three, four. One, two, three, four.

Over field and fountain, moor and mountain.

One, two, three, four. One, two, three, four.

Westward leading, still proceeding.

One, two, three, four. One, two, three, four.

Bearing a gift . . . of wrinkled, folded paper . . . she comes from afar.

One, two, three, four. One, two, three, four.

Following yonder star.

One, two, three, four. One, two, three, four.

Following yonder star.

Deep down, she knew she was losing it, that she was becoming delirious from dehydration and exhaustion, but her mind's musings were no longer in her control. She knew, though, that something was wrong. Nobody did that. Nobody followed a yonder star. Not anymore.

One, two, three, four. One, two, three, four.

Nobody followed the stars. Not anymore.

Chapter 18

"It's moved."

Maria looked up to see where Derek was pointing. The sun, already caressing the horizon directly ahead of them as they headed west, made it difficult to see clearly. She shaded her eyes with her hand. In the distance was a series of large, very large, circular concave-shaped structures—like satellite television dishes from the olden days grown to monstrous proportions. "Huh? What is that? What moved?"

Derek slowed the truck to a stop at the top of a small rise in the road on Route 60, about fifty miles west of Socorro, New Mexico. They got out and stood in front of the truck.

"The array. The configuration is different."

"I repeat, huh?"

"They're big old radio telescopes. They used to use them to listen to stars."

"Listen to stars?"

"You know, track their electromagnetic emissions—radio waves and stuff—then figure out what kind of stars they were and how fast they were moving, and whether they had planets. All sorts of scientific crap like that—space stuff that nobody cares about anymore."

"Okay," said Maria slowly, "but what moved?"

"The big dishes, they move. They can be put in different configurations to listen to different kinds of things at different distances or something. Look, I don't really know why they move, just that they can, or, at least, used to."

Maria squinted at the structures. "None of them look like

they're moving to me. Are they real slow?" She shielded her eyes from the sun again and peered at the monstrous towers one by one.

"Nah. I mean, yes, they move slow, but they're not moving now. They've moved since the last time I was here." He swept his right arm from left to right in gesture. "The configuration is different." He pointed toward the center, where the axis of the east, west, and north lines of towers came together. "They're more bunched up in the middle."

Maria turned toward him, her mind focused on matters other than the towers now. "So, you pass by here often," she said: a statement, not a question.

"Yeah," Derek confirmed. "Look, we're about a half a day from where . . . from where I planned to . . . send you back to Colorado."

"From where you want me to shoot you."

"Yeah."

"From where you can communicate with your superiors."

Derek swallowed hard. "Yeah."

"Look, Derek, I trust you, but my life is on the line here. Isn't it about time you explained exactly how your plan is going to work?"

"I was going to go over the whole thing when we stopped for the night in just a bit."

"Don't you think that this . . ." she gestured toward the rearranged array ". . . means we should talk now? Your buddies may be just down at the control building for the radio dishes."

Derek pondered for a few moments. "I don't think so. We don't pay this place much mind. Went over to it one afternoon years ago; it was all locked up. Can't imagine why anyone would want to be there. We always pass it right by."

"Well, then who moved those things?"

"You tell me. Mals, most likely."

"I haven't a clue," Maria replied, a hint of ice in her tone. "Just because there aren't many of us left, doesn't mean we all know each other."

Derek looked at the huge radio dishes and their attendant control buildings and then back at himself, Maria, and the SolarFord. Other than the hidden scanner and his old uniform and other items in his pack, all hidden away in the back of the pick-up, there was nothing to identify them as ConFoes. "Why not just drive up and see if anyone's there?"

Maria rolled her eyes. "Well, it's a good way to get shot, isn't it? Why not just pass the place by?"

"Except for the gangs in the cities—and they . . . aren't the problem they used to be—mals don't usually shoot other mals without asking questions first," Derek reported without emotion, verbatim from one of his training sessions. "Besides, I need to see if anyone's there."

"You need to? Why?"

Derek put his hands in his pockets and began to circle aimlessly as he thought. The sun set, providing a backdrop of fading crimson radiance to his pacing cogitation. Finally, he stopped in front of Maria, who waited with her arms folded and her hip thrust slightly to one side.

"First, it's my job."

Maria snorted lightly in disgust, but said nothing.

"Second, if they're hostile, I don't want them behind us . . . or in front of you when you're making your escape tomorrow."

Maria nodded lightly in appreciation, as if agreeing that this reason at least made some sense.

"And third . . ." Derek looked down at his feet, his hands still deep in his pockets. ". . . well, third, the plan's kind of risky. I was hoping maybe to find a better one and, well, you never know what you'll find 'til you look."

"They look like ConFoes to you?" asked Hank anxiously.

Ali leaned forward and peered through the tripod-mounted recreational telescope they had long ago liberated from the press office of the Very Large Array. "No, I do not think that is the case. The vehicle is an old civilian model and they are not in uniform." He deftly changed eyepieces for one of higher magnification and adjusted the focus. "Besides," he said, standing erect again and smiling broadly, "I do not believe the Conversion Forces include any women in active service at this time."

Hank's shoulders sagged in disappointment. "Damn. What do you think we should do?"

"Invite them in. They might be able to give us some information."

"Okay. But housing quarters only. Nobody gets into the data storage areas. That's sealed for perpetuity."

Ali nodded. "I quite agree. How do you think we should invite them? They may just pass by."

Hank rubbed his stubble and glanced about at the fading light. "Hell, turn on the outside lights. Doesn't matter anymore if the ConFoes see 'em. Hell, that would simplify things quite a bit, long as they do what they're supposed to."

"Bold, but simple. An excellent scientific solution." Ali stepped into the guest hut and threw a switch. "Let there be light," he murmured to himself. Three of the four floodlights on the exterior of the building crackled to life. He quickly rejoined Hank, who was now leaning over the eyepiece to the telescope, back outside.

Hank was chuckling as he watched the hilltop to the east in the dimming twilight.

"That got 'em moving."

★ ★ ★ ★ ★

"Jesus!" exclaimed Maria, as she saw the lights come on outside one of the buildings in the distance.

Derek whirled around to see what had happened, then turned back around and grabbed Maria's arm. "Quick! Get in the truck. We have to get down there before the ConFoes see 'em."

Maria and Derek both raced for the truck and jumped in. Derek had the vehicle in motion before Maria even got her door closed. He slammed the accelerator to the floor hard and kept it there, unmindful of the fact that the SolarFord was no longer charging in the dim light.

Derek was focused on one thing, getting the lights turned off before any ConFoes could spy them. His plan wasn't ready; he didn't even have the scanner set up. If the ConFoes showed up in the area now, Maria was a goner and he would be forced to finish his tour of duty.

Maria's mind raced. Why had she jumped in the truck? Who was down there? She could trust Derek—at least his good intentions, if not his unknown and possibly unworkable plan. Whoever was down there, though, might never let her go. She might never see Sanctuary again. The thoughts tumbled across her mind as her body was tumbled in the cab of the truck while Derek pressed forward. He drove as if possessed, at full speed, with no heed for the potholes in the ancient road or the deepening darkness of the night.

Maria wanted to slow him, wanted to think the situation through calmly, but had no opportunity. Derek abandoned the main road, making a sharp right turn into the entryway for the Very Large Array. Ignoring any directional signs, he headed straight for the lights, stopping only when he saw two men sitting in lawn chairs near a small telescope in front of the lighted building. He jammed the truck into park and bailed out of the driver's-side door, leaving Maria to turn off the vehicle to save the batteries. She quickly dropped the keys into her bra for safekeeping. She might need to make a getaway.

Derek charged toward the men excitedly. He had to get whoever was in charge of this place to turn off the damn lights.

"Take me to your leader," he shouted as he came up to the first lawn chair.

Hank looked up at the excited young man and smiled as broadly as he ever had.

"I've been waiting my whole life to hear that."

As a military leader, General Fontana had spent much of his life preparing for a battle that he had prayed would never need to be fought. Now it was upon him and he was immersed in the technical logistical details of men, materiel, and distance-to-objective.

The men (and a smattering of women) were trained. The weapons and rations and ammunition were broken out of storage, the canteens filled, the rifles oiled and cleaned. The objective had been debated and chosen and the approach route calculated and considered. Their target, though, was a long, long way away from their hideaway in the Colorado Rockies.

The troops referred to the upcoming trek as the March, but they wouldn't, couldn't, really march that far. It was too slow, too visible to the ConFoe satellites high in the sky. An army moving on foot can only move so fast, especially when it lacks an even more numerous support and supply chain to back it up. Without that, it would have to live off the land as it

217

traveled, reducing its already meager pace toward objective.

Fontana had confronted his troop's mobility issues long ago and done his level best in the intervening years to mitigate them as well as he could. He had, of course, assembled a motley collage of solar-powered vehicles from the oil-shortage years that preceded the Mandatory Conversion Act. There weren't nearly enough to move his troops, but they were useful for hauling the heavier equipment and bulk supplies, lightening the backpacks of the rank and file and, thus, facilitating more rapid movement of the assembled forces than would have otherwise been possible. Still, the Utah salt dome he had selected as their target was far, far to the west over rugged terrain. Too far to march his soldiers.

No, like many a war back before mankind decided to solve its problems by running away from them into an etched wafer of silicon, this war would depend on the railroads. And that meant he would start off in the morning marching his eager recruits away from Utah, east to Golden, Colorado.

The great diesel locomotives of the last century had been abandoned as conversion gained sway, the movement of bulk commodities becoming less and less necessary as the population dwindled and supply shortages were solved by conversion rather than freight. Fuel, itself, which had become so scarce as to be one of the motivators for mass conversion, became rarer and rarer. Eventually, the remaining reserves were seized by the government and allocated to the use of the ConFoes in enforcing the Mandatory Conversion Act. One by one, the powerful engines of the railroads, some of which had run continuously for more than twenty years between overhauls, alternatingly straining with heavy loads and idling on sidetracks or in enormous switching yards, fell silent.

The Believers could do nothing to awaken those diesel-fed

iron dragons, asleep and rusting at the termini of their last loads, but years ago a scout in Golden had discovered something along West 44th Avenue, behind the old Coors plant, that could make the rails sing once again. General Fontana had gone himself, with a crew of his best mechanics and engineers, and surveyed the find, the Colorado Railroad Museum.

The sign on the building read: "Delay Junction, Golden 2 Miles, Elevation 5,636 Feet, Denver 12 Miles." In the basement of the facility was an elaborate HO model railroad, with mountains, buildings, and gate crossings. But it wasn't the building or its contents that was of interest.

In the tall grass and weeds surrounding the squat building filled with books and displays about the Santa Fe and the Union Pacific and the narrow-gauge mining lines, were flatcars and boxcars and ancient passenger cars and cabooses. There were cars from the Denver & Rio Grande Western, the Denver & Salt Lake, the Colorado & Southern, the Union Pacific, and the Burlington railroads, among others. The museum boasted the old No. 1 engine from the Manitou & Pikes Peak Railway and a half-dozen or so narrow-gauge engines once used in now-abandoned lines in the mountains.

But most importantly, there was Chicago, Burlington & Quincy No. 5629, a giant, standard-gauge, steam locomotive, with a full coal car right behind it. The three-hundred-seventeen-ton behemoth had regularly hauled twenty-car passenger runs and much longer freight runs on the Denver to Chicago mainline. It could take the Army of the Believers anywhere standard rail lines would go.

The team had inspected the engine, fixed what needed to be fixed (using manuals and even some parts from the museum's displays), oiled what needed to be oiled, and stoked the boiler with coal. Finally, they lit the boiler and started the engine up one dark, stormy night when the ConFoes would be unlikely to hear or see what they were doing. With a horrendous, groaning screech of metal on metal, the beast moved forward in a sudden lurch.

The team fired everything back down and made the locomotive look as innocuous and decrepit as possible to dissuade others from investigating the site. Then, they celebrated their engineering feat by installing a bevy of nasty booby-traps to fatally discourage any others who might come this way to seek out the hulking transportation relics. Thus, the locomotive was saved against the Believers' time of final need.

Now was that time. An advance team was traveling during the night to Golden to prepare things for the arrival of the army that would march in the morning. Booby-traps would be dismantled, the engine stoked and readied, and temporary tracks laid across the road to connect the museum grounds to the Burlington Northern Santa Fe mainline. Then, with God's blessing, it would be Santa Fe, south and west across New Mexico and Arizona, then north, all the way to Utah.

There used to be a route, the old Denver, Rio Grande, and Western right-of-way, through the mountains, but he rejected the notion of taking it. Mountainous routes were exposed to landslides, had few industrial spurs where they might garner additional cars or equipment for repairs, and required more power for the steep grade and were, thus, much harder on the engine. No, to go west, he needed to go south.

The General whistled to himself softly, the toot-toot of the steam whistle of a locomotive rushing down the tracks, telling all the world to stand aside while it passed.

Chug, chug, chug, chug. Chug, chug, chug, chug. Toot-toot!

★ ★ ★ ★ ★

Kelly couldn't whistle. Her mouth was too dry, her lips too wind-burned and swollen, her tongue too thick, and her breath too ragged to whistle.

One, two, three, four. One, two, three, four.

Kelly pedaled on, surrounded now by ash and burned-out stumps as she approached Sanctuary.

One, two, three, four. One, two, three, four.

Even wracked with pain and weary beyond comprehension, she somehow still knew that she was supposed to give the tell-tale birdcalls: a magpie, a lark bunting, a Steller's jay. She tried to purse her cracked lips, but was rewarded with no sound, not even a meager toot, just a mournful wheeze in time to the thrusts of her searing, leaden legs.

One, two, three, four. One, two, three, four.

But still, her heart gladdened as she saw the entrance of Sanctuary down-slope. She was going to make it.

One, two, three, four. One, two, three, four.

The sentries should have known better. Kelly's return should have been anticipated. They should have been informed. But, they weren't. And, like most soldiers who pull late night guard duty, they were of the most junior rank. Simultaneously rattled by recent events and hyped up by the heightened alert due to the impending March, they could not really be blamed for what happened next. As Kelly shakily turned her replacement bike around the upper edge of a large boulder and headed further downhill toward the entrance of Sanctuary without giving the required birdcalls, a metal baton was thrust out from behind the boulder into the spokes of the unfamiliar, red mountain bike's front wheel to thwart the approach of the unidentified interloper.

One, two, three, four. One, two, three . . .

The front wheel stopped abruptly and Kelly was thrown

over the handlebars into the air and down the dark, ash-covered slope.

Kelly was too dazed, too uncomprehending to even wave her arms in terror as she found herself flying toward Sanctuary. But, whether from discipline or mere muscle-memory, her legs still pedaled as she flew forward.

One, two, three, four. One, two.

The first sanctuary ended just as had the first marathon.

General Antonio Fontana stared at the ancient, torn roadmap covered with scribblings in disbelief, his mind reeling in shock from the revelations it contained.

Lieutenant Maria Casini was alive.

She had killed all but one of the ConFoes that were responsible for the fire that devastated Sanctuary Vale.

The remaining ConFoe had acted with her in defeating the last of those killed and she was now traveling with him to an unknown destination.

Scout Kelly Joy Lanigan had received clues and communications from the Lieutenant and ridden from Sanctuary to Golden to Larkspur to Sanctuary in forty-eight hours. She had supplemented the Lieutenant's missive with her own explanation of events, apparently scrawled hastily in her own blood. But, Lanigan now lay dead, her head caved in by the rocky outcroppings of Sanctuary itself and her soul gathered to the ultimate sanctuary of God's bosom.

Denver was vacant, irradiated by ConFoe treachery, according to Lieutenant Casini.

Yucca Mountain had been emptied of its radioactive waste and now stood cool and silent.

And, of course, during the Lieutenant's absence, the Believers had decided to implement the Plan and march to the final battle, far from this place. But was it the right place?

Fontana blinked twice slowly, then suddenly handed the Lieutenant's map to his aide for further study and hastily opened up a map of his own displaying U.S. rail lines.

God had given him his sign.

Chapter 19

Only after Ali dashed into the quarters and flipped off the lights was Derek able to take a breath.

"Are you crazy, turning on floodlights? You could see that for miles!" Derek could breathe again, but he was obviously still somewhat excited.

Hank looked at the two newcomers with detached bemusement. He and Ali had avoided both the mals and the ConFoes for years, simply by holing up in a place with an adequate food supply (it had been stocked as a fallout shelter back in the days when it was mandatory for every county to have one) and good locks. Of course, it helped that there was nothing here that anyone but scientists would care about and that their own scientific habits allowed them to work easily at night, when they would be less noticeable—if they didn't turn on the lights.

"Actually," Hank deadpanned, "we depend on the fact that electromagnetic radiation, within and without the visible spectrum, travels quite a ways. Besides, I may be crazy, but I personally don't accuse someone else of insanity before I'm properly introduced." He held out a hand from his comfortable position in the lawn chair. "My name is Hank."

As Derek took his right hand, Hank waggled the thumb of his opposite hand in Ali's direction. "This here is my assistant and good friend, Ali."

Ali stepped forward and nodded to both of the newcomers in turn, before also extending his hand in greeting. "We are very pleased to meet your acquaintance. Please do understand that no insanity or hostility is involved in our somewhat dramatic invitation to visit us. We were simply desirous of meeting . . . fellow inhabitants of this area . . . who had an available source of transportation." Ali smiled broadly, his teeth white against his dark complexion.

The smile was genuine, as evidenced by the relaxed crinkles around Ali's eyes as he grinned, but Derek showed a flicker of apprehension at the reference to the truck. He shook both hands offered to him, before speaking.

"My name is Derek, Derek Williger. This here is Maria."

Maria stepped forward and lightly grasped hands with each in turn.

"The truck is . . . Maria's," continued Derek warily. "She's just dropping me off . . . in Arizona . . . then going about her way."

Hank leaned further back in his lawn chair, subconsciously working to reduce any threat his body language might convey to the tense young man standing before them. "Ali and me, well, I bet you already figured out that we're not some kind of gangbangers. Nothing like that at all, in fact. We're rational people, scientific people. Our work here," he gestured all around the area at the giant, silent dishes extending into the distance, "is done. We were just hopeful we might be able to barter or beg a ride elsewhere."

Ali chimed in. "It is a very hot, thirsty walk to anyplace from here. Transportation would be of great assistance."

Maria started to speak, but Derek cut her off. "What kind of work are you involved in?" he said to Hank, ignoring Ali in a way that Hank knew Ali had not experienced for a long, long time.

The slight to Ali put Hank off a bit, but he was not an excitable man by nature and if subtle ethnic prejudice was the worst they had to endure to secure transport, he would live with it. He knew that Ali, always polite, would also endure. "My colleague, Ali, and I are astronomers." He paused and looked straight at Derek. "We study stars."

Now it was apparently Derek's turn to be put off. "I know what an astronomer is."

Hank shrugged. "Education's not what it used to be. Being a dumb son-of-a-bitch doesn't matter much in the virtual worlds or in what's left of this one." He sat forward a bit in his lawn chair. "These dishes here, they used to be used to gather pretty extensive information about stars and galaxies and black holes—all that sophisticated, interesting shit— back in the day."

"So, you study far-away galaxies?" asked Maria.

Ali replied. "No, no. Not anymore. It would be very difficult for the two of us to conduct any meaningful research or analysis of that nature given our resources and our manpower. Alignment and maintenance must be very precise on the most distant observations. Several technicians would be needed for gain compensation filtering alone . . ."

Hank interrupted to bring the discussion back to the elementary level. "Basically, we just listen now to see if anyone out there . . ." he looked up at the myriad stars above, ". . . is trying to signal us."

"You mean like SETI?" asked Maria.

"Who?" queried Derek in bewilderment.

"SETI, the search for extra-terrestrial intelligence," replied Maria matter-of-factly. She had read something about it long ago.

"You are, of course, quite right," responded Ali with some glee. "The equipment here was not designed for such purpose and, despite some fictional accounts to the contrary in popular media, this place was not widely used for such purpose during SETI's most intensive years, but the array can be so used and we have done so. It was Hank's idea originally to do so."

"Yeah, well, almost five years of looking since we arrived and we didn't find a damn thing," interposed Hank, laconically.

It seemed Derek could not shake his lingering suspicions. "I thought you said your work was done. Does that mean you've proven nobody's out there? How do you prove a negative?"

Ali jumped to reply. "You are quite right that it is impossible to prove that there is no intelligent life elsewhere in the universe. We have merely been unable to discern any patterns in the electromagnetic radiation emanating from likely candidates which would prove that those star systems are inhabited by such creatures."

Hank decided to cut to the core of the issue. "Stuff keeps breaking that we can't fix. A bunch of the dishes don't track in parallel anymore. We tried to reconfigure to use a smaller array, but the tractor mechanisms are pretty bulky. Sand gets into everything hereabouts. We had another one freeze up a couple days ago. It was kinda the last straw. We can't get any more useful information, so we memorialized our research and are hanging up the towel."

"It is very disappointing," observed Ali sullenly.

Maria looked at the now-purposeless scientists. "Even though I don't believe there is anything out there for you to find, I am sorry that your efforts proved fruitless."

"Yeah," muttered Derek without much conviction, "we're . . . uh . . . sorry . . . er . . . for your loss."

"It is not your fault," Ali stated simply.

Hank turned toward Maria, one eyebrow arched. "What makes you think that there's nothing out there to find?" His tone was light, but there was an edge to the question.

Maria looked surprised by the question and a bit flummoxed. "I . . . er . . . well, because if there was someone out there, God would have told us about it." Her voice gained confidence as she spoke. "We're created in his image and it doesn't say in the Bible he created anybody else."

"Hell, God didn't tell us about bacteria or viruses or other galaxies or the atom, but they all exist. We just had to look to find them."

Maria didn't really appear offended—she probably had too logical of a mind for that—but Hank noted she was taken aback at the response. The religious types never really rationally discussed these things, he was sure. She gave the type of response he expected. "But, those things were made for us—they were necessary for our lives to work correctly, so He created them."

"Why not create others like us elsewhere?" He waved one hand in a broad, lazy circle above his head. "As they always said, otherwise it's a heckuva waste of space."

There was no hesitation this time; this one was simple. "God has us to worship Him and to extend His mercy to. Scientists like simple answers. Why would He need anyone else?"

Hank smiled and shook his head. "Look, Maria, I don't want to offend nobody, but why limit God's mercy . . . or his ego." That last slipped out before he had really thought it through. He didn't want to push too hard; they still wanted a ride. But it always perturbed him that the religious-types explained everything by saying God wanted it that way.

Ali interjected in a transparent effort to assuage any offense. "I think what Hank is saying is that the things that exist in the universe which make life possible for us would make life possible in many, many other places. It is a design, if you will, that would efficiently allow life to develop in many places in many ways. The universe is so infinite that it seems improbable that life and intelligence would not develop in other places in a manner similar to how it developed here. The math is undeniable."

"Hold on there," interrupted Hank with a brief wave of his hand. "My fault for starting it, but I'm going to finish it. Seems a mite impolite to lead off a conversation with heavy stuff like religion and theories of how the universe works and such. Why not work our way back to simpler stuff?" Hank looked at Ali and Ali nodded minutely.

"Fine," said Maria. "You said earlier you wanted transportation, but you never said where to. Where are you headed?"

Hank shook his head wearily. "Outta one fryin' pan, into another." He looked from Maria to Derek and back again, subconsciously moving his arms away from his body slightly and opening his palms to show they were empty. "Now, I don't want anyone to get excited or nothing, seeing how you are . . . shall we say . . . unofficial travelers in these parts . . . and you," he said, nodding toward Maria, "are probably dead-set against the whole notion, theologically speaking, but, well, we want to go someplace where we can turn ourselves in to the Conversion Forces."

Maria was startled. Sure, plenty of people—almost everybody who was law-abiding and had no theological concerns—had turned themselves in for mandatory conversion back in the early days, but no one did it now. Few mals even allowed themselves to be converted when captured, unless they were near death. You didn't live this long as a mal outside the law if you believed in the concept at all. Life as a mal was hard; life post-conversion was virtually a walk in the park.

By his look, Derek definitely shared her shock. "Really?"

was all he managed to say in response.

"Why would you want to be converted?" said Maria simply.

"Well, darlin', my whole life has been astronomy, especially the whole SETI thing. I can't do that any more. I can't do the science I was trained to do—can't even really do theoretical stuff anymore. Don't get me wrong. Ali here, he's one bright guy and we've had plenty of interesting discussions about things theoretical, but we're about all talked out. I need to go someplace to engage my mind or I'll end up killing myself."

"There are plenty of people . . ." Maria said, glancing furtively at Derek and blushing slightly, ". . . I mean, despite the ConFoe's efforts, there are still some people to talk to. You don't have to convert to find company or good conversation."

Hank grimaced lightly, turning it into a tight smile. "Meaning no disrespect, Maria, but talking science to a bunch of crazed gangbangers or simple-minded peasants or even to a group of . . . devout . . . fundamentalist Christians, well, it ain't exactly my idea of a good time. There's no scientific community anymore. They're all gone." Ali nodded silently while Hank continued. "Ali and I chatted about this and he had a good expression for it."

Ali responded to the prompt. "I called it a 'scientific rapture.' "

"I don't understand," said Derek.

"In Biblical terms," informed Maria, "the rapture takes place before the end of the world, when God calls all the Believers to Him and they suddenly disappear from this world, leaving the unbelievers and the less devout behind to live in an increasingly hostile world and fight against Satan in the last battle." She stopped, realizing suddenly how apropos the description of the rapture was to what had taken place in the real world—people leaving while some few were left behind to struggle. It was a particularly strange and somewhat disturbing thought because in the real world it was the non-Believers who had embraced conversion and vanished. The Believers had been left behind. Thus, the analogy made the Believers the ones who had been left behind in God's call to the faithful.

"Exactly correct," said Ali in response to her last words, not her last thoughts, starting to take up the explanation.

"You're saying," interrupted Maria, her concern lacing her voice, "that the virtual worlds are heaven and that my people have rejected the call."

Hank came to Ali's defense. "Actually, Ali there, he was just making an analogy."

Maria pursued Hank instead. "So, do you think that the virtual worlds are heaven?"

Hank screwed up his face and thought a bit. "Hard to say. Harder to know."

"If you aren't sure, why would you ever go?" asked Maria innocently.

Derek listened for Hank's answer. Maria had made this point before.

Hank got up from his chair and ambled back and forth for a minute, his hand rubbing his chin, as he thought about what to say. Finally, he turned toward the group, his head cocked to the left.

"There's an old joke. There's been a big flood and a guy is up on his roof to get away from the raging water. A guy comes by in a canoe and says 'Git in.' And the first guy says, 'No thanks. God will provide.' The water keeps rising and another feller comes by, this one in a row boat. 'Climb aboard,' says this feller, 'and I'll take you to safety.' But the guy on the roof says 'No thanks. God will provide.' Later, as the guy is clinging to his chimney, a helicopter comes over and they drop a rope ladder down to him. 'Grab on,' the people in the 'copter say, 'it's your last chance.' But the guy on the roof still refuses and eventually the water gets even higher and he is swept away and drowns. When he gets to heaven, he confronts God and says, 'I believed in you and you didn't save me.' And God says, 'What d'ya mean? I sent you two boats and a helicopter.' "

Derek laughed.

Maria looked at Hank coldly, a foot tapping lightly on the ground unbidden in aggravation. "Look, ma'am," said Hank in appeasement. "I don't mind you believing what you do, believe me. But as far as this world goes, the water's rising. I had something to do, so I held on, but now that my work here is done, I see no reason not to take the helicopter. It might not be heaven, but it ain't death."

The group stood silently for a moment. Finally, Hank spoke again. "Now that I've finished offending you all with my blasphemous beliefs and jokes," he said lightly with a tone of contrition, "Ali's analogy was really of a more minor nature."

Ali again took his cue to resume his explanation. "The analogy was only to say that conversion has had a rapture-like impact in the scientific community. Many, many of the smartest and brightest either converted voluntarily or quickly succumbed to mandatory conversion. Meaningful research was no longer pursued in the real world once conversion became readily available to solve the practical problems of disease and food production shortages. Funding for basic research dried up completely. The scientists, they have all gone to virtual worlds and we have been left behind."

"So, you're intellectually lonely?" responded Derek. The artificial lightness of his tone suggested to Maria that he was deliberately abandoning the analogy in an effort to ease the tension between her and the scientists.

"That is precisely the case," said Ali in confirmation.

"I suppose, then," said Maria, with a tone of confrontation, "that you want to convert, too?"

"Oh, no," replied Ali abruptly. "I want to enlist in the Conversion Forces."

"I wouldn't want to be one of them ConFoes when we get there," boasted a young Believer as General Fontana passed by his troops. This group was loading armaments and explosives onto the flat bed of a large solar-powered truck the Believers had liberated back when forays into the city were still safe. "They'll never know what hit them!"

"They'll know," replied the General in an enthusiastic, booming voice, reserved for rallying the morale of the troops. "They'll know that God has smitten them . . ." He raised his right arm up and brought his closed fist crashing down on a flimsy crate nearby, smashing it to bits. ". . . with his strong right hand!"

The troops cheered and redoubled their efforts to get underway to attack their enemy, the enemy of God.

They were going to meet the ConFoes and join them in the final battle.

Maria looked at Ali in disgust. The man seriously wanted to meet the ConFoes and join them in their battle against the mals.

Now it was Maria's turn, again, to be wary. "Why in the world would you want to do that?"

"Because, unlike Hank, I would very much like to remain in the world, in this world. I believe most fervently the time will come when our search here will be able to be continued. I choose to stay in this world until that time. To do that, I must become a ConFoe. All other choices lead to conversion or death."

It was all very logical and Maria hated the logic of it, the matter-of-fact calculation that ignored the morality of what the ConFoes stood for. "So, you're going to kill and torture people until you can pick up on your research again," she spat with venom and undisguised contempt.

"I do not think that I would be capable of such things. No, my thought was that I would volunteer to be a Converter. I have strong technical skills that could be useful in such regard and I could assist people, such as my friend Hank here, to move on to the virtual worlds. Eventually there will come a time when my research can be continued."

Derek looked at Ali in utter disbelief. He could not imagine anyone really wanting to join a ConFoe patrol, even in the relatively innocuous position of Scanning Equipment Officer. "Why not offer to use your technical skills for satellite tracking? It seems better suited to your background and you don't have to . . . get near to any fights."

"I considered that, but satellite tracking is not viable as a long-term position."

"Why not?" asked Maria in genuine interest.

Hank looked at the newcomers in amazement. "Hell, haven't you noticed? Not very many of them birds left anymore. Been winking out left and right for nearly a year now."

"How did you know that?" asked Maria in astonishment. Derek knew that this, this was information she would like to get back to the Believers.

Hank tilted his head and wrinkled his nose slightly. "How did you happen to stop your vehicle and start pointing at this place?"

Maria looked over to Derek. Derek looked at the ground.

"Let me guess. You've been this way before. The dishes looked different from the last time you were here. You weren't really looking for it, but something just looked different and you figured it out. We were worried that might happen, but decided a few days ago to chance it."

"Something like that," Derek said warily.

Hank waved at the sky. "That's all we do. We look at that. We set up the equipment and let it do the listening and the filtering, but between data runs, we got nothing much to do but look at that and jaw at each other. You really think we wouldn't notice when lights started disappearing? Hell, we have to factor out the interference they cause every time we calibrate a procedure."

"But why are they disappearing? Is someone shooting them down?" quizzed Maria, pressing for more information.

Hank snorted. "That would be quite a shot. Real rocket science stuff."

"There is no evidence of such," replied Ali with his usual precise enunciation. "We believe they are being destroyed by activation of their own self-destruct devices—installed to prevent catastrophe in the event of a launch trajectory difficulty."

"You mean," said Derek, "somebody got the codes and is sabotaging the satellite system?"

"Perhaps," responded Ali. "My personal theory is that the satellites are less and less needed as the unconverted population declines and that, accordingly, the satellites are being destroyed because they provide evidence of the technologically-advanced, sentient life on earth. Evidence which could be picked up by an alien civilization, such as those we seek."

"I don't get it," said Derek. "There are cities and highways all over the place. Any little green men that come visiting are going to know that someone was here."

"Ah, yes," said Ali, obviously warming to his lecture. "But these earthbound evidences will decay over a relatively short time, geologically speaking. Freeze-thaw deterioration, erosion, oxidation, microbial action, and the like. Space structures, while they may become non-functional, can orbit a significant time and can be detected readily from great distances. Their visibility is not obscured by atmospheric factors and they orbit with a periodicity that interferes with electromagnetic emanations, even the natural magnetic fields and light wave reflections of the earth itself."

"And the whole point of the ConFoes," extrapolated Maria aloud, "is to make sure no one is around, human or alien, to mess with the computers hosting the virtual worlds. Not now. Not ever." She looked over toward Derek. "It's a simple matter of self-defense." Derek glared at Maria, but neither Hank's nor Ali's expression seemed to indicate that this was any kind of revelation to them.

"But, if they are destroying the satellites, they must not need them anymore," said Derek, stifling a yawn while thinking it through. "Which means we . . . uhhhh . . . have to conclude that . . . they . . . think their mission is close to complete. So why is becoming a Converter a better long-term career choice?"

"I would be interested to know if you come up with the same theory I have," replied Ali with a twinkle in his eye. He frowned slightly, however, as he noticed the weariness in the faces of their visitors. "You are obviously tired though, from your journey. Please, rest the night and think of our discussion. We will nap a bit, too, so that we can move onto your circadian rhythm and schedule, in case you are willing to help with our transportation needs."

Derek perked up again at the reference to transportation, frowning involuntarily.

Ali responded to his look. "We would not have invited you, if we were not willing to be hospitable. Pick any quarters you like and secure them to your satisfaction if you feel unsafe."

Derek's eyes flitted briefly toward the truck.

Hank read his mind. "Maria grabbed the keys before she got out." He winked at Maria, but did not disclose more. "But, yeah, we could hotwire it if we wanted to." He smiled. "What kind of scientists would we be if we didn't know basic electronics?"

Ali smiled, too. "We do repair our own equipment."

Hank continued on, before Derek's concerns ran rampant. "If you feel your truck's not safe, just pop the hood and take some vital piece to bed with you. Odds against us being able to replace it with what we happen to have on hand are . . . well . . . astronomical."

"Parts are always a limiting factor with equipment," chimed in Ali.

Derek smiled tiredly. It was a good solution to his ingrained paranoid fears. He nodded curtly and ambled over to the truck.

Ali called out after him as he turned away. "Please, if you would be so kind as to remember how to replace what you took and not lose it."

Derek grabbed a part that looked important and was easy to detach, then shrugged his shoulders and headed for a room that would be near to the one Maria was beginning to move to. He had a lot to think about and it wasn't about Ali's career calculations. These guys could be the key to improving his plan. Even a good plan could always use a bit of tweaking, and his plan was workable, perhaps, but far from good.

★ ★ ★ ★ ★

Maria waited in the hall outside the dorm-like rooms that had once housed workers. They were all the same: sturdy twin beds and a simple dresser, chair, and mirror. Things were a bit dusty, but quite serviceable. Finally Derek returned from the truck, with what looked to be a voltage regulator in his hands. Maria caught Derek at his door.

"I thought we were going to talk about the plan," she said, softly enough that the science guys wouldn't be able to hear.

"We were. I just . . . need to sleep on it. I have to figure out if these guys can help."

"Why wouldn't they?" Maria replied. "They seem smart and friendly enough." She made a sour face. "They also seem sympathetic to your . . . world view."

"Yeah, but something's not quite right." She looked at him quizzically, but said nothing. He continued, "I mean, why are they here?"

Maria's eyebrows arched inward in minor consternation. "They said why they were here. SETI; they're listening for little green men. They'll never find them, but their reason makes sense from their point of view."

Derek shook his head. "Not to me, especially when they say that the idea of conversion seems logical to them. Nobody who believes in virtual worlds would be searching for intelligent life."

Maria snorted in laughter, bringing her hand up to cover her mouth in embarrassment. "I don't think you meant that the way it came out."

Derek tilted his head slightly to the left, his eyelids half-closed. "Yeah, well you know what I meant."

Maria became serious again. "Not really. Why wouldn't a . . . believer . . . in conversion not want to check whether someone is out there . . ." She waved vaguely heavenward,

". . . before they check out of the real world?"

Derek's head shifted up and back slightly in surprise. "Well, if you agree that going virtual is, basically, inevitable in any intelligent society because it eliminates the need for resources and solves . . ."

"Avoids . . ." she interjected.

". . . problems, then you know there is no one out there to find. Or, at least, you know that if anyone is out there you won't find them."

Maria folded her arms and pondered for a moment. She was getting tired; it didn't seem obvious to her. "And why is that?"

"Well," said Derek slowly, as if the answer were too simple to need explaining, "the time period between developing radio and having powerful computers is miniscule, cosmically speaking. And anyone who has gone virtual doesn't want to be found—it exposes them to risk of annihilation—so they won't be broadcasting on radio anymore. Heck, the ConFoes don't use radio anymore now, even though we could encrypt it and do it securely. Didn't you ever wonder why? I always did. But it became obvious to me tonight."

A look of understanding came over Maria's countenance. "Oh . . ."

"Anyone virtual isn't looking to be found. The odds of hearing anyone in the tiny window of time after they are technologically capable of broadcasting, but prior to radio silence being imposed when they go virtual, is beyond astronomical. It's a snowball's chance in hell."

Maria gave him a stern look. "It's slim, I admit."

He shifted the voltage regulator to his other hand and looked around casually to see if they were being overheard. He exhaled slowly—it was obvious he was weary, too. "Then why are they looking?"

Maria screwed up her face. "Maybe they're just not as smart as you think."

Derek shrugged and mimicked Ali's tone and precise enunciation. "I do not think that explanation seems likely." He reverted to his own voice. "Maybe. Look, I'll work on the plan. Maybe they can help with that anyway."

All the way to Golden, General Fontana had mulled the Plan over and over in his mind, confirming his thoughts and refining the technical elements that went with them. He made up his mind as the Army of the Believers marched and rolled into the yard at the Colorado Railroad Museum late in the evening. His advance team had been busy and it looked like things would be ready to go in five or six hours. That schedule would let the troops get a bit of a rest, but allow the train to move out and through the city still in the cover of darkness, even allowing a half-hour to pick up a few extra coal cars which had been abandoned with full loads behind the old Coors plant.

Fontana generally kept his own counsel, but now that he had decided to revise the Plan, there were some things that it was important for his commanders and the engineers to know yet tonight, so that they could fulfill the responsibilities of the Army of the Believers even should he fall (a ConFoe attack was possible at any moment; besides, even soldiers can sometimes die in their sleep of natural causes) and so they could understand why he had given certain peculiar orders. Certainly, soldiers are trained to follow orders without questioning them or understanding their role in the greater picture, but Fontana had always found that a little understanding up front encouraged the proper enthusiasm and prevented misunderstandings and mistakes in the actual execution. Accordingly, he called up his staff and laid the railroad maps out on a glass-covered display case in the museum. The day had been hot and the air was still in the musty building. Miners' caps lit the map while holding down the corners from curling.

"Before we leave at four a.m., everybody drinks a full canteen and replenishes it before boarding into the personnel boxcars."

"Yes sir," said his aide with unnecessary enthusiasm as the other staff members nodded in simple agreement.

"Personal emergency blankets are to be used to line the interior of the boxcars: floor, walls, and ceilings, but especially the floor. Reflective side should be out."

"Yes sir," repeated the unctuous aide while the rest of the staff eyed one another in unspoken confusion.

"We will also need several volunteers with the engineers in the train cab, prepared for extremely hazardous duty." He knew that, given the radiation, the train would be moving through as it necessarily passed through the city, it was really suicide duty, but he didn't call it that. The poor bastards would probably die in battle before the radiation got them anyway.

"To protect against attack by gangs, sir?" asked the youngest Lieutenant present.

"No," said his aide before Fontana cut him off.

"The gangs are all dead." Fontana motioned to his aide, who passed around Lieutenant Casini's missive, as he continued. "For the same reason we will need to move through Denver at the highest possible speed. Denver has been irradiated by the ConFoes. The longer we are in the area of radiation and the more exposed we are, the more we will suffer the effects of radiation poisoning."

The somber mood of the room turned downright grim. General Fontana filled the silence with further explanation.

"Boxcar doors stay closed until we are well south of town, no matter what. It'll be hot in there, which is why everyone needs to be fully hydrated before we leave. They may have to piss on themselves, but no one dies of heat exhaustion, is that understood?"

"Yes, sir," the group murmured in unison, looking up from the missive on the torn map delivered by Scout Lanigan at such tremendous cost.

"Will the blankets actually protect the men in the cars?" someone asked. "That radioactive waste can be pretty nasty stuff."

"It can't hurt," was all General Fontana said in reply. The pre-attack bravado they had all been sharing with their men evaporated into nothingness.

"What are the suicide volunteers for?" asked the young Lieutenant.

Gus Gerdemann, his chief engineer, the man who would be running the train and who had just realized, battle or no, he had a future life expectancy measured in days, spoke up. "I asked for 'em. Somebody has to run ahead and manually throw the switches if the signal arm indicates they are not where they need to be."

The persistent Lieutenant spoke up again. "Do we have protective clothing that could . . ."

Gerdemann cut him off. "They'll be on the ground and they'll need to move fast. Between times, they'll be on the access ladders on either side of the control room at the front of the train. They'll get plenty of dust and exposure to whatever's on the ground."

Fontana retook control of the conversation. "They'll have coveralls and painters' masks. We'll wash them off and give them some iodine in water as soon as we can once we're out of the city. That's the best we can do."

The group acquiesced in silence.

"Gus, here, has rigged one of our radon detectors to act as an audible Geiger counter. He'll monitor things as best he can."

One of the more experienced leaders began to trace his finger along the route to the salt dome in Utah. The man clearly thought ahead. "How many more major cities between here and Utah?"

"Albuquerque and Las Vegas. My guess is that Flagstaff is small enough to not be an issue. Of course, we're not going all the way to Utah anymore."

To a man, the staff turned to him in puzzlement. Even his aide, who had oozed smug superiority during the briefing, due to his earlier access to Lieutenant Casini's message, looked perplexed.

"Why not?" said the hapless young Lieutenant who had spoken up earlier.

"Because we're going ninety miles northwest of Vegas, to Yucca Mountain."

"What's in Yucca Mountain?" The Lieutenant would have to learn to shut up if he were ever to advance further in the ranks in the future—not that any of them really had a future.

"The point is, what's not in Yucca Mountain? There used to be tons of high-level radioactive material. The scientists put it there because they consider it to be the safest, most secure geological site in the country. But the radioactive waste isn't there anymore. Maybe it was never really kept there; maybe they removed it. Who knows? According to Lieutenant Casini, though, wherever it was, right now it's spread out over every major city on earth."

The General paused, waiting for someone to impress him, but no one did. Not his senior staff, not the cocky young

Lieutenant, and certainly not his aide. He spelled it out. "If you had the most secure geological site possible and if the rest of the remaining population on earth was scared to death to go there because they thought it was full of glowing, radioactive garbage, where would you hide the computers you never wanted anybody to find and never wanted to let the elements destroy?"

Fontana's aide let out a soft, low whistle until everyone glared at him and the underling shut himself up. Fontana continued.

"Billions of souls are in limbo in Yucca Mountain. I believe that to be the truth of the situation. And, with God's help, we shall set the people free."

Chapter 20

With the astronomers' help, Derek could set Maria free now. She could go safely on her way. He could teach Ali to use the conversion scanner by converting Hank. Derek would call in with the bogus story about the motorcycle gang, but add that he had with him a ConFoe recruit who was aiding him. Ali could shoot Derek (he hoped the guy could shoot) and start to convert Derek almost immediately. While the scanner ran, Ali could wash up and change clothes (no powder residue, just in case the ConFoes investigated the shooting) and wait for the ConFoes to arrive. The ConFoes would have a new recruit, already with some scanning experience, who had acted to save Derek. And, if the scanning was shown to be premature, well, the guy was just a recruit. They could hardly blame him for instituting the scan prematurely.

There was still some risk, but this plan was better. Certainly less of the risk was on Maria this way. Still, Ali puzzled him. If the ConFoes were about to win, wouldn't he be converted soon anyway?

Ali and Maria were greeted with a cornucopia of freeze-dried foodstuffs for breakfast. "No need to skimp," declared Hank. "Ain't gonna be here much longer."

Derek would have been content to ignore Ali's invitation from the night before to continue their discussion about why his desire to become a Converter made sense. It was enough that the fellow's desire helped with Derek's plan. Probing too much could disrupt that. But Maria had obviously been thinking about it; Ali's desire offended her in the most basic

way and she knew that a religious response would be ineffec-
tive in dissuading him. She had to understand the logic.

Over a mouthful of reconstituted apple crunch cake, she
suddenly blurted out in discovery: "Decreasing pool of recruits."

"Huh?" said Derek. He wasn't his best first thing in the
morning.

Maria turned to Ali. "Because so many people are converted and most ConFoe's tours of duty are approaching
their end, you think that there will be relatively long-term positions for Converters, because hardly anyone will re-up;
they'll choose to convert instead—and there aren't many
people left to recruit from." She waved her fork in triumph.

"Yes and, well, no," said Ali. "Certainly there are fewer
people to recruit. And certainly many current recruits will
chose to convert at the end of their tours. Logically, at some
point, there won't be anyone left to recruit and no one willing
to re-up."

"So, by then, we've accomplished our goal and everyone
converts and lives happily ever after," Derek said, pressing to
wrap up the discussion as he shoveled in a generous portion
of reconstituted scrambled eggs, liberally laced with ground
pepper and hot sauce. He stopped suddenly. "I mean that
that's what the ConFoes would say."

Hank's right hand fluttered in the air in a dismissive gesture. "Hell, no need to keep up the pretence. Thought you
might be a ConFoe last night." He reached under his chair
and pulled out Derek's old uniform. "Searching the back of
the truck confirmed things." He glanced over to Maria,
whose eyes expressed concern more than surprise. "I see the
lady knew."

Derek stopped eating for a moment, uncertain of what was
next to come, but Hank just tucked the uniform back under

his chair and picked up a slice of ersatz bacon. "Our cards are on the table. You being a ConFoe works just fine for what we want. The only issue is if Maria is forced to do something she doesn't want to do."

"No, the plan was for her to go her separate way soon anyway."

Hank nodded in brief acknowledgement. "Then everything's copasetic."

Maria's brow furrowed in puzzlement.

"Excellent, in good order," Ali explained.

"No," replied Maria. "I understood the expression. It was just . . . I mean our discussion earlier . . . they could never be sure, could they? They would always need to keep someone around."

"Huh?" said Derek. He really wasn't sharp in the morning.

"Maria is quite correct. They would always need someone around."

"I mean, we have . . . hidden . . . for years and years without detection," Maria explained to Derek. "Even if the ConFoes thought they had gotten everyone, they would have to leave someone to be on the lookout for stragglers, hermits squirreled away in odd places, or dedicated sects hidden in remote locations. The ConFoes have to remain alert indefinitely."

"The only other possibility," speculated Ali, "is that they have some sort of doomsday device—a series of precisely coordinated nuclear explosions that could be triggered to occur far from the site of the virtual world computers. These detonations could be configured to blanket the earth with enough particulate matter to block out sunlight completely in order to wipe out the ability of plants to photosynthesize and kill whoever's left."

Hank put down his fork long enough to snort gently.

"Hell, Ali, don't go back to that old theory. There's just no point to a doomsday device you don't tell anybody about. It doesn't serve as a deterrent to anything that way. And if it's not a deterrent and, instead, just a way of killing everybody that's left, why the hell haven't they used it yet?"

Ali shrugged. It was clear to Derek that the two scientists had been through this debate before. "Maybe nobody has the balls to press the button. Maybe they want to reduce the population first to maximize the possibility that no one escapes. Perhaps it is not a deterrent; perhaps it is just a way to eliminate whoever or whatever gets close to the computers when they do get close, whether by accident or design, decades or even millennia from now."

"Yeah, that protection from little green men theory is your strongest shot."

Suddenly Maria sounded concerned. "You mean you think there is a real possibility of a device that kills off the planet if the location of the computers is attacked?"

Ali shrugged again. "It makes sense. I would do it that way. But we are getting off the proper track of our analysis. Regardless of whether such a device exists, the ConFoes have a long-term need for personnel—a longer than lifetime need for personnel."

"What, you mean you think they breed their replacement recruits in some secret laboratory or something?" Derek asked.

Ali wrinkled his nose slightly, but was too polite to verbalize his true thoughts about such a theory. "Possibly," he said instead, "but that has many complications and uncertainties. Why not just use the recruits they have?"

Now Derek was concerned. "You mean they'll never let me out?" An infinity of ConFoe service was more than he could fathom.

"More like they will keep you in reserve."

"What does that mean?"

"Well," theorized Ali, "maybe a consciousness could be implanted back into a synthetic body or a robotic device that can accept a converted mind. When the time comes that ConFoes are needed, they are simply downloaded into the bodies or the robots and sent out to do what needs to be done to fight whoever or whatever may threaten the virtual worlds whenever that might be."

Derek was relieved. "So you're saying I might get called up from my virtual life in some distant future?"

Ali frowned. "Well, yes, except that you would not be much of a soldier after millennia of relaxation and soft-living. Reserve forces would be better soldiers if the converted personalities were kept in a training world, running simulations, keeping their wits and their edge by facing different foes and different situations."

"But wouldn't they get weary and burn out over time?" asked Maria.

"I sure would," said Hank. "But they would only get burnt out if they perceive the millennia of training. The same personality can get reinserted multiple times into a training world and, with a little editing here and there, could be fooled into not recognizing the amount of time that has actually gone by. The Generals, hell, probably the damn computers, assess the effectiveness of various tactics in various scenarios so they know which commands to give should that scenario ever occur. The poor grunts, they just get downloaded into one scenario after another and never even know they've been at it forever." Hank's eyes crinkled in obvious happiness to be theorizing on a new subject, or at least with new counterparts, for a change, and his voice boomed as he warmed to the lecture. "And one day, one day, they may just be released into the real world again. As long as you're happy in your job, then being a ConFoe is the only way to have a shot at coming back to the real world, ever."

"I don't know," murmured Maria. "Computers are fast, but they're not really creative. Wouldn't the training scenarios be obvious and unrealistic? I can't believe that they could fool anyone of any intelligence."

Hank looked at Ali and Ali smiled. "Intelligence isn't what most military outfits are looking for in a soldier. Besides, if they did fool someone, how would that person, by definition, ever know?" growled the older man.

Ali gave Hank a look like that given to misbehaving children and waved off his remark. "Pay no attention to him. He's just trying to scare you. But you are right about the lack of creative artificial intelligence, even in the fastest computers. That's why, if I was doing it, I would capture mals while they slept or were unconscious."

"Unconscious?" murmured Maria, a frightened look on her face.

"Yes, an unconscious mal would be optimal," responded Ali glibly. "That way you could convert them, without ever revealing to them that they were converted, and insert them into the training programs to do whatever they might do in the real world. That would generate some random creative input that the computer cannot generate of its own accord. The mals would just wake up and never know they were in their enemy's training scenario."

Derek dropped his fork on the floor with a clang. "They'd never know they were in a dream . . ." He felt an ominous presence in the room. He tried to move, but couldn't. "It would look real, just like it looked when they fell asleep . . ."

Maria joined in Derek's mutterings, ". . . but when you

thought about it later there would be clues, there would be things that just didn't seem right . . ." Her eyes flashed from side to side as her mind raced back to Greco and the house in which she had been tortured and held captive. She had always assumed the battle that had allowed her to escape Greco's foul clutches had been with a rival gang or, perhaps, the Believers. But now, just now, she realized with a shiver that all the sounds had been indistinct, the words muffled by the dull bark of the weapons fire; she couldn't know that the battle had not been with ConFoe forces. Her nightmare was more than she had ever imagined.

Derek's own nightmare was crashing down upon him. He broke out into a sweat as he continued murmuring to himself, "And if they did know they were dreaming, there's nothing they could do about it." He was frozen in place in terror—he could not force himself to move, to save himself, to wake into another world he could never be sure was real.

The train, dubbed the Limbo Liberation Express by the chaplain at its blessing before departure, chugged south and west, toward Yucca Mountain, at good speed. The history of the nuclear waste depository suggested that there would be a spur track off of the main line straight into the face of the mountain. The Plan was to disembark some miles short of their goal and unload their armaments, then send the train, along with two boxcars full of fertilizer-based explosives, chugging straight into the face of the mountain as their first salvo in the final battle.

It never occurred to Fontana, to any of the Believers, that doing so might trigger a Doomsday Device that would end all biological life on earth. Decent, God-fearing people just didn't think like that.

General Fontana smiled, the wind rushing through his hair as the train raced toward its destiny. Right or wrong, nothing could stop the Plan now.

Yucca Mountain was in sight.

Deep inside a secure facility, two techs monitored the situation. One leaned forward to push a button, but the other stopped him.

"Hell, let's see what they do. We've let 'em come this far."

The first tech shrugged and then both techs leaned back into their ergonomically engineered chairs and continued watching.

They were three miles out when they saw the first bones. They were two miles out when they saw the first signs.

The bones were bleached bare by the sand and the sun, scattered recklessly by scavengers before the bleaching had yet begun. Most were human, but there were some horses and indigenous animals, too. At first there were a few, but they increased steadily as the train approached Yucca Mountain. Soon, they were too numerous to count and Gerdemann slowed the train, halting it when he reached the first sign.

"*DANGER!!!*" it read, "*YUCCA MOUNTAIN NUCLEAR WASTE DEPOSITORY. EXTREME RADIATION HAZARD. ENTRY PROHIBITED. PROCEEDING BEYOND THIS POINT WILL RESULT IN USE OF LETHAL FORCE, RESULTING IN SEVERE INJURY OR DEATH. NO TRESPASSING.*" A second sign nearby made the same points with the use of pictographs of a dying man and a radiation hazard symbol. A third sign in the distance warned vaguely of "automatic weapons systems."

Fontana scanned the area ahead with his binoculars, while Gerdemann fussed superficially with the boiler controls.

"What do you think, Gus?" asked the General.

Gerdemann stopped what he was doing. "Is this intended to scare me away?"

"Yep."

"It's working."

"Sticks and stones . . . but words shall never hurt me." The General nodded in the direction of the mountain. "Could be a great camouflage effort, maybe there's mines, but I don't see anything but a few small outbuildings and the entrance to the mountain ahead. No troops, no tanks, no artillery. Nobody's on guard."

"What about the bodies?"

"Dumped there to scare us, maybe. The bodies of mals or even volunteers who have been converted."

Gerdemann reached over and grabbed his makeshift Geiger counter, switching it on and pointing it out the side of the cab towards the ground. It made more clacks than an infinite number of monkeys hacking away at an infinite number of typewriters.

The trainman lunged at the controls, throwing the behemoth into reverse. "Damn, it's hot here, sir."

The realization hit the General like the shock wave of a concussion grenade. The bastards, he knew, had irradiated the cities. Why wouldn't they irradiate the area surrounding their computers? Yucca Mountain was designed to be impervious to high-level radiation. It could hold it in for countless millennia. There was no reason it couldn't hold it out, keeping the vile computers safe, while anyone who approached would die.

Worse yet. The men were already showing signs of radiation sickness from the trek through Denver. Now they had been dosed again. He had led the entire Army of the Believers on a suicide mission, but there was no one to fight. Their enemy was inert, inanimate, unmovable, and lethal.

By the time the train had backed off a couple miles, however, Fontana had made his decision. Faith had brought them this far. He would not waver. The mountain would not come to them; they must go to the mountain. They would go forward with the Plan. They had almost no hope of freeing the souls trapped in Yucca Mountain, and they would all most likely die trying, but better to die for what they believed in, than to retreat. If they left now, they would not only suffer a crisis of faith, they would be picked off by ConFoes and converted as they lay weak and helpless from the radiation. Then their souls would be lost as well as their cause.

The soldiers disembarked and formed into platoons. Fontana did not tell them about the radiation they faced. There was no reason to dampen their spirit or undermine their faith by shoving the grim odds in their hopeful faces. Everyone who went to Vegas thought that they would be a winner. These soldiers were no different, except that they did not believe they played a game of chance. Victory was sure.

The demolition team readied the explosives on the train for its charge into the mountain. It didn't take long. Soon the train headed in toward the thick vault door that closed off the interior of Yucca Mountain from the real world. Gerdemann rode the Limbo Liberation Express alone, with no stops, coaxing every ounce of speed he could muster from the old iron beast straight through to the final destination.

Less than a hundred yards out from the door, the explosives triggered. The door, of course, had been configured to deflect and withstand sizeable explosions. What no one had contemplated, however, was that a giant locomotive would be propelled by a massive fuel oil and fertilizer explosion into the door—a six-hundred-thirty-four-thousand-pound cast iron piston slamming into the center of the reinforced steel and titanium door like the Right Hand of God and ringing it like the Bell of the Freedom. No. 5629 had completed her final run and she had delivered her biggest payload ever.

Two miles away, the Army of the Believers cheered and surged forward as the explosion rocketed the train into Yucca Mountain—an army of ants attacking a huge, granite boulder. It was, Fontana knew, heroic and noble and completely fruitless, but all of that didn't matter. It was a march of faith.

The two watchmen gazed at the tableau in bewildered amazement. They had only seen such a foolhardy display of faith once before. But their silent awe was interrupted by the blare of an automatic alarm.

Four eyes scanned the dials, screens, and read-outs. Four hands moved with speed and alacrity over the relays and controls. Finally, the alarm broke off and the two techs isolated the cause. Now their awe was compounded a thousand-fold.

They discovered that when old 5629 rang the bell, the force and the harmonics of the vibration had sent a thin crack branching out from the top of the door, spidering up to the arid, barren reaches at the top of the mountain. Too small to even be seen, it had been nevertheless been detected by the silent, smooth computer monitoring the situation. The tiny break would be enough to doom the contents of the mountain to destruction. Radiation would leak in through the rock's imperfection and degrade the computer code. Water and air would seep into the microscopic fissures and the cracks would enlarge. It would take time, but eternity tolerated no corruption.

It would be the end of Yucca Mountain.

"I'll be damned," said the junior tech, flabbergasted by what he had just witnessed.

"Not unless that's the world you choose," chuckled his boss. "That's why you run these things. Sometimes the impact of a variable just isn't intuitive."

"You can say that again," responded the junior tech.

"Now you know why I didn't stop things when that psycho mal chick ran out into the fire or when she slaughtered most of the ConFoe squad. You can just never tell. A good watchman knows you can just never tell." He shrugged absently. The excitement was over; it was back to the normal routine. "Time to reconfigure. Revise and reload the inputs and try again."

The junior tech reached forward and pushed a button.

Reset.

As the Army of the Believers surged over the bones of the damned to assault Yucca Mountain, there was a bright flash of light and the world disintegrated away.

The insipid ConFoe recruiting jingle looped merrily and endlessly through Derek's mind as he moved forward through the dry grass and tangles of the alpine valley.

"One Family. One Volunteer."

You'd think a pleasant walk in the woods wouldn't be so bad. It wouldn't, except for the fact that he was on point and there were people out there, mals, who wanted him dead. So he strained to put the incessant jingle out of his mind and focus on his job—checking for tripwires, searching for tracks, scanning the trees on the other side of the valley for movement or shadows that just weren't right.

It had been exhilarating at first, when he was a raw recruit, but he had been doing it for four . . . or was it five? . . . years now. He couldn't remember any more. It seemed like forever.

These days, he just endured his service as best he could. It wasn't easy. He grew to despise the Conversion Forces more and more with each patrol, to hate his miserable existence even more with each passing day. His duty in the Conversion Forces was like the stupid jingle—you just couldn't escape it, no matter how much you wished you could. You longed for a respite, a distraction, to take you away from it, but you never got a break. It just continued endlessly on.

It wasn't just the stress of the ConFoe patrols that he hated, it was the things he had to do and the things he had seen others do. Things they didn't really have to do, but seemed to enjoy.

"One Family. One Volunteer."

He took a step forward.

"One Family. One Volunteer."

Another step.

"One Family. One Volunteer.

One.

Two.

Three bursts of automatic weapon fire exploded suddenly from the other side of a small creek, ripping into the dirt at his feet and tearing through the branches of a nearby Ponderosa pine, sending a puff of yellow, powdery pollen into the air.

Derek dove for the ground and elbowed his way behind the imposing trunk of the nearest tree, his eyes streaming in irritation from the pollen and the panic that was rising in his mind. From the location of the attack and the sound of the weapons, he knew he had almost certainly fallen into an ambush by one of the mal religious cults. Now he was pinned down by coordinated fire, with no hope of saving himself. He just had to hunker down and wait for his squad—his miserable excuse of a squad of vicious misfits and apathetic recruits—to save his sorry ass.

He tried to calm himself down while he waited for his salvation by calculating the time left in his tour of duty, but he was too pumped up by the situation to think it through clearly. All he knew was that it wasn't forever. His tour would end in another year . . . two tops. Then he would go join Katy and his mom in Alpha Two forever. He would live in that world forever . . .

And life would be good.

And when he went to Alpha Two, this pathetic, miserable world would all just seem like a bad dream. He wished that he could wake up there right now, that he could move on to Alpha Two this instant, that he could see his Katy once again.

But right now he was pinned down by some unknown, sinister force.

He couldn't move.

It was a gorgeous summer day. The sun smiled warmly down from a cloud-dotted sky. A lazy breeze wafted over the sparkling, clear water of the forest lake, bestowing just enough of a hint of coolness to keep the assembled throng of guests, family, and friends from perspiring as they waited for the ceremony to begin.

Though there was always much joy in this place, the occasion of the gathering increased it, lifting the throng to a sense of contentment and well-being that they had once never believed possible. Indeed, the only hint of sadness came from the individual who was the focus of the day's activities, as she peeked out from behind the flower-bedecked trellis that marked the starting place of her short but meaningful trip down the aisle.

She had no real right to expect him to be here to give her away. The time had come and gone for her brother's return years ago. Still, hope knows no reason, no rationality. That is what makes it hope, rather than mere expectation.

Her mother kissed her lightly on the forehead as the music started, then preceded her down to the edge of the lake, before the assembled guests. A few moments later, it was her turn to make the brief journey. All eyes turned toward her.

Katy *walked* down the aisle alone.

Derek was not here. He would not give her away. He would not see her joy.

She had finally come to realize he might never join her and their mom on Alpha Two. Not today; not ever.

But he had given her a gift, not just for today, but for every day of her life.

Because of him, she *could* move.

It saddened her that she would never know Derek's fate. She hoped that, whatever had befallen him, his death had been quick and painless, that he had not lingered and suffered.

A few minutes later, Katy's union with her betrothed was blessed as she vowed to love him forever, 'til the end of time . . .

Or, at least until the sun goes supernova.

About the Author

Best known for more than fifteen years as the world's top-ranked player of classic role playing games such as Dungeons & Dragons, Donald J. Bingle is not only a writer of a variety of role playing adventures and gaming materials (Advanced Dungeons & Dragons, Chill, Paranoia, Timemaster, and more), but of movie reviews (in early issues of *Knights of the Dinner Table*), stories, and screenplays.

He has fantasy stories set in the Dragonlance world of Krynn in *The Players of Gilean* and *The Search for Magic*, a science fiction story in *Sol's Children*, spooky stories in *Carnival*, *Historical Hauntings*, and *Civil War Fantastic*, and whimsical stories in *Renaissance Faire* and *All Hell's Breaking Loose* (forthcoming). He is also the author of *Extreme Global Warming*, a darkly comedic screenplay about an environmental organization that is about to save the world, but doesn't want to get caught doing it.

He is a member of the Science Fiction and Fantasy Writers of America, the Role Playing Game Association® Network, the American Bar Association, and the St. Charles Writers Group. Don works as a corporate and securities attorney at Bell, Boyd & Lloyd LLC in Chicago. He lives in St. Charles, Illinois with his fun and creative wife, Linda, and their three puppies: Smoosh, Mauka, and Makai. He can be reached through www.orphyte.com.